W9-BJV-946

# NOT FOREVER, BUT FOR NOW

A NOVEL

# CHUCK PALAHNIUK

SIMON & SCHUSTER

NEW YORK   LONDON   TORONTO   SYDNEY   NEW DELHI

Simon & Schuster
1230 Avenue of the Americas
New York, NY 10020

First Simon & Schuster hardcover edition September 2023

SIMON & SCHUSTER and colophon are registered trademarks of Simon & Schuster, Inc.

For information about special discounts for bulk purchases, please contact Simon & Schuster Special Sales at 1-866-506-1949 or business@simonandschuster.com.

The Simon & Schuster Speakers Bureau can bring authors to your live event. For more information or to book an event, contact the Simon & Schuster Speakers Bureau at 1-866-248-3049 or visit our website at www.simonspeakers.com.

*Interior design by Carly Loman*

Manufactured in the United States of America

10  9  8  7  6  5  4  3  2  1

Library of Congress Cataloging-in-Publication Data is available.

ISBN 978-1-6680-2141-5
ISBN 978-1-6680-2143-9 (ebook)

# NOT FOREVER, BUT FOR NOW

## PART 1

# *JOEYS*

**1**

## OTTO MAKES US WATCH A NATURE FILM.

In the nursery upstairs, Otto sits me down to watch a film about Australia. About the wild animals of Australia. "Australia is horrid," he says, "the world's not all Winnie-the-Pooh."

We watch as a tiny baby joey creeps out of the mummy kangaroo's bottom. Its only hope of survival, according to Richard Attenborough's voice, is to climb the mummy's fur coat. The poor joey, just a pink speck of a thing, blind, hairless, clings with wet fingers to the mummy's fur coat.

The Australian Outback spreads out all around them, horrid and inhospitable, just red dust and awful homicidal maniacs and convicts. The outcasts whom England won't suffer.

The twee little joey crawls up the outside of the mummy's belly. Richard Attenborough's voice says she can't help it. She's merely a stupid kangaroo and has no idea the tiny joey is even there, clinging to her. You see, the mummy's forepaws are too short. No longer than the arms of a Tyrannosaurus rex. So even if the mummy gave a tinker's damn she's still fairly useless. As for the daddy kangaroo, Richard Attenborough says, no one has the foggiest notion where he's off to. The daddy kangaroo, no doubt, is having it off with a wallaby or a platypus down by the pub or he's out cottaging. Not that the daddy kangaroo gives a tinker's damn, either. It's just nothing but Australia for a million miles in every direction, and the blasted wind, and the tiny twee joey must go it alone.

It's not so much as a booger stuck to the mummy's fur. She won't miss it.

The squirmy, pink thing must rescue itself. It shall die unless it climbs up to safety in the mummy's pouch. Sticky joey, shivering little joey. In the pouch are milk and warmth and everything to meet the needs of a growing kangaroo. And if the joey falls off, Richard Attenborough says, well . . . it falls off.

Why, the bare, baked dirt of Australia must be fairly littered with helpless joeys that fall off, and the unthinking kangaroos jump smack on them, and the kiwi birds peck at them, but whatever the case the helpless things die straightaway.

Otto takes my hand, and we hold hands as we watch the gooey little thing stuck halfway between being born and growing up. I say that if the joey had any brains at all it would crawl back down, into the mummy's bottom. That would serve her right.

And Otto says, "It can't, Cecil." Otto says, "That's not how Australia works."

And we both watch the thing stuck in the fur like a messy piece of jewelry is all. And we both hate it, the weak puniness of it, and we want to see it dead if it can't muster the effort to save itself. It's just a squirming pink bug it is, stunned by the vast sunstruck Australia all around it. Otto and I hold hands and we want the joey to not die. And we both hate Richard Attenborough, his voice from somewhere off camera, who simply keeps whisper-talking about the cruelty of nature and the Great Barrier Reef and won't lift a finger to just pluck a tiny joey and stuff it in some mummy kangaroo's pouch to save its life.

No, Richard Attenborough, our Richard Attenborough, can't be bothered, Otto says. The same Sir Richard who always looks on while a pride of lions chases down a baby gazelle, and while a pack of hyenas pull a skinny, screaming baby giraffe to shreds. And Otto says the Right Honorable Lord Attenborough could do something. Shoot the lions, say, or clap his hands to scare away the hyenas, but Sir Richard never does anything. He merely lets the penguin chicks freeze to death in the Antarctic, and he lectures while birds of prey eat the freshly hatched sea turtle eggs in the Encantada Islands.

"And he makes us watch," Otto says, "the hairy old bastard."

I protest. Sir Richard is trying to teach us about the animal kingdom.

"No," Otto says, "Richard Attenborough just watches wee things die. He comes back to England, and he cashes the check." Otto says, "He's richer than Mummy."

The reason Richard Attenborough is always off camera is because while the wolves rend to pieces a tiny dik-dik, Otto says Sir Richard is breathlessly rubbing one out.

The joey falls in the dust and lies there like nothing more than a discarded bit of the mummy's wet insides. Stupid dusty thing. It hasn't the faintest idea it's even in Australia. It doesn't know it's alive except for an instant, before a condor eats it or a dingo gulps it down.

Otto says the joey must lie there with its mouth full of red dust while all the convicts and criminals of Australia have a go at it, and Sir Richard Attenborough cheers them on.

Richard Attenborough's whispery voice says, "Look, here a flock of vultures." He whispers, "Let's watch."

Otto says Australia is merely a big, great, dirty machine that makes baby kangaroos to feed to dingoes and baby lambs to feed us.

Before the baby joey can get anywhere in life, Otto turns off the film. He makes his voice hushed, and in a Richard Attenborough pillow-talk voice he says how sometimes the baby joey climbs all the way up to the mother's pouch and finds happiness. The joey finds milk and falls asleep, but then the mummy kangaroo reaches her paw in and snatches him out, she does.

"No," Otto tells me, "it's not like Winnie-the-Pooh, is it?"

If she's in one of her darker moods, Otto says the mummy kangaroo grabs up the joey and flings it onto the ground. Or she flicks it like a lump of nasty snot off her fingers. She looks at it with disgust, all dusty and dying on the ground at her feet because she's got a society club function to attend and she's got dress fittings, and really, she never wanted a joey, and if the daddy kangaroo can't be bothered then why should she?

The mummy is much in demand, these days. She's got such grand goings on.

Truth be told, the mummy kangaroo flicks it away because she hates its puny weakness. The damaged, feeble frailty of the horrid thing. You see, a mummy can always tell when a joey isn't like the other joeys, why it's always going to be a stunted pre-male. And she knows she'll be blamed, that she toilet trained the thing too early or loved it too much. That's what the other kangaroos will whisper. So to protect her social standing, she'd rather see the tiny thing got rid of.

"But then everything's better," Otto says, and smiles. "Because then it gets to go to kangaroo heaven. In kangaroo heaven the baby gets to eat jellies and iced cakes." He says, "Which is ever so nice."

Here, a look gets on Otto's face. It's like when a fire in the stove blazes up, so bright that it makes the rest of the room look dark by comparison, and all the light in the nursery seems to drain into Otto's eyes. A kind of fire, that if it ever got out of the stove it would burn all of us alive.

## 2

NANNY WATCHES ME COME DOWN THE BACK STAIRS FROM THE NURSERY TO the kitchen and says, "Hurt yourself, Master Cecil?" She asks how come I'm favoring one leg, and have I turned my ankle? The nosy old thing asks no end of questions. Listening at keyholes no doubt, trying to sniff me out. And when I ask if I might have my bath early, she pooh-poohs me and says, "I've got the tea things yet to polish. I've no time to bathe you, Master Cecil. You being a young gentleman, I'd guess it's high time you bathed yourself."

And when I insist she asks, "How'd you get all red down there?"

Poor nanny. To hear Mummy on the subject, this nanny can hardly shine a spoon. Mummy says that if we put her out no one else would bother to employ her. And after having filled the tub and taken off my trousers and jumper, nanny has only begun to wash me. As she works the flannel down my back, she says, "Why, you're near to bleeding down there."

I wince at her rough handling, and I tell her what Otto always taught me to say: How at school the bigger boys were ever so mean, and when we turned out for field exercise the boys in the upper forms would sneak up on a smaller boy, a twee, quiet sort of pre-male who's only toeing the line before our games begin. And those brash, older boys would yank down the boy's short pants with all the elastic banding and webbing and all the complicated pads and straps a boy must wear to protect himself during manly sport. And this pants pulling would leave a boy exposed for everyone's amusement, not simply exposed to the other boys but to the headmasters and the laborers who mow the pitch and roll the tennis courts, and it's such a sensation to have even weak sunshine falling on skin that's never felt sunshine, and to be buffeted by laughter, that the task of bowing down to collect all the elastic around your ankles and dragging it up and to refill the net parts and to strap back the stretchy parts, well, the process takes so long that sometimes a really wicked, bigger brute will be so bold as to sidle up and have it off.

Plain as day I tell nanny this, just as Otto rehearsed me.

According to Otto, the truly wicked boys can always suss out the timid, precious sort they can have it off with. Otto even says Christopher Robin and Winnie-the-Pooh have it off. With Piglet and Eeyore. Every chance they get in the Hundred Acre Wood. And Otto ought to know because he went to Sandhurst.

That's how I've come to be so red back there. If nanny must know, the old busybody.

Here, a look gets on nanny's face, the same look as got on Mummy's face when she told us not to look. That was a different day. On the train we were, on some bleak morning that would otherwise be lost to us had Mummy not been looking out the compartment window and said, "Cecil, Otto, boys, you mustn't dare look." So we all looked. There amidst the rushes and gorse a one-eyed tosspot was having it off with a three-legged dog. The three of us, Mummy and Otto and I, all looked with a slack-jawed interest in seeing how the business would finish, only the train continued its chugging along until the bucking of the tosspot and the ecstatic slathering of the dog's long pink tongue were now obscured by a copse of hornbeams. At that Mummy sat back in her seat, took out her diary from her bag, and began to write a letter to the president of the rail line. "Dear sirs," she whispered as she wrote. "You ought to provide more edifying scenery and not be exposing your passengers to the spectacle of an inebriant having it off with a crippled animal." The steel nib of her pen scratched angry little hissing sounds across the page.

Here, just such a look gets on poor old nanny's face, shriveled nanny, red-faced nanny, and she gets up from her knees. She stands next to the bath, drying her old hands on her apron.

But she must bathe me, front and back, I say. Here I laugh and splash her with a handful of tepid water. I threaten to climb out of the tub this very instant and sit bare-bottomed on Mummy's settee in the music room, and nanny will be all day with a toothbrush and peroxide trying to get up the stain.

To this, nanny says, "Master Cecil, I've no business washing you. Why you and Master Otto must weigh twelve stone apiece and stand all of eighteen hands high." The poor thing is boo-hooing now. "With all that hair down there," she boo-hoos, "and a man's arms and legs you've got full use of." She lifts the hem of her apron and mops the tears from her face.

Unmoved, I challenge her to quit us. The cake of soap floats in the water between my hairy knees, and I flick it with my fingers to make the soap spin and bob. My fingers toy with the hair on my chest. My hair is none of her beeswax. Mummy says being hairy is the Welsh in me.

I tell nanny to pack her bags and leave us if she finds her duties too arduous. But she need not ask for a reference. Perish the thought. Mummy would never write her a letter of introduction. If nanny is to be of neither use nor ornament in this household she had better hit the bricks and beg passersby for her daily crust.

Be gone, I tell her, or she'd best soap me up and get on with business. It's common knowledge that many people bathe themselves. I can well learn to bathe myself and zip my own zippers and even cut my own steak if need be.

And that troubled look gets on nanny's face, and her voice falls to a whisper when she asks, "Is someone hurting you, Master Cecil?"

By now the water's gone quite pink with blood, and I splash her with pink water and tell her no, and call her an old sow for good measure.

Otto says we once had a nanny who did it with her mouth. I don't remember, and I shouldn't want that now. Not from this nanny, at least.

The smell of silver polish on her, the petrol smell is sunk into the wrinkles of her face and hands. Mummy won't venture within an arm's length of the old girl, but Mummy would never say as much.

No, Mummy would call me out here, for being so awful, but nanny is only an old char lady. No one would miss her. No one else will have her, and if I'm heartless it suits her right for spying at keyholes. And it will make things easier if she hates me, whenever Otto decrees we have to do her in.

**3**

OTTO SAYS, "NO ONE IN HELL SUFFERS MORE THAN THE DEVIL." HE SAYS IT IN his Richard Attenborough voice. Today is horrid and drippy, one of those days when the sun starts to set from the moment it's up. Today we must need be bury the dead yard boy.

You see, Otto and the garden boy were great friends. Until the yard boy got his throat cut. The most terrible look had got on his yard-boy face, Otto told me. Very much like the look that got on Mummy's face when she found the nanny who did it with her mouth at the foot of the back stairs, all in a heap at the foot of the stairs. "Her spine had shattered something awful," Otto said. "Her head twisted all around on her neck." He said, "Like a chicken."

Otto says, "Like an Alfred Hitchcock, this is." Ghastly, just ghastly. Mummy makes us go to see him buried. A boy of no importance, like that. The boy hired to tend the garden, that's all he was.

We pay our respects as near as we know how. His people burn a horrid cloud of incense, and we're not high church. They set out a great lot of food in the church basement, and Otto takes my hand and tells me we have to eat first. Just awful stuff. Mince tarts and gooseberry trifle, and Otto gobbles down great heaps of the foul stuff. Custard topped with dried currants. Nasty stuff. Sweetbreads poached in milk. Pickled duck eggs.

At the casket, the boy's people stand aside. Country people, cowed to see us young gentlemen paying such respects to their dead son. Brute that he was. A brooding, brutish lout was all.

Otto can hardly speak for belching. Gooseberries have never agreed with him. We hold hands, we two, and look down on the yard boy in his casket. A lot of country flowers are tucked in around his dead body, weeds really, and his hands are folded across his chest, wrapped all around with rosary beads.

His people seemed to care a great deal about him once he was dead. A rough, wicked boy like that. Mummy gave them one of Otto's old suits, a suit of clothes Otto never wore, but still it belonged to Otto and he didn't want it buried in the churchyard on some dead yard boy. Some rotting-away lad. So Otto put up the biggest fuss.

You see, the yard boy had taught Otto how to play Winnie-the-Pooh, and they'd made their secret clubhouse on a soiled army cot in the potting shed. There with all the pruning hooks and trugs.

A boy of his low station, he'd asked how we made our fortune. Of all the gall. Otto told him the dinosaurs had gone extinct because the Hudson's Bay Company gave them blankets infected with smallpox, and the cheeky boy believed it. Otto told him that Mummy's Christian name was Urethra, and he swallowed that, too. Nonetheless, Otto tagged along after him in wet weather and fair. A brute like that, with no education, always in his shirtsleeves and baggy trousers. Strutting around always smoking his pipe as if he owned our garden.

Otto only soured on him when the garden boy talked to me. Asked me, he did, would I like to learn to play Winnie-the-Pooh? The yard boy gave Otto a wink, and said that Otto was awfully good at having it off, and that he'd taken a lot of snaps and sent them around, the yard boy had. And Otto could go into the trade if he so chose. Pots and pots of ready money could be made in letting a lot of strangers have a go, but Otto failed to see this proposal as a compliment. You see, Otto wanted to be the Richard Attenborough and speak in a hushed voice from behind the camera, and not be the spotted fawn dragged screaming from the tall veldt grasses.

It's after that Otto wouldn't give the yard boy the time of day. And it's after that Otto found the boy dead.

A yard boy on his way up, Mummy had called him. A credit to the Empire, he was. With a fine head on his shoulders. A boy no one expected would get his throat slashed in our potting shed by a person or persons unknown. The constable held an inquest, but nothing came of it. The boy makes quite a picture in his casket, all done up in Otto's old suit of clothes. The garden boy had great bushy eyebrows, but someone had put pomade on them to make them lie flat. On his lip, just the fuzz of the faintest blond mustache.

Otto, sad-eyed Otto, frowny-faced Otto, looks into the casket and says, "You think someone is going to be Pericles or Agamemnon, and then he's not." Otto gazes down upon the garden boy with his garden-boy chin tucked down and his collar pulled up to hide the stitches. A face as perfect as a Greek bust in a museum, and the boy's hair curling against the pillow like a victory wreath of blond oak leaves.

Otto says that as soon as people fall in love they're already looking for a reason to hate each other. Because everyone you love is just another fragile pink joey, and cancer will eat them, or wolves, so no matter how much you hurt you'll need to still look down at their dead body someday. On that day, your only comfort will be to say, "At least I won't have to smell your horrid armpits anymore." Or, "Thank goodness your ugly feet died with you."

A ready-made suit it was. Of terrible cut and just awful, still Mummy had no business to give it away to a dead boy who'd pruned the tree peonies all wrong so they didn't flower after that.

Otto tells me, "When you think it's love . . ." He says, "Often, you just want to have it off with their stylish eyeglasses or their clever haircut." He uses his hushed Richard Attenborough pillow-talk voice.

And here, here it is that one crystalline tear falls from Otto's eye. It dots a dark, wet spot on the boy's white shirt. At the sight of that Otto is sick. First a mouthful, and then a bellyful of regurgitated offal and bile spill out all over the boy. The way a mother bird feeds her babies. Otto spews gooseberries and custard sick, all into the open casket. All over the flowers and the yard boy's dead face, mincemeat and tripe. Oh, just buckets. Until the casket is almost brimming. Oh, the stink of it. Sweetbreads, too.

# 4

OTTO IS ALWAYS SO CLEVER. HE TELLS ME SO ALL THE TIME. HE'S ALWAYS writing letters and getting letters from interesting people. Otto says, "If you're Christopher Robin, then I'm Christopher Wren."

All interesting sorts of people write to Otto. His pen pals are people who've pulled off home invasions and pistol-whipped whole families and disposed of them in shallow graves. They're hammer murderers, pitchfork killers. Of course they're all incarcerated in prisons or committed to asylums for the incurably insane, but they're ever so lonely, and Otto writes to them, and they write back. Oh, just reams and reams. Really interesting letters about how they've used a machete to take apart someone by the arms and legs and put a torso into a suitcase and then got pinched trying to check their bags through at Heathrow. Just fascinating things.

Otto eggs them on, writing back that he's madly in love with them, and they write back with all the exciting ideas they have for when they get out. How they're going to take a guard hostage and shoot him with his own service weapon and dash across the countryside until they find Otto and do the worst they can imagine to him. Otto writes back that they should stop sending such sordid abuse, but his heart's not in it. He's only telling them no so they'll try harder. They write back with even naughtier ideas, and the letters fly until everyone is very stirred up.

Otto writes, *I really can't fathom that I'm in touch with the Buckinghamshire Hatchet Killer, and that you're really you* . . . And the pen pals draw all sorts of pictures of the things they'd do to him with ropes and broom handles. He reads these aloud and we have a giggle.

Other times, Otto asks me to read the best letters to him in a hushed Richard Attenborough voice while he has it off. Both of us hoping at any moment that an escaped criminal or convict will come bursting through the nursery door. Most times it's only old nanny. Sniffing at the keyhole, she says, "Master Cecil? Master Otto, what reeks in there?"

Otto asked this nanny, the shriveled nanny, would she shave me all over, my whole body, to make me look more like a Page Three Girl? Otto takes pics and sends these to the criminals and convicts. All sorts of naughty poses, he puts me through, and these pics are a massive hit, and we get even more brilliant letters, and it's a lark to know that armies of stirred-up serial killers are having it off to our pictures and know our address. And we have a giggle over the fact that Mummy hasn't the slightest notion that we're a lodestone for every escaped homicidal lunatic, our house is, and any prison break could release hordes of escaped sex killers who'd descend on our little family in a heartbeat.

"Cecil," Otto says, "you know we're playing with fire, don't you?"

He's very bright that way. Otto sighs over the most recent letter from a cannibal serving a life sentence, and he says, "Cecil, do you know that it takes a truly, genuinely demented person to write an inspired love letter?" The cannibal carries on and on about how he's going to chop Otto to bite-sized morsels. Bone him like a kipper, he will, and guzzle his blue blood. Such an exciting prospect!

These horrible criminals and lunatics, they're the jackals and sharks while Otto is the silvery little minnow. "Should they ever have the chance," he says, "they'd gobble me up in one bite."

Otto shows me the newspaper pictures he collects of his pen pals. We two sit cross-legged beside the nursery stove and moon over the lot of them. Nightmares of phrenology they look to be, with cobblestone brows and lantern jaws. The faces of cinema monsters sprouting cauliflower ears, to boot. Teeth as tilted and mossy as tombstones in an ancient churchyard. Sniff these letters, we do. Paper gives off such a stench, a quality that elevates the crudest page above the most eloquent of emails. We inhale the heady reek of stale sweat and drool. The undercurrent of damp concrete and rank urine.

Among Otto's favorites is a great brute named Felix. Felix, a computational wiz besides whom Turing looks a moron. Brilliant Felix, panting Felix. He's flushed ever-so-many victims down the toilet of his bedsit, and now he aches to have a go at us. He writes that our pics have put terrible mileage on his wanking hand!

Otto commands me to take a letter, and I sit ready to write as he speaks.

"Dear Felix," Otto dictates. "Thank you for your most recent snap of your fully exposed private bits. I'd expected a bit more. To judge from your photo in the *Times* and the *Guardian,* you're a brute overall. Perhaps that's the reason your bits look so small. Or perhaps you have an endocrine disorder. You might have some tests run . . ." Here Otto stops.

I ask if he wants to watch the wee dik-dik get shredded and have a go. And he says, "No."

As of late he's been in a muddle. You see, Mummy and Otto have locked horns. Mummy keeps pushing him to leave the nest and pull his weight. She fears he's going to sink us, if all he does is have it off all day and watch Richard Attenborough animal snuff films until the nursery reeks. She's issued the ultimatum that either he goes to university or he enters into the family firm. She's being so hateful, Mummy is, and says she's going to stop his allowance.

A look gets on Otto's face like the time he got his hair cut, and complained that his head was too cold, and Mummy said, "Just take care not to get chilblains." And Otto laughed a merry laugh because he heard her say *chilled brains.* And we were all so jolly back then, chuckling away, with Daddy and Daisybelle, before the nanny who did it with her mouth and before the butchered yard boy. Before it all, life was nothing but having it off and having a go. Daisybelle frolicking in the back garden. Daisybelle, the very model of the ideal Boston terrier. Daisybelle, a lovely one-stone dog with the spirit of an animal ten times her size. Just one twitch of an old smile gets on Otto's face, but then it's gone.

Here I ask if Otto wants to play Winnie-the-Pooh, and this time he can be the honey pot. And he says, "No."

I ask if he wants to do the shriveled nanny in. We could garrote her and make it look like an accident. And Otto shakes his head, no, and this worries me.

There's really nothing left to us. Nothing we enjoy so much.

Here, Otto continues, "Dear Felix . . ." He asks, "Where were we?"

I read what's written.

And he dictates, "Felix, as for your heated threats to go off your medications and to break out and stove my head in with a cobblestone while you have it off, and to have another go on my dead body, well, we both know that's a load of rubbish." Otto says, "Because you're a moron and a brutish ruffian with cretinous, stunted private bits, and you'll never escape anywhere, much less find my comfortable home at 1057 Briar Hill Lane in Buckinghamshire and have a go on my corpse." Otto says, "So good-bye and sod off, you bloody pervert."

On an envelope, Otto writes the address for the Buckinghamshire Asylum for the Homicidally Insane.

In a big, bold hand, I write Mummy's name at the bottom of the letter.

This gives Otto a smile.

We fold the page around a pinch of my shaved-off Welsh hair, seal the thing, and rush to make the afternoon post.

# 5

ALL I RECOLLECT OF DADDY IS ONE TIME. HE HAD BEEN EMPLOYED BY THE government then, by Scotland Yard, where his job was to sit on a computer all day and pretend to be a Christopher Robin sort of boy. A really winning boy, a truly ripping boy.

This was after Daddy had fallen out of Grandfather's good graces. Not to get too far out ahead of myself, but Daddy had muffed the Princess Di Job, hadn't he? And he'd failed to drop Building Seven of the World Trade Center. You see our family does such things. Someone must. And since our family firm had no further use for him, poor Daddy, Grandfather had pulled some strings and secured him a position at Scotland Yard. And even that light duty had swamped the man.

According to Daddy, ever-so-many boys running around the internet are actually old toffee-nosed duffers looking to have a go with tykes, and Daddy's mission at Scotland Yard was to catch them at it. The nonces of England won't suffer. Otto says once the Crown pinches them, they all have to go to Australia and have it off with the convicts there in the dust and the heat.

Daddy saw this mission as a calling. He wouldn't just stand aside and whisper in a pillow-talk voice while predators pick apart their prey. No, Daddy wanted to save the little spotted fawns.

At issue was this other detective. The other Scotland Yard detective was having a massive success as a fake schoolboy, and he'd rather fished the oceans dry. So Daddy came to Otto and asked him how to be a better little boy. More winning and popular. Here, Otto showed him, and told him.

To give credit where it's due, brilliant Felix, predatory Felix provided invaluable advice on all matters computational. Message boards and whatnot.

Point of fact, Daddy feared his position had become so precarious that he faced being dismissed. He claimed that we stood to lose our lovely home and lose our staff, and be compelled to relocate to a council estate or an attached house, and Mummy would have to go on the National Health, and we could bid our governess and tutor good-bye, not to mention the spotted pony we kept at the bottom of the garden.

It wasn't really cricket that Daddy's fake little boy didn't warrant an online hello, while the fake little boy of some other Scotland Yard detective, he roped in just oodles of real-life cabinet ministers and solicitors who were panting to pop by with condoms and beer and have a go.

Otto sat Daddy down and told him the National Geographic facts of life. That everyone is disgusted by spindly weakness. And when they see a twee, fey little pre-male with his head in the clouds they must run him down. They all must have a go at him and have it off before they tear the boy apart. And that's the Law of the Jungle. Otto says that certain boys, the crippled, fey, feeble little boys, they go looking for hungry grizzly bears and mountain lions who'll do them in. A sort of mercy killing, it is. Such boys court the predator animals who linger in chat rooms and on something common people call social media, where they message back and forth with other grown-ups like Daddy who pretend to be tykes. And then the predator animals show up at your family's flat with beer and condoms and want to have a go.

Otto advised Daddy, "Tell the chat rooms that you're damaged in some small way. You're not like regular boys." Otto said, "If you're not a killer yourself, they'll want to kill you. They'll crave killing you, even if it means motoring all the way from Calais through the Chunnel and hunting you down in bloody Buckinghamshire."

Otto said, "Be the one they want to kill most."

It doesn't matter so much who does what. The predators must prey. The prey must be predated. They only wish to be preyed upon by someone who'll do the job properly.

Otto lectured Daddy that online people don't want a great, hale fellow well met. They don't want healthy rough-and-tumble footballers. It's like in Richard Attenborough, where cheetahs look for the crippled Tiny Tim to cut from the herd.

You see, Otto's very clever that way.

"All the frail, crippled, sensitive animals that cry often and wet the bed," Otto said, "the other hearty, apple-cheeked animals with ambition and pluck, those self-starting animals want the frail ones dead."

All the fey, twee, wee little flawed things.

The mincing, lisping, scrawny, pigeon-chested things.

"Once the breakable things are broken," Otto said, "then everyone can relax."

It's all in Darwin, he said. Otto told Daddy that any boy who truly wants to be destroyed must promise he'll do human toilet. And that he'll do rusty trombone and dirty Sanchez, whatever those things are. What matters is that a predator's very faint of heart so the prey must debase himself to put the predator at ease. Otto said, "No one is as needy as a predator." This is all from the National Geographic Society.

Here, Otto said the strangest thing. He said, "All whores take to hell every man they've had inside them, they do." He said, "That's why Satan makes whores, Daddy."

At the time, Otto was smaller than I am now. And such wisdom!

And here, a look got on Daddy's face, like when we'd been motoring to the strand for a holiday and a woman we didn't know from Adam had thrown herself across the bonnet of Daddy's Bentley. At a red traffic light, it had been. With her face mashed up against the outside of our windscreen, the woman had looked at Mummy. The face had shrieked, "James, you never told me you had a wife and child." All shrill. And from the backseat Otto had corrected her, saying, "Two children." And this strange woman, God only knows what she'd been banging on about. She'd yelled, "James! You promised." Weeping.

Straightaway, Daddy took Otto's advice. Back in those glory days, a steady stream of duffers and punters were always popping by the house, and when Daddy was at home he'd pinch them. When Daddy and Mummy were away, Otto would need be get on with it. Otto felt ever so happy to be useful. Even if the people who popped around only had in mind to have a go and have it off. Otto felt desired, really deeply desired. The way a drooling puma desires a baby goat. And how the flocks of carrion birds will circle for hours waiting for their turn to strip the bones. Otto felt special. And what he no longer felt was alone.

Daddy took Otto's advice and rose in the ranks to become the best fake boy at Scotland Yard. He had had the lunatic woman pinched and put away, where Otto can only write to her.

Within a month, Daddy had Pakistani grooming gangs waiting in long queues around the block to have a go and get pinched. Broken-down duffers, out-of-repair punters. And he had predators flying in on private jets from Dubai, and Daddy was reeling in all sorts of big fish. And after that Daddy was gone.

All I can recall of Daddy are the veins in his forehead. Veins you could see, on either side of his forehead. And how when he thought his thoughts the veins would twitch. They'd pulse like little lightning bolts under his skin. Those veins would bulge or jerk sideways, then disappear back into his brains. Fleshy and awful.

No one's ever asked how that insane woman had known Daddy's Christian name.

# 6

ON CHRISTMAS EVE, SOGGY CHRISTMAS, SOPPY CHRISTMAS, WE GRAB DEAR old Grandfather by both hands and drag him to a chair by the fire. With wind slanting the rain sideways, raindrops running down the front windows, we squeal. "Tell us about Elvis Presley!" And, "Tell us, again, about London."

We sit at Grandfather's feet to gaze over the great hillside of his knees, his bearded face and red nose up above us. On the telly, Dorothy sings "Somewhere Over a Rainbow." Our favorite Christmas song. His smoking jacket belted across his belly, Grandfather closes his eyes to remember: "The twenty-second of June 1969," he says. After a beat, "Cadogan Lane."

We call out, "London!"

He recites by heart the parts we hear by heart.

In his day, Grandfather was the spry young man. He tells how he'd itsy-bitsy-spidered his way up a downspout. Climbed handhold by toehold up some brick wall to reach a dormer window on a roof. As a cat burglar, no one could touch him. Spidering in the half-light, he'd climbed to a window he'd never fit through nowadays. In those bygone times he jimmied the window. Tied to his belt, a string dangled, the string trailing down to the mews, to a valise on the sidewalk, a valise he could later drop off a bridge into the darkest still water of the Thames, if need be.

From inside the window the smell of cigarette smoke hit him. That younger him who'd yet to become anyone's grandfather. In the dark, the bright end of a cigarette tapped ash into a sink bolted to one wall. The cigarette traced a line to where it flared, sucked bright, to reveal a blue-veined hand, twitching like a buzzing tube of neon. A face as smooth as burlap painted white. A head of bootblacked hair. Two eyes glittering, as if from the bottom of two dirty ashtrays.

That mouth like nothing so much as somebody smeared red lipstick round the pucker of a very pretty, very dainty pink bunghole. The skin tented over the cartilage of her crone's nose.

Grandfather stepped his whole skinny self in through the window and stood on the tile. He looked at that skeleton person perched on the toilet with one skeleton leg crossed over the other at the knee. Wearing the ghost of a white nightgown, silvery, sagging empty for the most part. Hunchbacked, shoulders slumped, she looked back at him like he was Christmas morning. Like she'd waited her whole life for him to crawl in through her window.

Well past halfway through that night of 22 June 1969, young Grandfather touched two fingers of his Grandfather hand to his forehead by way of a hello.

That young Grandfather, skinny Grandfather from before our mama was even a dream, it crossed his mind that Dorothy had grown into the Wicked Witch. The cigarette tapped ash into the sink. And it crossed his mind how every Dorothy turns into the Wicked Witch. In effect, Dorothy was always killing herself. And he pulled the string, where it trailed out the window, looping the string around one hand, to lift the little valise up from the sidewalk.

Inside our TV the poppies put everyone to sleep. The turpentine smell of our Christmas tree bleeding to death. A log popped in the fireplace. The rain.

We tug at Grandfather's sticky fingers. Sniff the pitch on his hands. His fingers gummy with sap from putting up the tree, busting the blisters of sap that bubble under the skin of the tree trunk. We smell the pitch handled from Christmas tree trunk to Grandfather to us, and we ask, "Did you do Princess Diana?" Another London story, only in Paris.

Our own fingers still sticky from having it off.

And Grandfather ho-ho-hos at our question and says, "Your own sweet Mummy," he says, "it's she who eventually did the Lady Di Job."

Here at this point in the story, here he gets on his Grandfather face a look, such a look, the same look as got on the one governess's face when she read aloud Otto's poem and started to cry, crying so hard she had to be led out of the room, and we'd had a new governess for what was left of that year. Maybe the goiter governess. Grandfather makes a face like something hurts. A face that feels pain, and his voice goes quiet, the way a fire sounds so quiet until it's grown out of control.

The same as the time we drove past a front yard. Somebody's front yard. A house decorated with blow-up Santa Clauses and the Holy Family and Three Kings, only unplugged so the blowers weren't blowing, and the fabric of everyone was asleep. Frosty and the shepherds were resting, heaped and layered across the green grass with their faces looking up at the sky, and their hands and sandaled feet just limp and flat on the ground. The long hair of the Three Kings, lank and spread on the grass. And looking as we drove past, Grandfather had nodded at the peaceful sight and said, "Otto, Cecil, look."

He'd told us, "That's what Kent State looked like." He jerked his head for us to look and said, "That's how Jonestown looked." And it's family moments such as those that form the core of our Christmas tradition.

More of our Grandfather's work. The family trade.

Those misdeeds that need doing. The tasks that proved so beyond Daddy.

People say, some people, that we live nothing after the age of, say, seven. After that we only relive the first time we fell in love. The first time we felt left behind. Or our first dog getting her front paw mangled in the chain of the chauffeur's motorcycle and dragging along until she's half rubbed to mess against the blacktop and still not dying after getting her home, not until we put her in bed, the half of her still alive, and tucked her in under the covers with her head on a pillow, and even when she was all dead we left her there, sweet Daisybelle, lovely Daisybelle, and not even Mummy made a peep about the stuck-together sheets and how the mattress underneath would be good for nothing more than hauling to the curb.

That woman, the woman on the 22 June 1969 toilet, yellow showed on her fingers when she took the cigarette to her mouth. There, she asked, "Is it Franky? Did Franky send you?" She laughed a slow-motion face, a laugh that ended up a cough before she shrugged, shrugged her boney shoulders and said, "I guess if the Chairman of the Board wants you dead, who am I to argue?"

In his story, young Grandfather saw the way she must see him. His reflection in the mirror over the sink showed just the dark Grandfather shape of him outlined against the half-light of the window. The London, outside. She wasn't his first, but she was his near-biggest to date back then. His shape in the mirror grew.

Here, a look gets on Grandfather's face like when he stepped through Judy Garland's 22 June 1969 window. Judy Garland had asked, "So it's not Sinatra?" She'd asked, "Well, then who the fuck wants me dead?"

And Grandfather, skinny Grandfather, young Grandfather had asked, "Do you know what $(C_2H_4)_n$ is?" He'd opened his valise and taken out his signature enema bag.

Judy Garland had tapped the ash off her cigarette into the sink. She'd shrugged. "Should I?"

Young Grandfather had unpacked the phenobarbital and champagne from his valise. He'd asked, "Are you familiar with $(C_2H_4)$n?"

Judy Garland had asked, "Can you bother to explain it?"

Young Grandfather had asked, "How much time do you have?"

And Judy Garland had pointed with the two fingers holding her cigarette, had pointed at the enema bag, and asked, "You tell me how much time I've got."

# 7

**HERE WE MUST GO BACKWARD FOR A BIT. DADDY HAD ONLY JUST VANISHED,** so Mummy had to play breadwinner and venture off to Paris to complete the Lady Di Job, and Seattle to do the Kurt Cobain Job. You see, Otto would stand by the nursery window all day and watch for Daddy's return, and when Daddy was not forthcoming Otto would itsy-bitsy-spider down the ivy at night and toddle over by the village pub for a look. In case Daddy might be tipping a pint with that mess of mugs and tossers.

The gang of them, those snockered yobs and bullies, they'd get Otto up on the bar, and him only just out of nappies. They'd slip off his jumper and paste postage stamps on his wee nipples so to make him not starkers, and pull off his trousers. The louts. Once Otto was down to his linen, they'd bid him parade up and down the bar while they cheered lustily and pounded their hands together and stamped their boots. Him being a fine young gentleman, it made for ready sport. They'd ask, did he know any songs? "Do you know to sing any songs, Master Otto?" they'd ask.

Back then the only song Otto could sing was some Carmen Miranda. That "Chica, Chica, Boom, Chic" song by Carmen Miranda. And here he was all of knee-high singing and high-stepping up and down the Crested Eagle for the pleasure of a herd of cranks and bog men. Singing "Chica, Chica, Boom, Chic," he was. The Crested Eagle being our public house, hereabouts. Where all Otto wanted was to be told he was a good boy. All he wanted was to be petted and praised by jolly, cheering men. And if "Chica, Chica, Boom, Chic" didn't do the trick he'd learn to wink one eye in the saucy style of Carmen Miranda and to work his tiny shoulders and cut his eyes from side to side.

You see, to Otto's young mind he'd made a great success.

All the while Mummy was off to Australia to do the Michael Hutchence Job.

It was hard work, it was. Every night down at the Crested Eagle Otto had to bring a bit more to his performance. To wear Mummy's lipstick, say, or shake his tiny chest as if to make the postage stamps fall off. He was high-stepping between the pints in a pair of Mummy's high heels, all this effort expended just to rope in the attention of slobbering drunkards who'd grab at his thin ankles and sing along to the "Chica, Chica, Boom, Chic" parts while they smoked their ciggies. It was a merry pastime to watch the boy scion of a great county family make such a shameless display of himself.

As for Otto, he saw this as love. He saw getting set up on the bar by the spotted hands of the working class as great, grand affection. Every night he was all the louder singing "Chica, Chica, Boom, Chic." Every day Daddy never came home. But every night Otto could swing by the pub and enter by the alley door and do his makeup in the toilet and be up on the bar, by now with some bananas balanced atop his head, by now high-kicking between pints and ashtrays, a bit later with bananas and an apple on his head like the heroic boy from William Tell, the boy the man tries to shoot with arrows to lay the foundation for the Swiss Confederacy. And Otto was a great sensation and a brilliant success, he was, all three stone of him blowing kisses and shimmying his wee hips, singing "Chica, Chica, Boom, Chic" until that one night.

That one night our nanny popped round to put a stop to Otto's twee bit of happiness. She'd found his half of the crib empty. She'd been frantic. Searching high and low, she'd been. Our nanny came frantic-like stumbling into the Crested Eagle saying how the young master had been kidnapped. Panicked nanny, appalled nanny. And here was Otto leading a rousing chorus of proles and thugs singing "Chica, Chica, Boom, Chic." A grand thunder of drunken voices.

Bang inside the pub door not two steps, and nanny put a stop to Otto's stardom. "Master Otto," she shouted, she did. "Climb down from there, you wicked, filthy imp!" Addressing the tossers, she shouted,

"You're all wicked, the all of you are. To treat a wee lad like a harlot for your own amusement!"

Seeing as how I was at home in diapers at the time, this scene comes secondhand through Otto.

The nanny, that same awful nanny who'd later tumble down the stairs and snap her neck, she slapped the paint off Otto's little face and yanked down his linen and paddled his bare bottom, right there in the Crested Eagle. The pub fell to silence as Otto wailed. The nanny ripped off his postage stamps as he blubbed in front of the entire silent village, and she stuffed him back inside his clothes and got him home and to bed. This being the nanny, Otto says, who did it with her mouth. This went on while Mummy was away on the Chris Farley Job or the John Denver Job, and when she was home she had to look after the tenants' well-being, didn't she? Busy Mummy.

For the longest time that nanny slept in the nursery. If Otto so much as put one banana on his head she gave him what for. It's within the realm of possibility she did it to Otto with her mouth out of some misguided good intention. To make a real boy of him, or some such. But the lessons never took, so when Mummy was home—on one of her few returns—and she caught Otto high-stepping with a pineapple, it was agreed by all that he should attend Sandhurst. Not that boarding at Sandhurst did him much good, not with a small regiment of older boys always keen to have it off.

Before this story goes another step forward you ought to know that "Chica, Chica, Boom, Chic" passes for the best part of Otto's life, such as it was. A happiness he shall never see again. And he's never since put so much as a grape on his head.

People say, some people, that we live nothing after the age of, say, three. After that we only relive the first time we danced near naked atop a pub bar. Or the first time our nanny paddled our bare buttocks under the gaze of illiterate yeomen and barmaids. So before you pass judgment, please know that Otto had never had an easy go of it.

At Sandhurst Otto found himself just another thumb-sucking joey cast down in the red dust. Behind stairs he was very popular. If not forever, then for now. An ever-diminishing margin of returns, so be it. And with that he just had to soldier on, didn't he?

You see, nice as it feels, we won't any of us be that near-naked infant strutting up and down some public house forever.

Wicked or not, Otto's never had a soft option.

# 8

OTTO GOES TO THE CUPBOARD IN THE NURSERY AND OPENS A DOOR AND digs out something from underneath the folded underpants. He shakes the thing, and it rattles. Pills in a pill bottle. The name on the bottle is a governess we had, oh, just governesses and governesses back.

Otto had found a pill wedged between the cushions of Mummy's settee so he had a fair idea there were others to be had. Tongues had already wagged, after Otto was sick at the funeral. Mummy was having a beastly time keeping staff, so when she'd hired our most recent governess, Mummy had been compelled to scrape the bottom of the barrel.

Otto went into this new governess's room and was idly sorting through her knickers when he came across the most frightful needles. Hypodermic needles. And pills. And it was good fortune he did.

Otto asks, "Do you know Mummy's superpower?"

I tell him no. I say my bleeding has stopped so he can have a fresh go.

Here, Otto goes out the nursery door to the stairway landing. He leans over the handrail and shakes the bottle. The pills rattle. The rattle sounds vast and echoes on the stairs. He shakes the bottle again and whispers, "Hush, Cecil. It can wait."

A look gets on his face like when I found the nanny all tangled at the foot of the back stairs. The nanny who did it with her mouth, you know. When she looked up at me standing on the top step, her eyes looked, oh, horridly glassy like a doll's eyes, and she said, "Master Cecil, please help me." Her arms and legs were in a terrible state, all over blood with the shattered ends of her long bones stuck out every which way. But already Otto was kneeling next to nanny's head. Half of her was on her back and half on her front, that's how knackered her spine was.

Otto lifted her head from the kitchen floor. Cradling her head in his arms, he said, "Poor, poor nanny."

And it didn't hurt, what he did, or she'd have cried out, wouldn't she? But Otto cradled her head and held it close to his chest. The day was dripping wet, and nothing had gone on. And as if he were wresting a football from a much bigger boy on the pitch at Sandhurst, Otto jerked his entire body to one side. Oh, the bones in nanny's neck made a most awful racket.

It was rather like when the chauffeur put our Bentley up on jacks. The chauffeur said we two boys could stand by and watch as he crawled under to tinker with some component with only his legs sticking out from beneath the car. In the garage, it was. The chauffeur asked Otto to hand him a spanner out the tool box, and instead Otto kicked away a jack. The full weight of the Bentley tumbled off the remaining jacks and crashed down, coming to rest on the chauffeur. So much so that his legs kicked and thrashed something awful. To help sort things out, Otto undid the chauffeur's belt and took down his trousers and tried to have a go despite the violently kicking legs, and Otto could hardly have it off before the weight of the Bentley made the chauffeur's skull give the most horrid pop.

That's the sound nanny's neck made. That pop. And the look that got on Otto's face then is the look that gets on his face now as he shakes the bottle of pills at the top of the hall stairs.

The rattle echoes in the vast front hall. Presently a voice calls up, "Do my ears deceive me?" It's Mummy's voice. "Do I hear OxyNorms?"

Otto leans farther over the rail and shakes the bottle once more.

From closer, as her footsteps ascend the stairs, Mummy says, "Twenty milligram size, unless I'm mistaken."

Otto shakes the bottle. The pills rattle. We're all the way at the top of the house.

From the sound of her voice, Mummy must be to the third floor by now, calling up, "And don't tell me. Let me guess." She says, "There are thirty-seven capsules."

Otto shakes the bottle.

"No!" she calls up, closer. "There are thirty-nine in the bottle."

Otto throws me a smile and shouts out, "Clever girl! Such a clever old girl!"

That's Mummy's superpower. She arrives on the top landing and her greedy hands snatch the bottle from Otto. Her eyes scour the label. For the expiration date, no doubt. And she says, "These are not suitable for little boys." She twists the cap off and holds the open bottle to her nose and sniffs. And Mummy smiles. "Wicked, wicked boy," she says to Otto, "for not telling Mummy you had such things."

Without casting her eyes my way, she says, "Cecil, would you go down to the kitchen, please?"

Otto says, "Ask nanny to shave you again. You're getting somewhat prickly." The pills are a peace offering. These pills are clearly a bribe so that Mummy shouldn't make Otto leave the nest. I should very much like Otto to live at home, and perhaps assume a role in the family firm. If Otto was sent away, well, then I would be the poor soul who had to find Mummy's veins for her.

Otto and Mummy are thick as thieves as I take my leave.

In the kitchen, the shriveled nanny sets aside her darning egg. She draws a bath and works the razor against the leather strop. She foams the shaving soap in the mug like Daddy used to do. None too happy, she undresses me and tests the bathwater with her elbow as I stand by, shivering. Anymore, she can hardly reach my collar button.

I ask after cook.

As she shaves me in my bath, my arms and legs, all my prickly Welsh hair, nanny says, "Cook's calling on the shops to collect our supper." She says the tradesmen have a mind to no longer call at this house. "Master Cecil, tongues are wagging," nanny says. She says a lot of rot. The townsfolk are a superstitious lot. But that's to be expected. They're Catholics.

"It's just all the misfortune," says nanny. She means the yard boy getting himself butchered, and the one nanny twisting her neck on the stairs, and the chauffeur getting his head knackered under our Bentley. "Folks see you with the new chauffeur, still driving that car," says nanny, "and they cross themselves, they do." She looks a bit knocked back.

What a bunch of skint mugs and gits, townsfolk are. I tell nanny that every household of quality has its own share of governesses who pitch out of windows, like our last one did. And footmen who get themselves set on fire while tending a stove. And parlor floor maids, like ours, who fall facedown in a tureen of leek consommé and drown themselves. That's how Australia works, I say. I splash nanny with some tepid water and tell her it's all in Darwin.

Silly nanny, poor nanny, she says, "But Master Cecil, there's more to it, innit?" In a whisper she says, "It's spooks, innit?"

Mummy says servants aren't paid to have feelings. There's no hurting them. They're simply not clever enough to be hurt. Mummy says servants are servants because they're dull from birth. That's how come they're always getting themselves gobsmacked by toppling-over bookcases, and twacked under falling chandeliers in the morning room.

Still, nanny being nanny, she's having no part of it. She draws Daddy's razor up the inside of my leg, saying, "Word is, around the whole of the county," says nanny, "that this house is haunted, Master Cecil."

It strikes me as somewhat tiresome and threadbare, the idea of ghosts. A gaggle of old slags are jumping at the sight of their own collective shadow. That's how come tradesmen won't stop around. It's how come cook must fetch our supper. A look gets on nanny's face like when she found the old butler twacked by the chandelier. At the time Mummy took Otto and me aside. Mummy told us that nanny might be going mad. Mummy said that some people have a second childhood.

And without rancor in his voice, Otto, sensible Otto, practical Otto, looked down on the old butler and said, "Only the ones who had a first childhood."

Haunted. Our house is haunted. I suppose it is, but only by Otto.

# 9

TRY AS I MIGHT TO CLARIFY THE GOVERNESS SITUATION TO DATE, IT REMAINS a bit of a mixed bag. They rather run together in one's mind. Aside from the pill-popping, scag-shooting governess, we've employed a wide range. These include the aforementioned one with the goiter, a great goiter in the shape of a red cabbage on one side of her neck. During that stint, Mummy made scant visits to the nursery, so put off was she by the sight of that goiter. Not that any successive governess fared any better, I suppose. We'd suffered the one with halitosis, hadn't we? She brings to mind the governess afflicted with albinism. A marvel she looked, if one could get past the red eyes of her. And somewhere in my memory we'd taken on one who wore a monocle. A great stork of a person with a stork's legs and a stork's long neck, she was, with her monocle always slung on a long chain around her neck. Some became quite chummy with Daddy. Always sharing a slap and a tickle with him in back hallways or on the filthy army cot in the potting shed. Mummy had only to catch wind, and the governess in question would find herself served a bad oyster or an unwashed stalk of asparagus and she'd expire in the throes of some great gastric distress. More than a few were sniffed out and met their end due to Mummy serving them something undercooked or out of season. Otto tells me of a governess who retched blood all over the music-room piano. So much so that all the stained ivory veneers had to be redone and the warped soundboard replaced.

Among the governess hordes, only the brill one stands out. The picture-book one Otto liked too much. Lush governess, tidy governess. You see, Daddy had his predator's eye on her. It was only a matter of time before he'd have sunk in his claws and she'd meet a dire end like all the rest. She'd had a way about her, hadn't she, a sweetness.

In contrast, Otto says, the monocle governess was a mannish sort who was always running at Mummy until Daddy took to twitching curtains, nosy Daddy, and snipped the brake lines of the old girl's Morris Mini-Minor. Otherwise, we learned our maths and conjugation and planted beans in cut-down milk cartons with a wide variety of girls, which included the governess with one wayward eye. The governess who said pish-posh in response to everything. The governess who spoke not a word of Latin. The governess allergic to Daisybelle, whose body the constable later fished out of the well at Tishingbeck.

Then there was the year the maid got herself killed. Don't ask me which.

Not the one year, but the other. The year Otto gave out Tide Pods for Trick or Treat.

A look got on nanny's face because the parlor floor maid asked how come there was blood on the private bits of the jaguar in the library. She asked it in the servant's hall with Otto standing by, she did. The maid had had no professional training in the safe removal of blood from the stuffed bits of a jaguar. Funny this was, she said, but the blood always came back. And this maid couldn't help but wonder if the jaguar was poorly preserved and still fresh and bleedy inside. Or, her voice hushed, the maid wondered if this was some jaguar miracle like the statue at St. Perry's who was always bleeding from the eyes and the Sacred Heart on feast days and High Holy Days, it was, and, if this was some jaguar miracle, might it be a sacrilege for an earthly maid to be on her hands and knees scrubbing away at the blood with borax and a toothbrush. The maid asked if perhaps Father Caswell ought to pop round and examine the jaguar on behalf of the diocese. Besides, all that scrubbing was hardly doing the jaguar's stuffed bits any great favor.

Here it was a look got on Otto's face, and nanny saw that dark, brooding look, and told the parlor floor maid to just leave the jaguar be. Let it alone. But the maid said that at times the jaguar dripped on the carpet, and the missus was such a stickler about clean carpets. And it wasn't two days went by before the parlor floor maid got her head caught in a tureen full of leek consommé and drowned herself. And didn't a soul bring up the jaguar at the inquest, and nothing further came of the matter.

It's since then the staff has been walking on eggshells. And all this talk of ghosts.

## 10

OTTO HAD GOTTEN ME NAKED AND POSED ME UNDERNEATH THE JAGUAR
with my bare bottom smack against the jaguar's stuffed bits. Otto was
taking snaps to send to his pen pals. To really stir up their incarcerated blood.

As I struck my pose, Otto said, "You know Mummy doesn't love
us, don't you?" He drew a bead on me with his little camera and said,
"She only thinks she loves us. It's a lie she tells herself."

According to Otto, Mummy knows that Otto and I are runty, skinny,
sissy things, just useless to the Empire, but she tells herself we're not.
"And to *not* know something all the time," he said, "well, that takes an
awful toll on her. The poor old girl." He said she feels stuck with us.

Otto fiddled with his little lens and said, "They already hate us."
Us fussy, mewling man-babies, he meant. "So we must do things, awful
things to earn their hatred."

He told me to arch my back more, despite me still being so raw.
Otto told me to say, "Oh, Pooh, you silly old bear!" And I said the
words just as Mummy walked into the library to return a Pearl S. Buck
novel, and a sour look got on her face. Otto tried to explain that we
were only playing Jungle Book, but Mummy turned on her heel and
left in a huff. As for me, I was still trying to extricate my naked self
from under the stuffed jaguar.

Otto followed her to the garden room. A maid was only then setting out our tea, and Otto tried to explain more, but Mummy cut
him dead, saying, "I'll hear no more of your truck." So Otto slipped
a pill into her tea and passed the cup to her, and she drank it down.
Otto crossed his fingers that she might die, but her mood brightened
immensely.

As of late Mummy never rallies or comes into her right mind unless Otto slips a pill into her tea. After that, she's so cheerful she might ask him for an injection. It's after an injection that a look gets on her face, a smile like Daddy's ghost has just kissed her. She invites us to sit with her in front of the drawing-room fire, propped on silken cushions. Mummy reclines and speaks in a voice almost nodding off between words. Otto pets her hand. One languid hand hangs where Otto can pet it and kiss the back of it. And kiss the palm. Otto lifts the perfumed hand and runs her limp fingers through his own hair. He says, "Tell us about when Daddy went to heaven, please." Otto holds the hand for me to kiss.

A fleeting look gets on Mummy's face. That look that got on her face when that lunatic lady flopped on our windscreen. That day we motored onward to the strand, to a hotel bang on the ocean, a windy and drippy place it was, where the weather drives sand into mountainous dunes. And these slow-motion tidal waves of sand creep about and bury everything in their path.

Those great rolling waves of golden sand pull a grave over the top of everything.

Mummy and Daddy tucked us into our hotel bed. Just the pair of them, they'd gone down to a late supper for two with candlelight and wine. The low moon in the sky was making love to the shimmering moon in the ocean. The same moon that wolves howl at and mountain lions yowl at. On the beach, under the night sky of history, Mummy and Daddy leaned into one another and walked along in slow, deep footprints of sand.

Here, Mummy tells us about the ghost forest. I kiss her hand.

On the strand, Mummy and Daddy, tipsy Mummy and tipsy Daddy, walked to where the dunes had half buried a grove of trees. A *ghost forest*, Mummy called it. The trees dead, standing silver-white against the night. You see, the sand does this, kills trees, and they bleach to standing driftwood colors. A Hundred Acre Wood, except dead. Reaching out stubby, broken-bone branches. A forest of such towering ghosts.

Mummy kicked off her shoes and ran plodding, sinking steps up the loose sand into that forest dead as Stonehenge. And Daddy sprinted after her. They played What's the Time Mr. Wolf? with Daddy chasing Mummy between the tree trunks. Daddy following her foot-prints in the sand, and the moon making it all an old photograph.

And after a bit Mummy stopped to be caught, and when he didn't catch her, she backtracked in search of him. Mummy followed her old footprints back to his, back to where his prints stopped. Just one final footprint, and he was gone. She craned her neck to look for him up a dead tree and saw no one.

His footprints stopped, and Daddy was nowhere to be found. It looked as if the heavens had opened up and Daddy had flown away. Mummy looked down at his last footprint on earth. She called his name. She walked back to the hotel, hoping he'd gone there. But he hadn't. Unreliable Daddy, unfaithful Daddy had taken a powder.

Here, reclining on silken cushions in front of the fire, Mummy falls asleep.

Otto whispers to me that a second injection at present would leave him and me orphans. He says, "It's not beyond the realm of possibility that Mummy had Daddy bumped off, Cecil."

Otto rather fancies the idea of us two in a haunted castle with only a skeleton staff of servants. He says Christopher Robin and Winnie-the-Pooh did away with their parents.

Asleep, a look gets on Mummy's face. It's like the look that got on the governess's face after Otto had nicked her pills and needles. Barmy governess, dodgy governess. She could hardly report such a crime to the authorities, could she? No, the unhappy girl feigned an illness and retired to her bed. Sweating and shaking, she was. In such a fevered state, she flew up the stairs to the top of the house and flung herself out the nursery window. The silly thing dashed herself on the stones in our forecourt.

Here Mummy begins to snore, a ragged death rattle of a snore. I suggest we get a hand mirror and hold it beneath her nostrils, but Otto pushes me down on the cushions and has it off.

## 11

AS FOR BIRTHDAYS, WE'VE NO NEED FOR THEM. NOT SINCE DADDY'S vanishing act.

Here my heart goes all bump-bumpy in my breast. You see, a look had got on Mummy's face at the hotel where Daddy had taken a powder, the morning after their tipsy walk in the ghost forest. Even as the local constabulary searched high and low for clues as to Daddy's whereabouts, Mummy had rung for breakfast in our rooms, and she'd decreed that henceforth we were neither to wind clocks nor to replace the ever-yellowing calendar hung on the wall in the kitchen near the zinc tub I'd near to outgrown for my baths.

Time, for all intents and purposes, was to stop in our household.

Already Mummy and Otto had begun to argue on the regular, but on this point they were of like mind. That morning at the hotel, Mummy had decreed that the age we were then would be our age going forward. And we've aged not a day since.

"Birthdays," Otto says, "are suitable only for mean clerks and two-a-penny workmen and the like, those paid by the clock tick, who hurry their lives toward an idle, infirmed old age." Per Otto, all birthdays do is grow a person old. It's having too many birthdays that kills most people, it is.

Mummy, the lush figure of her, her splendid tresses must be protected at all cost. She need be remain the pink-and-gold sort. A fashion plate. To that end she declined to wear mourning, not so much as a jet brooch, and she was loath to burden our impressive front doors with a black wreath. Daddy had merely stepped away, she told the staff.

To Otto and me, she said that treats such as inflamed cakes and sweets-stuffed piñatas need not be doled out only on a miserly, annual basis. If a person wished to avail oneself of a gaily wrapped toy, he had merely to make the request.

No, we'd have no more birthday teasing and tomfoolery. In place of birthday wishes we were to have eternal youth, we were.

Clever Mummy, ageless Mummy.

## 12

ON SOME BLEAK DAY, A SOGGY, SOPPY DAY THAT WOULD'VE OTHERWISE
been lost to memory, a man arrives. Mummy is out of the house. A
broken-down duffer rings our bell and asks the footman if Otto is
receiving callers. Straightaway Otto meets the man—a bounder from
the internet roped in by Daddy some time in the past and ready to
have it off. Beer and condoms at the ready, this nasty nonce, he's prac-
tically slobbering to have a go. But Otto says his mother is about. The
man and he will have to retire to some safe place. The nasty ruffian
says he has a car. And Otto asks, "Will you play What's the Time Mr.
Wolf?"

Otto acts quite the coy, cutesy sort. He winks and giggles until the
man agrees to drive to the strand, to the old hotel bang on the ocean.
They two park and walk to the dunes. The ghost forest. Here, it's a
drizzly, drooping afternoon, with the sun scarcely shining through
low clouds.

Otto asks the duffer, "Will you be my daddy and chase me through
the Hundred Acre Wood?" He says, "And when you catch me, you can
have a go."

You see, Otto is experimenting. A scientist, he is, like Richard Attenborough. And he dashes off, dodging between the half-buried
trees. The trees bleached driftwood-white with broken bones for
branches. All like Mummy said it would be. Where Daddy vanished.
The old duffer pants along in hot pursuit, he wants to have it off so
bad. Otto sprints, each step throwing up a little spray of sand, and
Otto always just out of the man's reach. Otto's the baby peccary running for its life, and the old duffer is a greedy panther needing to
make a kill. And Otto runs patterns around trees until half the time

he's chasing the duffer, and then the duffer turns until they almost run smack into one another, but Otto pivots fast, pivots and bolts in a new direction.

This darting, dodging, dashing routine gets the bloke's blood up. Red-faced old punter, puffing old punter. And he throws his ancient hands around great armfuls of air as he tries to snatch up his prey. He means to collar Otto and have it off and strangle this twee, frail, flighty boy. But Otto executes his best zebra leaps and springbok double-backs and feels this puffing, blundering death always a long stride behind him. And just when Otto's legs begin to fail him and he loses his wind, Otto looks back and finds no one.

Otto pants to catch his breath. He follows his own small footprints. He backtracks to find the much larger prints of the duffer, stamped much deeper in the sand. And just as with father, those footprints simply stop in the middle of nowhere.

It strikes Otto that the awful man might be up a tree, ready to pounce like a panther in National Geographic, but the ghost trees are bare and empty.

Otto tells me all this over the phone from the hotel and asks if the chauffeur, the new chauffeur, can bring the car around to collect him. I motor out to meet him, and the new chauffeur runs me up to the ghost forest. I get out and meet Otto and see where the duffer vanished. A mystery it is, indeed.

We get back in the car and Otto has a go with me in the backseat while the chauffeur spies on us in his mirror, and a look gets on his chauffeur face like when Mummy walked into the library with her book of Pearl S. Buck and clocked me faking a go with the stuffed jaguar. And at home cook has jam tarts ready for tea, and the postman has brought by six new letters from lunatic serial killers and the sun breaks through, the sun actually makes an appearance in our rainy lives, and nanny cuts my steak into bites so big a lion couldn't eat them, the old sow, so I make her cut them again, and quickly enough all the events of that strange day are lost to us.

**13**

GRANDFATHER COMES FOR A VISIT. LOVELY GRANDFATHER, DARLING
Grandfather. Mummy had asked him to have a stiff chap-to-chap chin
wag with Otto before Grandfather had her bundled off to Switzerland
for a rest. Otto's idle boyhood must needs be end, Mummy said, and
he must steel his resolve and gird his loins and assume a stodgy role
in the world at large.

Grandfather doesn't love us, either, Otto says. Grandfather told
Otto that we two are hardly a credit to the Empire, two sulky, pre-male
tykes stuck halfway between being born and growing old. It's queer
and revolting what we two have been up to, but Grandfather's here to
make a proposal.

He's half a mind to smother us in our bed. Instead, Grandfather
tells us thrilling stories about Jim Morrison and Jimi Hendrix and
Janis Joplin. In his glory days, Grandfather was a regular double-oh-
seven, always fielding calls to retire some celebrity who was damaging
his or her brand. Once the powers that be are invested, really deeply
in a hole, and the person's poisonous behavior is hurting the bottom line, why, the investor calls someone who calls someone who calls
Grandfather who jets in to do damage control.

In the library, among Grandfather's stuffed jaguars and trophy
animals, sits a vitrine. Protected behind the glass sits a row of small
boxes filled with cotton. And atop the cotton in each is a stumpy
little stick of sorts. Some look a touch shorter than others, but all
are the same dead color, like the trees in the ghost forest. Like nothing more than driftwood twigs, they are, except one is labeled *Jim
Morrison's Pussy Finger*. Another is labeled *Jimi Hendrix's Pussy Finger*.

*NOT FOREVER, BUT FOR NOW*

Another, *Janis Joplin's Pussy Finger*. All the labels written in the same scrolling calligraphy. A wide-ranging collection of the fingers famous people once used to have it off. All Grandfather's wizened trophies, these are.

Grandfather pops up to the nursery to have a serious sit-down with Otto and tell him what for. He winces at the smell and shoulders open the window where the governess made her plunge.

Otto asks, "What was Marilyn Monroe like?"

Here a look gets on Grandfather's face, like when he caught sight of the awful craters in Mummy's arms where Otto had tried the same vein too often. Now Grandfather has come to be our appointed guardian. While Mummy recovers.

He says, "Miss Monroe was very compliant."

He says that when he climbed through her bedroom window she was already a bit pissed, and she lay in bed like a racehorse who's broken her beautiful leg and knows what comes next. And the sweet old nag looks happy to see someone with a valise climb in the window and take an enema bag out of the valise and begin to fill the enema bag with secobarbital and phenobarbital and champagne, and the old mare only wants to see the job done properly, and to not suffer in pain any longer. And that's the only method for making so many pills take effect so fast, before the housekeeper comes knocking or Bobby Kennedy pops around for another go. It's really for the best, you see, and as Grandfather's apprentice, Otto will get the hang of ever-so-many tricks of the trade, and meet celebrated persons at the moment when they need him the most.

Grandfather says, "It's all well and good to wring nanny's neck and smoosh the chauffeur's head, but it's time to put those talents to better use."

Grandfather tells about taking Miss Monroe by one lovely ankle and gently turning her over, and as he was administering the enema, she said only one word, "Jack," and these old war stories are by way of showing Otto what a wide world of adventure awaits him when he joins the family firm.

"I'd like to do what I can for you," says Grandfather. "It's not your fault that you're an abomination before the eyes of God." He glances about the nursery, at the twee wallpaper full of happy tigers and prancing zebras and no troops of baboons having it off with baby impalas while Richard Attenborough pillow-talks and rubs one out.

Grandfather tells Otto that it's fine to be a wee baby Bambi and loll about in a cradle all day in the hope that the biggest brutish Godzilla will do you in; however, a fellow can have an even better time being the Godzilla. Other grandfathers take you by the hand to go out of doors and search for fairies in the garden, but not ours. Today, a soggy, sopping day. Mummy off in Switzerland.

Otto, the Otto who wrung nanny's neck and kicked the jack, he regards Grandfather with a cold eye. Otto puts on a nature film. Sir Richard tells us that prey animals such as rabbits and sheep have eyes on the sides of their heads by way of watching for predators. While predators have their eyes in the front, to focus on the kill. Grandfather watches the nature film with us. Upon being dragged from its hiding place in the sedge, Grandfather asks, wouldn't it be lovely if the baby peccary could shoulder, say, a German-made Heckler & Koch MP5 Model L92A1 submachine gun? Grandfather says, "Wouldn't old Richard Attenborough take notice then!"

The baby peccary could jolly well blow away those pesky hyenas *and Sir Richard.* Blast the Honorable Lord Attenborough into a bloody, squealing mess, he could!

And here, a look gets on Otto's face, like when I found him in the potting shed with a pruning hook in one hand and the garden boy bleeding profusely from his slit throat on the soiled army cot that served as their secret headquarters, and Otto had wiped the handle of the pruning hook on a tail of the garden boy's shabby tunic and hung the hook back in its place and said, "Such an undistinguished boy. I should never have allowed him a go." As the garden boy glug-glugged on the vast, endless torrent of his own blood, stupid garden boy, dirty garden boy, Otto said, "I never loved you." And Otto had it off with the garden boy's half-warm corpse.

And if our house is haunted, it's haunted by the sound of the chauffeur's skull popping, as well as the pop of nanny's neck. Not to mention the ranks of pussy fingers preserved behind glass in the library. And here, Otto turns off the nature film and takes Grandfather's hand and asks just what such an apprenticeship in the family firm would look like.

# PART 2

# *DAISYBELLE*

## 14

OTTO SAYS NOT TO BE SCARED. THERE ARE NO GHOSTS. WHEN THE CHAUFFEUR got himself crushed he went to chauffeur heaven. The nanny went to nanny heaven. Likewise, the yard boy went to smoke his pipe in his own soiled heaven. Otto is clever, he is. In whatever heaven a person goes to, you get lots of wonderful slices of sandwich cake, and ices, and lovely puddings, and you can have a go with anyone you fancy at any time even without asking. And a person never feels a mite glum like when he's just had it off and the world seems to offer no joy or possibility beyond eating something sugary and having another go. And you lie in your bed halfway through the night and wish a great grizzly bear would pop in through the window, or an escaped hatchet killer who'd grab you up like a baby koala bear and rip off your school uniform and play Winnie-the-Pooh until he loses interest, then open a valise and mix you phenobarbital with champagne in an enema bag and take you by one ankle and gently turn you facedown.

You see, Otto finds me with a bottle of stolen pills. The ones he brewed in tea to put Mummy in a gay mood. Otto shakes the pills and asks, "You don't see any fey, weak baby peccary trying to off itself, do you?" We all find ourselves stuck to the mummy kangaroo's fur, but that's no reason to fling yourself down bang in the hot and dust of the Australian Outback where all the local tradesmen and fishwives will file past your open casket and whisper their vile rumors to your dead joey face.

A look gets on Otto's face like when the governess stormed into the nursery late one night. Sweaty governess, screeching governess. And she accused Otto of nicking her private property, her most precious personal possessions she couldn't name and there was no calming her down, so Otto had to shove her out the window straightaway.

And if our house is haunted, it's haunted by the crunch of the governess shattering all her bones on the stones of our forecourt.

Otto says, "Cecil, you can't off yourself." He says, "That's not how heaven works." According to Otto if you off yourself you go to heaven, and if you off yourself in heaven they only send you to a better heaven. "Heaven," he says, "is about making you happy, isn't it?"

It's fine that Mummy hates us, he says. It's a bit of alright that Grandfather feels disgusted by us. Because people put too much stock in love. If one settles for being loved, one must always be at the beck and call of others, and stay out of their black book, and thus retain that love no matter what the cost to one's freedom.

Here, Otto puts on the Australia film and says, "You don't see the baby kangaroo pitching a tantrum because Sir Richard doesn't deign to kiss it and save its skinny, scrawny neck." No, the wee joey must soldier on no matter how much the local tradesmen whisper filth about him. It's no good wallowing in self-pity. If a wee joey finds himself in the dust he must do without milk and warmth and bring himself up. Milk and warmth are all well and good, but Otto says it's much better to eat a mouthful of noxious red mud and remain one's own master.

Here a new look gets on Otto's face like when the one governess read his poem aloud, the poem about how he planned to prick her with pins and scorch her with a candle and have a go at her trussed-up body. All because he loved her. Otto only wrote that poem because he loved her and wanted to give her a heads-up so she'd take her leave and not become just another ghost in our lives. She was pretty, that one was. With a sweetness about her that brought out all the twee, tiny, fragile, feeble, lisping Christopher Robin in Otto.

A look had got on the governess's face as she read the poem, just like the look on Otto's face as he'd looked into the casket at the dead yard boy wearing that secondhand suit of clothes. Before the one teardrop fell and the sea of gooseberry sick what had drowned it.

You see, when Otto found me I'd pulled off the bedclothes and struggled to turn over the mattress, and I was touching the red stain of where Daisybelle had died with her head on my pillow.

A look gets on Otto's face like when he found Daisybelle dragged along the road with the chauffeur not having the foggiest, and little Otto was forced to carry her home in his arms. Arms as stumpy and useless as a mummy kangaroo's. Suffering Otto, weeping in front of all the tradesmen and fishwives, weeping and wailing, in plain sight of tosspots and sneering nannies, the National Geographic world of laughing Richard Attenboroughs. All of them watching and snickering at Otto with tears running down his cheeks and the alive half of dear Daisybelle cradled in his arms, and even as she dies she's licking his face, licking the tears from Otto's face.

All the while, the villagers heckled him, shouting, "Look at Master Crybaby!" And, "'Tis a pity about your wee dog, Master Crybaby!"

And even once all of sweet Daisybelle was dead Otto begged Mummy not to toss our mattress, but just to turn it over so Daisybelle would always be with us in spirit, and seeing and touching the stains there, the old look gets on Otto's face. And that's how come the nursery reeks of old blood and offal. Here, he's all over a little boy again with dog kisses and tears, on his knees and begging creation not to kill the second half of his dog. And the yard boy had laughed about digging a proper grave for a stupid dog, and it wasn't two days before he got his throat cut open. A chilling coincidence, I suppose.

Inside a week we stood by and heard the chauffeur's skull pop.

And standing next to Daisybelle in her open grave, Otto had said, "She was a terrible dog." He said, "And I'm glad she's no longer getting her muddy paws on my nice things." Because the instant one falls in love one must find a reason to eventually hate the beloved. And already Otto is hating Daisybelle for not being Pericles or Agamemnon, but being just another fragile twee creature filled with nothing but bones and blood. From the look on his face it's as if Daisybelle and the governess he loved, he now despised them both. If they were still here he'd kill them both. And the tradesmen and alewives who saw him weeping and smeared with blood, he wanted them all dead also. He'd enjoy to watch and narrate in a Richard Attenborough whisper as piranhas gnawed them or killer whales chomped on them.

You see, dear Daisybelle had comforted Otto even as she herself was dying.

To this day, the villagers call him Master Crybaby because he wept over a broken dog. Master Crybaby, they call out in the singsong voice you might use to comfort a baby, a queer, twee, wee, fey little baby you'd never dream could cut your throat during Winnie-the-Pooh.

Here, Otto introduces a motion. He proposes that either I eat the red dust and soldier on with him as an apprentice to Grandfather. Equally attractive is the second choice: that I gobble down all Mummy's pills and when I'm half in the bag Otto will straddle my Christopher Robin face and have it off bang in both my eye sockets so all the village louts and ruffians can badmouth me and spew gooseberry sick to swamp the eyeless sockets of the corpse in my casket.

Otto takes the pills for a moment, but here he gives me back the bottle. He goes into the nursery bathroom and fetches out a tumbler of water. "Mind you take them all," he says. He gives me the water and says, "You'll want to be stony cold when I have a go at your eye sockets."

Me sees Otto means business. Me thinks he'd deliver on his promise.

Otto draws back the bedclothes to reveal the red outline of dead dog. And he pets the stain as if it were her. "It's no use brooding," he says, his voice as hot and distant as Australia. I'm only feeling punk is all. Punk and peckish, what with Mummy off to Switzerland. He says, "What you need is to gobble some scones while nanny gives you a good going over with a fresh razor."

Once I'm raw and pink as a Page Three Girl, I'm to return to the nursery so Otto can slap me all over with witch hazel.

Just for the record, Mummy says we're not to have a new dog. She says she's turned that age. The age when she won't adopt a next dog because she'd never outlive it. Silly Mummy, vain old girl. She says that when you get to her age it's like puberty never happened.

## 15

HERE'S ANOTHER DRIPPY, DISMAL EVENT THAT WOULD BE LOST TO MEMORY if not for the arrival of a stranger at our door. A veritable yob, a great brutish yob comes knocking. A great shirtless beast, he is, wearing only drawstring hospital pants and paper ward slippers. The whole of him dotted with the blood of prison guards he's slaughtered or asylum orderlies, his head is shaved down to Welsh prickles, and he clutches a flapping sheet of paper.

Peering nose-close to the paper, he reads, "Is this 1057 Briar Hill Lane?" And before the footman can respond, the great stranger cranes his muscle-knotted neck to examine our natty front hall, and he shouts, "Urethra!" He shouts, "It's your Henry, Urethra, I've come to fetch you!"

Otto and I watch from the landing at the top of the house. This half-naked bounder is no doubt an escapee from some institution for serial killers. He fairly dwarfs the footman, why, the footman's head hardly comes up to the man's barrel chest of coarse, matted hair. A sight Otto can hardly resist, this is. And Otto undoes the top three buttons of his shirt and finger-combs his hair and bounces on tiptoe down the stairs as if he were a rubber ball. A twee, spritely boy with lovely hair and lovely bright eyes.

The hulking yob sweats, his skin shines oily with sweat despite the chill weather, the sweat only a genuinely mad man can sweat, goatish sweat, glandular sweat, and he shouts again, "Urethra!"

Otto reaches the bottom of the stairs and says, "She's not at home to visitors." The silly footman grows quite pale, what with the brute's great bare chest already pushing its way into the house, and the foot-man's hardly been in our employ for a few weeks and already he's caught wind of our household's unsavory reputation, and now he finds himself barring passage to a lout who drips salivate from both corners of his mouth, and who's got one ear off, and whose face is hash-marked with knife scars.

Otto excuses the footman, who's only too glad to flee to the basement kitchen. Otto turns coy. The lout on our doorstep might not be Pericles or Agamemnon, but he'll do. Otto tells him, "The lady of the house is away at present. You see, she's a naturalist." Otto says Mummy is at the beach, birdwatching for snowy owls, and he offers to accompany the stranger to locate her whereabouts.

The brute shows us the letter with Mummy's fake name forged at the bottom, and Otto rings for the chauffeur, and Otto winks at me and says, "Cecil? Will you ask cook to set an extra place at dinner tonight?"

Otto and the escaped monster motor to the strand, to the ghost forest, and along the way Otto says Mummy will be thrilled to have a suitor because it's been ages since she's done rusty trombone and human toilet, and it's clear Otto's racy talk is stirring up the monster to no end.

"Mummy hasn't been herself," Otto says, "since Daddy went away."

In short order it's just Otto and the monster standing ankle deep in sand at the edge of the dead trees. They tromp sliding, skidding footprints into that forest of bone-white trunks. Those tombstones of standing driftwood broken off at the sky. The seaside muffled by the roar of ocean waves. All the world dappled with mist.

The caveman shouts, "Urethra!" He berates Otto, demanding, "I mean to have it off, you know. I was promised, I was, that I could have a go."

As Daddy and Mummy entered the ghost forest so long ago, Otto and the brute wend their way among the skeletal trees. The sun might be anywhere in the overcast sky. Any direction might be north.

Otto knows the way out, but the caveman loses his bearings and asks, "Where the bloody hell are we?" He slogs after Otto, shouting, "Don't you ditch me, you little shit."

And Otto feels giddy to be pursued by this staggering monster, who's primed to have a good go. Whatever the outcome, to be stalked by this moronic caveman is a marked improvement over the nursery and Australia films. Otto calls out, "Mummy! Mummy, your Prince Charming is here to meet you!"

The puffing, slobbering yob stays always one long reach behind Otto. In that, the ghost forest where Daddy disappeared. You see, the sand-staggering, great, deadly lummox means to throttle Otto now. The monster means to have a go, then bury Otto's body among the trees without so much as a *by your leave.* Not one lunge behind Otto, the shambling caveman fairly stinks of needing a tiny gazelle to munch.

And it's the greatest feeling, it is. To be the wee hind that's about to meet its end in the tiger's maw.

The caveman calls out, "Urethra!" but his voice cuts off with a yelp. And the yelp cuts off to silence.

In the retelling, Otto turns and looks back. There, the deep-pitted footprints of the caveman just end. A small ways off, a paper ward slipper sits abandoned until the wind catches it and carries it off between the trees. Otto retraces his footsteps, but the man is simply gone.

And it strikes Otto that perhaps he's not the wee, twee, bewitching little thing he imagines himself to be.

# 16

IT'S NOT A PRETTY PICTURE TO BE A BABY PECCARY WELL PAST ITS SELL-BY date, yet still trying to look delicious and tender and lure some disinterested panther into the bush to have a go. Otto brushes his hair over the nursery sink. Then he counts the loose strands that fall out. He says, "Cecil, are we a bit long in the tooth to be baby anythings?"

To lift his mood I suggest we enlist nanny to dress us in a grand assortment of Mummy's evening frocks and do our makeup and we two can have a promenade around the high street and back. We can wear Mummy's high heels, and this smashing plan will provoke a slew of predatory hod carriers and lorry mechanics to catcall us with foul language and come back to assail us with verbal brickbats and circle back, pissed on lager, to climb into a dustbin with us and have it off for a quid. In the dark middle between two streetlights, Otto can still carry it off. He's quite fetching to the tossers who get booted out after last call.

In front of the looking glass Otto studies his naked body, pushing flesh this way and that with his hands. An expression gets on his face like when he'd walked into a train station loo and a menacing gaggle of yobs and hooligans had got him surrounded, and Otto had felt done for as the circle closed. He'd been the teensy baby seal that all the Siberian tigers would all risk missing their trains in order to bite. They desired him more than anything at that moment. Even as they'd barred the loo door and reached overhead to unscrew the bulbs of the electric lights, Otto felt deeply wanted in a way he'd never felt. Needed. Truly necessary to the survival of some species. If not forever, then for now.

And what the lions and tigers and bears coaxed him to do, why, they'd taken their time to coach and mentor him in a way no grown-up ever had, and time had stopped because the whole world was about

Otto back then, and everyone wanted nothing more than to praise him for a job well done, to praise his pretty skin and hair, and pet him, and see that he accomplished everything to utter perfection. A lovely long grooming, it was. Such men, they'd give out great cheers as if they were cheering at a football match where Otto had scored a goal on the pitch, and all this being celebrated and admired had lifted Otto to a state of happiness he'd never dreamed was possible.

And for the first time in his memory, Otto had not felt ugly or ignored or left out.

As the flesh pressed in upon him, Otto felt that this was the pouch he'd been climbing fur for his whole life to find, and he could at last remain a baby joey here and suckle milk and be pressed in upon from all sides by some gentle, warm, hairy heartbeat. And that's the expression that flits across the face in the looking glass.

A regular look gets on Otto's face now, and he says, "Cecil, do you know there are a million tiny baby dik-diks born every day?" He says, "I don't fancy being some ancient trollop shambling along the high street the rest of my life in the hope that some pissed tosser will give me back a wee taste of my glory days."

While looking at his naked self in the mirror, Otto says there's nothing in Mother Nature more sad than a baby anything that just sits in the tall pampas waiting to be eaten and no one bothers to attack and the baby just grows old there, alone, and dies uneaten.

Deep in the looking glass Otto catches sight of me. I'm standing near behind him, and he catches my gaze reflected in the mirror and asks, "Cecil, you won't abandon me, will you?"

At that point, someone knocks at the nursery door. It's the tiny footman, having carried the tea tray up four flights, and here's Otto without a stitch on. The cook's blessed us with jam tarts and iced scones. These scones are really spot-on. And that's the problem with servants, because the footman looks at Otto all bollocks-out starkers, and he suggests Otto cover his nakedness with a dressing gown. You see, servants rather run your life, they do, and we're all-the-time forced to move into the next moment when we've yet to complete the last.

## 17

**THIS MORNING THE POSTMAN BRINGS THREE DELIGHTFUL DEATH THREATS** from serial killers, lovely, long tales spun with white-hot branding irons and such. But Mummy's also written. From Switzerland, she says she's gone and married her massage therapist, a great brute out of Bavaria, who rips the towel from her naked flanks and pulls her ankles apart with Teutonic authority and fulfills her with his knobby hands. She can't speak a word of Swabian German, nor can he any English, so they play charades that they're in love. Grandfather, it goes without saying, is not in favor of the match.

But there is no love, not according to Otto. There is only having it off. The powerful and the powerless. Otto says, "Cecil, old thing, perhaps what we felt for Daisybelle was love." He falls silent for an instant. "But that's all the more reason to steer clear of that feeling." A horrid feeling, love is.

It boggles the mind, our Mummy pulling in double harness with some hulking Schwarzwälder. All of this echoes when the old butler and Mummy almost married, and what a stroke of luck it was when the morning-room chandelier put a stop to him.

This new entanglement is a lurching, blond gorilla, I've no doubt. Rawboned masseur, robust masseur. Some beast with nothing more than his long strands of DNA to recommend him. And it's all the more a shame because we've only just got the morning-room chandelier back in working order.

In the nursery we read Mummy's letter aloud. Otto takes my hand, and his sweaty fingers feel sticky, as if with Daisybelle's blood. And we two hold hands as we read, then a look gets on Otto's face like the afternoon we heard the crash. The house shook from cellar to weathercock. And everyone dashed to the morning room and stood goggle-eyed. Our poor chandelier was smashed all over the butler, with the butler trapped there not dead, not yet. Writhing butler, bloody helpless butler. And Mummy knelt beside the poor mangled chandelier, the butler wounded in countless places from shards of lead crystal. And Mummy took his red butler hand and kissed it and said only, "Oh, Shadle."

Mummy gave Otto a look. A very arched look, the butler's blood shining on her lips. The butler died, and she said nothing more that day. The look on Otto's face then, it's that same look that gets on Otto's face now at the mention of Daisybelle. As if he's still covered in her dog kisses.

Whoever this new masseur husband is, I expect he'd best watch his step. Lest he become just another household ghost.

Here Otto rallies. He says we're to have a tutor. A tutor to drill me in Greek and geometry. A Jesuit, a Jesuit brother, Otto says, the church hires out. Some sad frightened thing that's consigned himself to taking vows and living in chastity and poverty.

Religion, Otto says, is merely what people invent when they wake late at night filled with the ancient terror of being found out in their little nest of grasses and torn to shreds by the inevitable.

Whoever this new tutor is, he's the same disgraceful, twee weakling as are we. There's no vast gulf between the lame, crippled fawn and the sanctimonious, self-righteous fawn. In truth, it's more fun for the lions and tigers and bears to flush out the latter sort and have a good messy go. You see, the tutor is all saintly and has renounced his physical body.

And we, Otto and I, must convert him to our own practices.

## 18

OTTO AND I SIT IN RINGING SILENCE ACROSS THE NURSERY TABLE FROM OUR new nemesis. It's Otto's notion that we take a butcher's at this one.

Our would-be tutor, he is. The thing looks to be lower than bog-standard as tutors go. Why he brings to mind no more than a bit of old scran, his face does. This pre-male Jane Eyre. The poor sad thing wears an Eton collar, no less, a wilted Eton collar. His hair's a bit of bad luck as well. Not to mention his weedy gob. As for his voice, it's Geordie layered over with Manc attempting a lot of plummy rubbish until he's made a pig's ear of his accent. He says, "Forgive my surprise, but I hadn't expected my charges to be so—" he wrinkles his beastly nose—". . . mature."

Such a slender, skin-and-bones, skeletal thing, he's like an idea wearing clothes. And rather grotty clothes, no less. Mean as cat's meat by the look of him.

"Nonsense," Otto tells him. "I'm a mere five years old." He adds, "και είμαι σε αυτήν την ηλικία τα τελευταία τριάντα χρόνια."

The thing stands no taller than sixteen hands, and can't tip the scale at more than ten stone.

Otto has been a five-year-old longer than the would-be tutor's been alive.

Here, I say, "And I'm three." Adding, "मया च ज्ञातव्यं यतोहि अहं गतत्रिशित् वर्षाणि यावत् त्रयःअस्मि."

An expression gets on his face to prove he knows bugger all about ancient Sanskrit.

Our would-be tutor says, "I don't follow." He says, "You two are hardly boys, are you?"

A knock sounds at the nursery door. Here, a footman delivers our tea, and Otto goes to pour. A lovely array of cakes and biscuits, it is. Otto asks milk or sugar, but more to reality he spikes the tutor's with any number of OxyNorms. He hands over the cup, saying, "Drink up." In a jiffy we'll have him dispatched.

Him with his grotty necktie. A dressed-up bog rat, he is, and Otto means to have a knees-up time once the pills kick in. Otto means to undress the ting and snap pics in ever-so-many lurid poses. These are to reward Felix, programming-genius Felix, who grasps the ins and outs of algorithms and C++ and JavaScript and endless coding. Lovely Felix serves as the brains behind our new project, Tyger.

More on Tyger soon. Our bold move into predation!

Yes, Felix continues to reside in the clink, sent down for all his sexual psychopathology. Felix with his stunted private bits. But he's a wizard at all things computerized.

The tutor sniffs at his cup but fails to take a sip.

Sizing him up, Otto asks, "με ποιον θα διάλεγες να κάνεις σεξ: τον Άδωνη ή τον Άρη?" He's just making small talk, Otto is.

The specimen tucks his chin as if he's taken offense. "You're a bit long in the tooth to be Ganymede," he says. "Don't you think?"

The specimen has yet to lift his cup to his weedy gob and sample his tea. To judge by the expression that gets on his face, he's got bugger-all Greek.

Otto asks, "*Qui erant parentes Tros?*"

The tutor's silence speaks volumes. It's clear he hasn't the foggiest about Trojan lineage.

By way of an interview Otto asks, "If there were a fight between St. Gerard and the Greek god Oceanus, who would prevail?"

The tutor pulls a face and makes no reply. The thing needn't jig about, but he needn't sit there such a stick, either.

Otto continues, "In a fight between St. Casimir of Poland and the Roman god Vulcan and a meat-eating bull mastodon, who would win?"

The tutor rolls his eyes and casts his gaze at the nursery ceiling. A look gets on his face like got on Otto's face one time. You see, I'd once asked Otto how it was that we'd no grandmother, and Mummy had no mummy, and Otto had pulled this same sighing, rolling-eyed expression.

As Otto had explained it, Grandmother was a bit of a non-starter. She hadn't the mettle nor the pluck to be a good consort to Grandfather. Simply not a team player, and all that. The one time she was dispatched to bump off Bob Crane—some scally American film actor—all she needed to do was have it off with him in a motel room and strangle him with an extension cord. Light duty, if you ask Otto.

After Grandmother proved herself incapable of even bludgeoning an actor, timid Grandmother, custard-hearted Grandmother, she went to our library to fetch a Pearl S. Buck novel. As luck would have it the massive free-standing bookcase—a great carved example of late-Jacobean case goods—the bookcase had become untethered to the floor. Quite unstable, it was. At Grandmother's gentle touch the combined works of Dickens and Pliny as well as the sultry, steaming novels of Elinor Glyn, they crashed forth and Grandmother found herself quite mashed to hash, didn't she?

Otto tells me that mashing Grandmother was Mummy's first go in the profession. That Grandfather had decreed it. Mummy had done in her own mummy.

Here Otto's tiny telephone chimes to signal a letter. It's from Felix, who writes, *01001111 01110100 01110100 01101111 00100000 01101101 01111001 00100000 01100010 01100101 01101100 01101111 01110110 01100101 01100100 00100001 00100000 00100000 01010111 01101000 01100101 01110010 01100101 00100000 01100011 01100001 01101110 00100000 01001001 00100000 01100010 01110101 01100111 01100111 01100101 01110010 00100000 01111001 01101111 01110101 00111111?*

In gleeful response, Otto keyboards, *73 110 32 116 104 101 32 97 114 115 101 44 32 111 102 32 99 111 117 114 115 101 33!*

You see Felix can only speak binary. Otto can only speak ASCII. Why, they're a regular Romeo and Juliet.

Meanwhile the tutor folds his arms. Smug tutor, superior tutor.

Otto presses on, asking him, "If faced with St. Drogo, the Greek god

Ares, and a Bengal tiger with great venomous fangs . . . Who would you kill? Who would you wed? And who would you have a go with?"

The tutor lifts one spindling wrist and looks at his watch. "That's just silly," he says.

Otto turns to me. Triumphant Otto, victorious Otto, he says, "What did I tell you? The imposter knows nothing of theology!"

Clever Otto, he informs me that a footman or nanny might tell you what to do, but a tutor . . . a tutor tells you what to *think*, no less. He worms his way into your mind for what remains of your life. To maintain our mental autonomy we're compelled to resist this know-nothing nobody. All of this Otto says aloud as if the tutor weren't present.

Eyeballing the frail man-baby, Otto cants his head near mine and whispers, *sotto voce*, that we ought to have the bugger's head off and peel away the pale skin. We could give the peeled head to cook to make a nice jellied calf's head. Everyone fancies a nice bite of jellied calf's head. Otto says, "I know I do."

Otto says there is wisdom. And there is what can be taught. The two are mutually exclusive.

Here the tutor rallies, "I do know that your grandfather has put me in charge." He puffs himself up to full height. "And if you object, it's best you take up the matter with the great man himself."

And just when it seems the day is sunk, the sanctimonious thing sips his tea.

## 19

OTTO PUTS THE SMALL END OF A CASHEW NUT INTO HIS EAR. HE LODGES THE cashew in place and wears it as if it were a hearing aid. Grandfather's pink plastic hearing aid. And he demands, "Speak up, Cecil!" He shouts, "Don't mumble so, my boy!"

I play Judy Garland sat on a pretend toilet on 22 June 1969, and Otto pretends to light my invisible cigarette. We act out the story we know by heart. In Grandfather's plummy accent, Otto asks, "Miss Garland, might I inquire which of your fingers you consider your pussy finger?"

All the while I puff on my pretend cigarette and tap the ash into a make-believe sink and say, "You leave my private bits out of this, buster," in a Judy Garland slightly pissed voice. Pretend to adjust the strap of my nightgown over my pretend boney shoulder, I do.

As make-believe Grandfather, Otto talks about the swooning, fey, tight-pants crowds of young men who flock to Miss Garland's concerts, and how such fops are a political powder keg waiting to explode, and how Miss Garland's death must be timed to exactly tonight, 22 June 1969, because already a hired troop of mercenaries has been recruited from among the cutthroats and blackguards of the world, recruited and dressed in sequined gowns and azure wigs, these great murderous hired assassins, and they're being trained to lip synch to recordings by Barbra Streisand and Diana Ross, right this moment in a 22 June 1969 United States warehouse in the borough of Queens. These shock troops are learning stage choreography so that in six nights they can tussle with the police at an obscure bar in the Greenwich Village neighborhood of New York City.

I smoke my invisible Judy Garland cigarette and say, "Come again?"

Pretending to be young Grandfather, skinny Grandfather, Otto says, "Had the anogenital distance not shrunk to a crisis point, my dear, we'd not have to do you in."

According to script, I ask, "Anogenital what?"

Here Otto touches the cashew in his ear just as Grandfather presses a finger to his hearing aid, and he explains the detailed background of PCB-based finishes on wood floors and the parabens formulated into vinyl shower curtains and whatnot, and how exposure to those chemicals has condemned a generation of men to a stunted, mincing state as pre-everything man-babies who only want to eat sugared cakes and have it off with one another. A mess of pre-males with undescended testicles and piddling sperm counts and the like. And thanks to the chemicals industry these avid Judy Garland fans are at best sexless drones born to live and die with only the compulsion to have a useless go with their fellow defectives, so already a casket is waiting at the Frank E. Campbell Funeral Home on Manhattan's Upper East Side, with flowers to be delivered on 26 June, and her body is needed in the casket for a big public viewing on the twenty-seventh, so in the wee hours of 28 June the phalanx of cutthroats posing as female impersonators can tussle with a contingent of similar mercenaries made up to look like 1969 New York police officers. And in such a manner will history be made.

As per our script since Grandfather first told us the story, I tilt my head in pretend Judy Garland confusion and say, "I don't follow." I don't ask if future busybodies won't question how the florist knew to craft *Rest in Peace Judy Garland* wreaths before she was even dead. And won't people in years to come wonder how the funeral home knew to print programs with her name and the date of the death while she still lived, happily wed to her fifth husband? But I don't ask these questions. They're not part of the script.

And pretend Grandfather smiles in pretend sympathy and circles back around. "Let's start afresh." He asks, "Which is your pussy finger?"

Here I hold up a finger. A finger that represents the driftwood-white finger nested in cotton in a small box in the library vitrine downstairs. The real Judy Garland finger. The fingernail still painted red.

# 20

TODAY A LOOK GETS ON OTTO'S FACE LIKE THE RAINY, WRETCHED AFTERNOON when the footman walked in on us. Bold as brass, the footman had entered the nursery without knocking. He'd walked in just as Winnie-the-Pooh was having it off with all the stops pulled out. The footman's hands were too full, what with handling the tea tray, he said. All the while Otto was having a go and whispering in Sir Richard's voice about what a good baby peccary I was, and how no panther could want for better. And how tasty I was, while a National Geographic film played in the background and baby bunnies were pulled from their burrow by a savage red fox. And it's only once Otto had it off while biting the side of my neck that the footman made his presence known.

Seeing us, the footman had said, "No wonder it stinks like a zoo in here." Here he set down the tea tray with an excessive rattling of cups.

What's more, here the footman said the forbidden. Said it under his breath, he did. Said, "Master Crybaby," as he turned to go without so much as a *will that be all sir?*

Clear it was, that Otto would always be that disgraceful weakling weeping over his broken dog. And here, the footman had stumbled, stumbled and fallen bodily against the nursery's blazing-hot stove. To describe the stove: blue-and-white tiles cover the outside, lovely tiles, Delft tiles showing windmills and wooden shoes, a stove brought over from the Continent. A great, tall thing stoked with coal and too hot to go near.

The nursery stove was a gem until the footman took a tumble and landed his face smack against the searing-hot tiles. Clumsy footman, oafish footman. His forehead and cheeks stuck with the sound of cook braising lamb shanks, and he planted both hands against the stove to shove himself free, only his palms and fingers stuck, those tender, pale insides of both hands, so now he was stuck in three places to the blazing hot. The smell smelled better than one would imagine. Better than the nursery had smelled for some time. Rather like when some Irish footman fell headfirst into the library fireplace while roasting chestnuts one Christmas. Northern Irish is all. When that particular footman had scolded Otto for shaking Christmas packages and then by accident, sheer accident, had plunged into the library fire with a smell like roast mutton. Not dying, not totally, but not staying on, either. In a care facility in Belfast, I believe he is to date. A living monstrosity.

In the nursery, the footman had launched himself free of the stove, but not without leaving behind half his face and at least one eye stuck to our nice Dutch tile. A mess that took the bedroom-floor maid ages to scrape clean.

That footman was rushed to hospital where he contracted a bacterial infection and died straightaway, didn't he? A footman so young he still had spots. Hardly anyone's first choice. Merely another ghost for locals to whisper about.

And getting that old, familiar look on his face, Otto says we must make due with the tea-drugged tutor, moron that he is. The tutor with no knowledge of theology or meat-eating bull mastodons! There's no dodging, I suppose. That's unless he dies.

## 21

THE DOTTY, SCRAN-FACED TUTOR PROVES NOT TO BE ANY GREAT SUCCESS, a bookish, pale product of St. Swithun's, but Grandfather tells us that, with the checkered reputation of this household, beggars can't be choosers.

Most days Otto's off with Grandfather, learning the ropes at the family firm. For example, how a person can inflate a merry bunch of Mylar balloons, a jolly collection of helium balloons, and set out to where the main transmission lines of the electrical grid traverse overhead. And simply by releasing those Mylar balloons you can tangle them around those overhead cables. And mind you run straightaway because the Mylar will short out the lines and burst into dripping flames, and the adjacent lines will smolder and sizzle until power is cut off to half of England. As are communications via cell towers. And only then is Grandfather free to put an end to almost anyone he wants, isn't he? At least in those blacked-out districts.

Grandfather has decreed that Otto carry a wee telephone. A telephone no larger than a playing card and as thin as toast. Why, Otto says such phones are common among common people, who use them to snap pictures and tell time and do calculations and do everything except talk to each other. By touching the tiny buttons one can even send letters.

"It's called *texting*," says Otto. The screen offers any number of lovely places to touch. "Icons," Otto calls them. *Applications.* With no more than the tap of a finger, one can order anything from take-out curry to a fiancé. And when Grandfather needs an errand run he sends a wee note, and Otto's out the door regardless of the hour, day or night.

As for my stick of a tutor, Otto says he's a boy spinster sort. Priggish tutor, prissy tutor. The boy spinster tries to busy me with a packet of work. All Aristotle and geometry. With a face cobbled together out of flints and slates, he looks to be the aging peccary type who's set his cap to say no to every flirt after a lifetime of having a go with all and sundry. As if any self-respecting predator would have him now. You see, now that no one wants him, he must consider it a great victory to reject everyone before they can reject him. All prim and pristine he is, with his Aristotle and Descartes. He drills me on the Jacobite Rebellion and the dissolution of the monasteries and no end of useless muck. He might not be a Jesuit, not yet, but he moves in that world. The shabby thing doesn't splash out for decent clothes but only wears one of the two suits he owns.

In his brittle voice, the tutor says, "$Y = 8z3 - 13z5 + z - 23$."

With his see-through skin and his wispy hair, he's ugly enough to be a member of the aristocracy. Maybe not England's, but the aristocracy somewhere.

Otto says that once you're that old and ugly and no one wants to have it off with you, then your only refuge is to pretend you're chaste. But I tell the tutor that his eyes are azure pools. Wine-dark eyes, lapis eyes.

And a look gets on his sissy face like got on Otto's when the yard boy would light up a pipe, and Otto would offer to turn the garden for him and the yard boy just watched Otto work and plotted his next go.

Here the tutor says, "Σεσίλ, δεν πρέπει να φλερτάρεις."

The jumped-up son of a tradesman, he is. With no people to speak of. His Greek is terrible, and if he's waiting in his nest of rushes and gorse for some jackal to sniff him out and praise his lovely hair and pet his lovely skin and to gently get him around one ankle and turn him over and slowly ready him for a good, long go, well, this specimen will be waiting until the end of time.

Otto says my task is to enrage him. To get his blood stirred up. So when the tutor's got his back turned I grab great handfuls of his suit coat and tear it straight up the back seam. Just as Otto told me, all the way up to the collar. A dreary, off-the-nail jacket it is, all machine stitched. A look gets on the poor, prissy thing's face. He's near to blub-bing at the sight of his ruined coat. His best suit of clothes, to judge by his stricken look. And the poor nelly thing, vexed he is.

Once the tutor is enraged, I open my trousers and linen just as Otto told me. And I demand that he put me over his knee and spank my bare bottom just as Pooh must sometimes bend Piglet over his lap and spank and spank at Piglet's bare bottom until both animals explode in pent-up excitement.

It stands to reason this silly tutor has neither given nor received a proper caning because now I'm compelled to snatch the eyeglasses off his face and stomp them underfoot before he's sufficiently en-raged to cast aside my trousers and linen and bend me over his knee and give me the swats I'm after.

It's quite exciting, this next part. To convey this next part to Otto. Because the bookworm begins to whale on my backside full-force, and I've goaded him from being a fey herbivore to becoming a true meat eater, and once he catches hold of himself he stares, bewitched, at his raw hand and at my bottom the color of steak tartare, and he begs, "Master Cecil, can you please forgive me?" and "Master Cecil, can you find it in your heart?"

And here I get to my feet, and he sees the mess I've made down the front of his pants. Nothing vexes a tutor more than when a boy roars loudly and has it off, especially a boy of our good size, Otto or me, all down the front of the tutor's lap and spoils the tutor's already shabby trousers. After much more of this, the tutor will be down to wearing his cricketing flannels.

I laugh and say I couldn't help it. What with him being so forceful and all. And besides, this is how Australia works. And now the poverty-stricken thing is in a state.

Him with his sham piety, he's just a grotty old kangaroo baby who pretends he can still get any dingo he fancies. And now because no predator will have him, this tutor embraces grand ideas. What does he know? Otto says I must act the predator and put this tutor back in his low station and not let him get above himself with a lot of lofty Greek and differential equations.

Otto says all the Latin and trigonometry in the heavens is nothing compared to having a good go.

So now the tutor's living under our roof and taking his meals with us in the dining room. His shattered eyeglasses, glued and taped together. Smashed specs, knackered specs. And tonight cook's made a stupendous rack of lamb, and Otto's spilled a full glass of red wine all down the front of the tutor's last remaining jacket, and with that the silly punter's retired to his room. No doubt to have himself a good cry.

## 22

UNDER GRANDFATHER'S TUTELAGE OUR OTTO'S PROVED HIMSELF A REGULAR
sneak thief! Why in two shakes of a lamb's tail, he can knick anything
on four wheels. Or two legs, but I'll not get ahead of myself here.

Otto says the outside world's not altogether beastly. The world outside our pleasant house. On no particular evening he'll pull up in a
Lamborghini Aventador.

That, the make and model of roadster that calls for your immortal
soul just as the down payment. Somebody's dream set of wheels, it is,
only as Otto puts it, "Ain't no piece of ass you won't outgrow." Not in
his Sir Richard voice, mind you, he says this with an American twang.
A symbol of his rising importance in the world.

Here's the end of a ragged day, when the sky is so shot through with
bands of orange and red that if you put it in a painting people would
laugh. Otto says people will believe only the most banal of goings on.

His custom is to come collect me in the gloaming. Otto will rev
to the curb, sat behind the wheel in some flashy predator magnet. A
window-tinted Ferrari Portofino, for instance. Or one time a Maserati
Quattroporte, barely street legal with an extra pair of latex gloves for
me to wear. Otto will punch it, that extra-everything synchromesh, to
get big air over ordinary speedbumps. Otto, he'll sling that million
horsepower around corners faster than carnival rides.

We race past the punters and tosspots who get put out at closing,
and they ogle us, slack-jawed, marveling at how two such twee, feeble,
measly boys could've got hold of such a magnificent car, these hod
carriers and farmers, and they shout after us. Great shambling yobs.
They'd like to interfere with us, they would, and spoil our fun, but
Otto says not one of them looks worth the trouble.

Even as he drives, Otto leans sideways to place his cheek against mine, and he uses the tiny phone to snap a photo of we two making cow eyes. This he dispatches to Grandfather with no more than a click.

Not one clock tick later, an old tosser stops us in the road. The dotty thing doffs his cap. He holds the cap with both hands, bowing a mite, and asks, "Begging your pardon, sirs?" He asks, "Could you two fine gentlemen see to giving me and my crippled mate a ride home?" Here, he turns to look at a tosser leaning on a cane.

And Otto blows them a kiss. Otto stomps the gas to generate an ever-increasing force of G's that makes me, his baby brother, swallow my caramel-coated butter toffee. Not just for Grandfather does he do this. Not just for that cash money paid by rich drivers wanting insurance payouts for new rides, Otto cranks the steering wheel to kill that always-moving part of himself that all young people need to kill. That reckless, restless you who you don't want to be anymore by old age.

Here Mummy would say, "*Whom* you don't want to be."

Otto feels a kinship with these lovely cars that rich men want to be rid of. It's of no importance that Otto can't drive except to pop a clutch and steer a Lamborghini bang into Stonehenge and then fight to find reverse and hightail it across the moors and heathery downs before a gaggle of National Trust blue-hairs catch wind. It's Otto's new career, it is.

Otto says no one actually falls in love because you never meet the people driving the same speed as you. You only meet the boring slow-pokes or the crazed speed demons, and when you marry one or the other, you can kiss romance good-bye.

Be it unsavory, two wee, weakling, feeble brothers having it off, but it's on a par with Otto's car analogy. Of the anyone-else we might have a go with, there are only the two sorts. Either the speed-demon yobs who want to throw you in a dustbin and have a messy snog before they're off down the road with their mates. Or the slowpoke spinster boys who want to drag you through the whole of the British Museum to gape at Mesopotamian relics and never dare to pop into the loo and have a slap-dash go with their fellow art lovers. At least Otto and I are cars traveling at the same speed.

Otto skids the tyres down to canvas trying to leave a good half-mile of vintage Mercedes-Benz 60833 Cayenne Orange or Tesla Midnight Silver Metallic scraped down a motorway guardrail.

I've got to hand it to Otto. The nighttime is lovely, with never many people around, and the ones who are, they're up to no good. Perhaps our future is outside the house.

You see, the tutor has given Otto a fright. Knackered eyeglasses and all. To meet this doddering spinster boy, whose only happiness lies in ancient history, well, Otto fears meeting the same fate. To become some would-be cleric not halfway through life and already mooning over his thimble-full of sherry and engravings of Achilles. The fear of this makes Otto downshift too fast, exploding the compression in the engine cylinders so we wake everyone in every sleepy village we bomb through.

Otto steers the car bang against ancient rectories and whatnot. He says, "It's not pretty to be a used-up old tart trying to cover your sins with a mess of talk about the Peloponnesian Wars."

As Otto sees it, there's no margin in being a baby joey forever, always forced to choke down a mouthful of some stranger's red mud. Better we should raise ourselves up to be great giant kangaroos that do battle with polar bears and have it off on their dead-bear bodies.

"And we must accomplish the feat ourselves," Otto says, "because no one will help us."

## 23

WHETHER WE DOUGHNUT CHURCHYARDS OR DEMOLITION-DERBY AGAINST traffic stanchions, every night ends the same, with a muffler-dragging, fender-dented limp down a dirt backroad to Otto's secret lake. An ordinary lake past midnight with milfoil and a concrete boat ramp that slants steep into deep water.

Otto revs the engine at the top of the boat ramp and tells me to get out. He sets the stereo to play "Nearer, My God, to Thee" and turns on all interior lights. With the transmission in gear, he eases out and shuts the door and says, "I, Ottfried Wilhelm Oskar Coyner, hereby christen thee *S.S. Lamborghini* . . ." And here he allows the vehicle to seek its own watery grave.

Standing by on the shore, Otto gives the car a brave salute. And I follow suit.

Like all the others, this car bolts the short distance to bury its bonnet in the water. It floats a ways, engine running, lights bright. Poor dented thing, bashed by stanchions, scraped by gravestones. Its bonnet and front bumper sink first, and it tips up with its boot in the air. "Nearer, My God, to Thee" still blaring from within. The engine sputters and dies, but the lights stay bright as the whole of the car stands on end, floating a short ways off the ramp, but drifting, drifting until it's above deep water. It's a straight-up finger that points at the moon. At last, air bubbles forth from the door seams and the undercarriage, and the whole of it slips lower, then sinks under the surface to plunge down, down to the mossy lake bed.

Otto's secret lake. There must be a parking lot on the bottom. Lamborghinis and Rolls-Royces and Aston Martins. The lake where no one ever wants to come up for air.

Not since Otto drove up to our lovely house in a 1968 Stingray convertible with a supermodel riding shotgun. A ginger you'd have to look at a good long time to tell wasn't flesh and blood. Otto says, "Cecil? Meet Red." Otto gives the ginger a sock in the skinny shoulder and says, "Red here is a custom job. Insured for twenty-five big ones."

On closer inspection Red's skin feels the same as latex gloves. Inside her skintight miniskirt she's a lipsticked, manicured, girl-sized condom, all plastic parts, and Otto's marching orders said to collect her from an unlocked house. The wee phone chimes, and once more Grandfather has issued a new mission order. On our next stop we jimmy a bedroom window and make off with a bikini-clad statuesque blonde. Two more stops and we're full up, bombing around town with another blonde and a stunning Black chick.

It's then Otto says it. Almost to the secret midnight lake Otto tells me, "Ain't no piece of ass you won't outgrow, kid!" In his all-American accent, he says it.

Plastic girls in lace nightgowns. Girls in sequin thongs. They all float for a ways when Otto shoves them off from the shoreline. Blue eyes, green eyes, smiling faceup at the moon. Lips open just a smidgen. Their long hair fanned out across the water, they float to the center of the lake. They sink.

To create a mystery no one wants solved because everyone wants to sink there.

At first, some weekend skin diver splashes over backward off a boat in this very same lake. Daytime. That hobbyist, he never comes back up. A search party sends down a team of divers, and those divers never come back up. A recovery team goes down and those guys never come back up.

Unknown is why nobody swims up to the surface for more air. Down there, reclining on the mossy bed: all those redheads and geishas and centerfolds are settled on their backs with their legs splayed open. Settled on their fronts with their plastic butts in the air. Underwater in-the-air with their miniskirts rucked up and rippling. Beauty queens who spiraled down, tumbling through the murk to land on their sides with each head turned just so to give a come-hither look over one latex shoulder.

That's how the divers must find them. Lace negligees and feather boas floating around their breasts. Their long hair slow-motion floating in the cold, underwater breeze. What yob could stop himself? What duffer could settle for just one? Rapture of the deep. Another one always beckoning, a prettier one, the one he hasn't had.

Like Aesop's dog with the stolen bone. Who drops his bone in the water, you know?

So it is with the secret lake. Anymore, our Sirens aren't alone. Haunting those waters are the randy spirits of weekend divers and Special Boat Service warriors still trying to get off in the afterlife. The only submerged sound, the rasping in and out of heavy breathing.

According to Grandfather, that's what it's called when your blood oxygen runs too low: rapture of the deep. A feeling so giddy you forget you're suffocating. If any diver notices, it's too late. Still, nobody raises a stink because everyone dreams of taking his shot. Every man thinks he'll make it out alive. The nitrogen builds up in your blood to give you a dick that won't quit.

An underwater wonderland of Bugatti Divos and Land Rover Defenders and Aston Martin Vulcans. Arrayed among them, Junoesque courtesans and pert coquettes and busty showstoppers.

To kill a man, any man, Grandfather says, you only need to tell him the location of one of our secret lakes.

## 24

SOMETIMES OTTO STANDS OVER MY BED, HE DOES. PAST HALFWAY THROUGH the night I'll wake, and there's Otto looking down upon me. Sometimes, a look gets on his face like the afternoon he walked out of that train station loo and told me about having it off with a mob of rotters and reprobates, and how they'd all had a go, and how Otto's face looked like a different person after that, a stranger. That same expression gets on his face now, tonight, as he stares down on me in my nest of bedclothes, and Otto says, "The only reason I don't do you in, Cecil, is because I don't want to be alone."

Otto says, "If I held any suspicion you'd leave me, I'd put a stop to you in an instant." And in his eyes is the fire of the nursery stove when it blazes up behind the thin glass.

An expression gets on his face like when he ferrets out a plastic girlfriend with her bendable arms and legs and her Page Three breasts. Like when he finds her hiding in the back of a closet, where she's buried herself under soiled laundry when she hears the crash of Otto and me housebreaking. Otto finds her wearing only her Victoria's Secret and perfume, that perfumed hair of hers, and her soft, white teeth. The something loveable no predator wants to flush out of hiding. The objective of our night's mission.

It's struck Otto that the longer he loves someone, the more painful losing them will be. As Otto sees it, in our work for Grandfather we rid people of what they've loved too much to be rid of themselves.

You see, the yard boy had arranged Daisybelle the way she's always slept, curled nose to tail to make a soft, furry wreath. And he'd wrapped Daisybelle in a soft blanket and placed her in the grave and tamped the soil down very lightly. He'd replaced the sod and suggested he and Otto cut some roses to place there, and when they'd gone into the potting shed for a pair of snips Otto had cut the boy's throat. Not because the yard boy had treated Daisybelle poorly, but to stave off how much more Otto would hurt in the future if anything should happen to the boy.

"Something was going to kill him someday," Otto says. "So, wrongheaded or not, I wanted that thing to be me."

And now the yard boy and Daisybelle are in heaven partaking in boiled sweets and black sausages and heaps of chocolates. In hindsight it struck Otto that the yard boy wasn't being beastly when he'd called Daisybelle an old dog. He'd merely been trying to get a rise out of Otto, to spare Otto some pain.

As he stands at my bedside, a look gets on Otto's face like when he had to sink a smiling princess. All golden hair, all button nipples. He shoved her out from the boat ramp, but she only back-floated to the center of the secret lake and lay there smiling at the moon, arms wide, legs spread, offering her two pale breasts to the moon. Meanwhile, Otto whisper-shouted, "Sink." He hissed from the shoreline, "To hell with you already!" Otto stooped to collect a stone from the ground. He threw it.

The stone flew in a slow arc that splashed next to the girl, shimmering the water in the moonlight. The girl wore diamond earrings. Heavily insured earrings. Real diamonds on a plastic girl, which sparkled in the moonlight. And a necklace of real emeralds insured for twice again its value. A princess going to her watery grave with all her riches, so much beauty someone wanted to liquidate in order to stalk new beauty. The smile, the jeweled lights, the innocence of her hovered there on the surface. A miracle out of the New Testament. Someone strolling across the Sea of Galilee or a witch who would not be ducked. And Otto hissed, "Cecil, we must scuttle her!" And he motioned that we grab up rocks and dead branches and fling them splat at her. To the effect of merely rippling her golden hair. Rocks plunked only to dapple her clear skin with pebbles of moonlight.

You see, daybreak wasn't a clock tick behind the hills, and there she floated: a ravishing maiden no one wanted, wearing a king's ransom. A dead giveaway, certain to arouse police interest, and something sure to displease Grandfather. Lovely Grandfather, not someone in whose black book you wanted to end up. Not unless you had a pussy finger to spare for display in our library vitrine.

Here Otto shucked his Sandhurst blazer and kicked off his shoes. From the prat pocket of his trousers he produced a slim handle that flipped open to become a long knife. A spidery long thing, it was. A silvery tooth in the starlight. Otto staggered down the concrete boat ramp, wading into the water toward the fate of so many Ferrari LaFerraris and Mercedes-Maybach Exeleros and cheerleaders, until he heaved forward to dog paddle with his head held above the surface, the knife clenched between his teeth. Otto paddled and sputtered out to deep water, the deepest part where the perfect, unsinkable girl glittered.

And this moment was just like in his poem. The poem he'd written to ward off the one governess. The fit one, the tidy one. About how he'd planned to prick her with pins until she died in our nursery, and as she'd read it aloud Otto had opened this same knife and used the tip of the spidery blade to clean under his fingernails. A sight so unnerving that the governess had stuttered and swallowed. She'd repeated her words, never taking her eyes off that knife, not until the footman had put his coat over her head the way you'd blinker a spooked horse to lead it past a snake, and the footman had ushered her out of our lives forever.

And here, dog-paddling Otto, knife-clenching Otto, arrived at the raft of floating beauty and jewels and he heaved himself atop her, and straddling her waist he panted and gasped as if he'd just had it off with her. Otto took the blade from between his teeth and raised it overhead in one hand. For an instant the fist and knife were outlined inside the white circle of the moon. Then the hand swung down, swung down, swung down to give her the death promised to the governess. Wounds too many to count, like the lead crystals plunged a million places through the butler by the morning-room chandelier.

Quite disturbing, maybe, but I forgot myself while I looked on. If you've a mind to shed your cares for a moment, Otto's the one to watch.

And, no, we weren't inventing art and architecture, not exactly, but Grandfather had assured us we were taking part in winning some vast, secret war.

Whatever air was trapped inside this beautiful princess, it bubbled out, didn't it? The poor girl sank so that only her face and diamond earrings shone back at the moon. So Otto planted the knife there, in one beautiful blue eye, and whatever idea was trapped inside her head, that vapor escaped as the swamped, lifeless what's-left-of-her capsized. Keeled over. She settled her way toward the mossy lake bed where the ghosts of so many Royal Navy heroes waited to have a go at her.

And here, tonight in the nursery, Otto holds no knife, but he's got something, somewhere, he has. So I tell him to let me sleep. If he wants to go it alone, so be it. I tell him to kill me or let me sleep. There's the tutor I've got to antagonize in the morning. Not to mention nanny to bully. Between the two, I've a full day of it, haven't I?

Otto's too clever to put a stop to our cook. Her poached pears are reason enough not to cut her throat. And no one can touch her Dorset sole almondine.

Do me in or don't, I tell Otto, but let me get my night's rest. And as if it weren't obvious, I tell Otto I'm here. If not forever, then for now.

And here a look gets on Otto's face like the day when he found a packet of hundred-pound notes in with the scrap paper for recycling. Stacks and stacks of banknotes mixed in amongst the shirt cardboards and old newspapers, all ready to be recycled. And how we came to grasp that some old scullery girl, daft old girl, barking-mad old bird, had been sniffing out our paper money and sending it off for waste recycling.

With that, the tense moment is got through. I take Otto's hand and wet two fingers in my mouth. I spit in his palm and roll facedown and play Lady-in-the-Lake so he can have a go and get on with it. We've both heavy days ahead.

# 25

OTTO TAKES A CASHEW NUT AND STICKS THE SMALL END IN HIS EAR. IN A pretend Grandfather voice he says, "Did I ever tell you two boys about the bloody awful time I had putting a stop to that Dorothy Kilgallen woman?"

In a pretend Richard Attenborough voice I suggest, let's watch now as the savage grizzly bear has a go at this tender, infant panda. And I push down my pants and linen to my ankles and turn facedown to play Lady-in-the-Lake, but there's no throwing Otto off the scent.

No, he forges ahead. Touching his pretend hearing aid, Otto drones on about *The Voice of Broadway* and some 8 November 1965 townhouse at 45 East Sixty-Eighth Street in New York City.

In response, I merely cross my fake Judy Garland legs at the knee, lift one fake-skinny leg and sling it over the other so I can jiggle my fake foot in its make-believe Judy Garland house slipper. I use two fake fingers to pinch a shred of pretend tobacco off the tip of my Judy Garland tongue. Too nearby, in a box in the vitrine, is one of those actual fingers at present in our downstairs library.

Romeo and Juliet this is not, but it's nice that a man's shinnied up the drainpipe to crawl in the bathroom window and keep company even if he'll eventually flush out my bum with champagne and phenobarbital. That young, skinny 1969 Grandfather looked a dapper picture with his colonel's jawline and patrician brow, but beautiful or not, there's no part for me to play except Judy Garland. Whether that Dorothy Kilgallen yelled out the window or smote him with the fire irons, Grandfather never taught me her part. So I continue to play the only script I know until Otto pays heed.

I make a looping gesture with my pretend cigarette, a get-on-with-it gesture, even though the end of Grandfather's story signals my fake murder. An expression gets on my Judy Garland face like gets on Mummy's face when she had places to be and no time to coddle a spoiled, frail, delicate baby guppy that does nothing all day and night but soil its nappies and now it's taken a header down the back kitchen stairs, it has, and knackered its guppy arm, busted the bone in two by the look of it, the way the arm only hangs there and the baby guppy wails such bloody, blasted wailing. And Mummy's head is already ready to split, isn't it? So she tells nanny to pop the thing round to hospital. Mummy's waited a fortnight for this dress fitting, and she's not to be a no-show because some bloody baby can't manage to not fall down the blasted stairs.

It's that look that gets on my face, and Otto's fake Grandfather follows suit.

And I say *guppy* here because guppies get on with what needs doing, don't they? They don't strike poses and spout a lot of high-minded speech about the duty one owes mankind to raise up truly exceptional offspring. No, guppies just off and eat their young.

I posture one skinny, nelly arm to showcase the scar where the tiny bones had stuck out, and I bring my invisible cigarette to my pretend lips.

Otto shrugs. He chalks it up to a bad toss, and says in plummy pretend Grandfather tones, "Miss Garland, have you any questions?" He asks, "Or shall we make a start?"

I fake Judy Garland scratch my head and ask, "What's all this got to do with me?"

Here, fake Grandfather fiddles with his invisible enema bag and says that great powers have decreed she must die so a great troop of paid hoodlums can dress as degenerates in stockings and wigs and pantomime her songs onstage at some low place called the Stonewall Inn. Among their ranks will be Grandfather himself, after he sagely escorts Miss Garland's very dead remains over the pond to New York City. Grandfather will deliver her to the Frank E. Campbell people. He'll oversee the hordes of well-wishers who file past her open casket, and by the small hours of 28 June 1969 he and his hired ilk will be

NOT FOREVER, BUT FOR NOW

posing as silly shirt-lifters and overturning police cars on the streets of Greenwich Village.

Legions of cutthroats have been marshaled to masquerade as fake female impersonators. A trick of fake fakes faking their fakery, all these illusions Grandfather says are to cover the biggest crime in human history. Their script says they're to besiege a cohort of fake coppers who arrive to pinch the fake ladies for deviancy. The fake deviants must corral the fake coppers inside the Stonewall Inn at 4:00 a.m. on the dot. You see, it's all been worked out with bits of masking tape stuck on the ground, every bit of stage business, so all and sundry can hit his mark.

Every beauty spot and beaded lash has been worked out for months: Miss Garland expires. A multitude of twenty thousand pass in single file to pay their respects. The police attempt to apprehend the gaggle. A riot ensues. History, Grandfather tells us, is always planned out well ahead of time.

Otto asks, "Do you follow, Miss Garland?"

As per the script, I ask, "What the hell is the Stonewall Inn?"

And Otto says, "Why it's the birthplace of an entire political movement, isn't it?"

And here, I fake stubbing out my cigarette and pretend Grandfather playacts lighting me another. In my best Judy Garland, I say, "You're about as clear as mud, buster." I give my best vampish wink and roll a pretend Judy Garland shoulder and ask if he's interested in having it off. "One for the road," Judy Garland says, a little slurred, still a bit pissed.

Pretend Grandfather checks his make-believe wristwatch and says, "Just so long as you're stony cold by 11:00 a.m. when Mr. Deans is supposed to find you."

Judy says, "So Mickey's in on this, too?" Pretend crestfallen.

A look gets on Otto's face like when some Form Five boy lingered too long in the changing room at Sandhurst, until it was just he and Otto, and the boy loitered there bollocks-out, starkers, pretending to relace his trainers until he gave Otto this look, a look that spoke volumes, just a weighted glance backward over one bare shoulder it was, and without so much as an *Oi!* Otto pushed the boy down on a reeking heap of the lad's own filthy kit and football gear and had a great, messy, grunting go.

There it is. Form Five boys and Page Three Girls, why, they're Otto's whole world, aren't they?

And, heigh-ho, Otto's shedding his shirt, headed my way to stop our farce and have a very real time of it.

## 26

IT'S OTTO WHO SAYS WE SHOULD INVITE THE TUTOR ON OUR OUTING. THE boy spinster wearing his knackered specs. Our mission is Buckinghamshire Hall, some massive National Trust pile. Built by the Earl of Everything, Otto explains, who pledged his support to Charles I in the battle of Wimpole Street and consequently was awarded all lands and titles and so forth and so forth for perpetuity. Once a lofty symbol of position and royal favor since the dawn of the reign of the monarchy, now no one will have the place. A noble house such as that, once so beloved, now it's quite the opposite. Someone actively de-loves it to the extent that they're paying Grandfather's firm a tidy packet to have the place got rid of.

Clever Otto continues to rise in Grandfather's iron-ribbed esteem. From sinking cars and dolls to torching landmarks. All on account of Tyger, but more about Tyger later. More about Tyger, soon. Felix it seems is still tinkering with the app.

This brand of insurance fraud goes off far more than people care to grasp. Ask Grandfather what he was doing in the weeks leading up to 11 September 2001, but only if you've got a few hours to sit and hear about squibs and using plasma torches to slice through structural steel members, as well as greasing the skids for some radical patsies to think they'd pulled off the caper by crashing a couple jetliners. Granted, old Buckinghamshire Hall didn't carry the heft of the World Trade Towers, but Grandfather says Otto's an apprentice and one can't start at the top.

A look gets on Otto's face like one day when a boy popped round. A prole he was, he came knocking to ask do we need the loft looked after or the chimneys swept. A scrawny twig of a youth, hat in hand.

A ratcatcher's son, by the look of him. And Otto talked him up to the nursery where the lad's coveralls came off straightaway, and this lad had slicked himself up, hadn't he? He'd been so pawing to have a go he'd gone and slicked himself up the bum with awful greasy stuff already. The kind of self-starter the whole Empire admires. And Otto was smack at it, but not halfway to having it off when the lad started blubbing and says, "Please, sir, I don't like this." And, "I promise I won't tell nobody." And, "You're hurting me, sir."

It crossed Otto's mind that the lad might be revisiting some buried trauma. Or that this dirty prole with his ready slicked-up bum might be able to feel pain. Trouble was, by that point Otto had had too much blood in the wrong places to make a compassionate decision. All this blubbing and rubber-chinning brought Otto off. As it did the lad, who afterward copped that it was merely his way. He needed to get his back up and pretend to suffer. It was his only way to have a go, it was, to play the teensy tot what's being preyed upon. Otto was so smitten he never saw the lad again for fear he'd kill the boy. Otto loved him so much.

Ever since, Otto's fancied a touch of the choirboy in his goes. And here, I suspicion the tutor strikes his fancy. In regard to the tutor, monkish tutor, unworldly tutor, Otto has gone to the man's room and idly sorted through the undervests and stretchy elastic pants and says the tutor's more fit than he lets on. The man only looks the slouch due to his sloppy ready-made clothes. To judge by his linens, the thing's got a remarkable figure. It's not all hair shirts and scapulars and banded collars for this boy spinster.

Nonetheless there's nothing to testify to a secret life amongst the man's things. Only the evidence to suggest the man's fit and trim and worth having a look at undressed. The wiry sort, he is, who always looks so big around when he has it off.

You see, Otto's not all nobs-versus-proles. If anything, he'd just as well have it off with a burly hod carrier as one of those toffee-nosed toffs from Sandhurst.

No, the tutor's hardly the strapping, bulky sort. But he looks to be a ripped, milky specimen, says Otto. He throws me a bone by adding,

"You're not to feel threatened, Cecil." By way of a slight, Otto says, "The man's clothes are all a bit of naff. It's irksome enough how he's always waffling on about Charlemagne."

About aged Buckinghamshire Hall, fabled Buckinghamshire Hall, it boasts mullioned windows and crenellated turrets and polychromed knights carved of pre–Magna Carta oak that buttress the vaulted ceiling of the wedding banquet chamber, and a flagstone courtyard large enough to muster an army within . . . and it was all to be gone by daybreak so our client could put up a shopping plaza with ready access to the motorway.

Despite all the English Heritage good intentions and blue-haired docents, Buckinghamshire Hall was for all intents and purposes a goner. Same as Dunsland House in Devon in 1967, and Witley Court in 1937. Not to mention Judy Garland.

Otto lobbies we bring along our tutor, he of the glued-together eyeglasses. To his discredit, Otto somewhat fancies the thin-lipped boy spinster. What a lark it presents, to nab a Jaguar XJ Ultimate and ferry our tutor through the night countryside to the gates of this historic landmark, there to produce a key and usher our friend inside to gape and marvel around the grand setting, the witness-to-history the place was, where kings and knights of old had it off. That's until Otto and I set to smashing up the place, the hand-carved polychromed everything of the place, before putting its tapestried majesty to the torch.

Grandfather said to give the elegant pile a quick and dignified death. But Otto says otherwise. As of late Otto and I are a topic. Villagers cower as we walk past, and they turn tail lest our shadows fall over them. Two fey, puckish, wispy jessies such as us, why a strong wind would blow us over. Yet stolid ironmongers and alewives cross themselves at the sight of us roaring past in a doomed Rolls-Royce Dawn Drophead. Even tonight as we fishtail our million horsepower through town squares to batter cenotaphs and rattle shopwindows, the dried-up tutor is slung side to side in the rear seat of the car like the shuttle in a crofter's loom. Why the poor thing's all black and blue, isn't he? And us not near halfway to our destination.

Moonlight falls upon the hedgerows and stiles. Starlight shines over the stone walls, and all that's little more than a blur as we race past. Mill towns and market towns and tow paths along canals. Otto giggles as he cranks the wheel to one side to sideswipe a hayrick. Forage and silage and haylage, Otto lays waste to ever-so-much barnyard foodstuffs. His hand finds my hand across the void between our two bucket seats, and his fingers twine with my own as he throttles fast and gears down to cut deep ruts in a truck farm field of fennel and sunchokes. Our rear wheels throw up a great wet rooster tail of knackered ramps and fiddleheads smack in the face of some shit-faced dosshouse tramp.

Here Otto loops back to maybe have a go at this fallen-down tosser, but the man's more to reality a loathsome thing.

Otto says, "Cecil, my love, give us a whirl," and he removes both hands from the steering wheel so's to prompt me to lean over and safely veer us around rookeries and dovecotes and wickets galore. Meanwhile our ride-along boy spinster with his busted specs suggests we respect the property of others.

Peevish tutor, sullen tutor, he sulks in the rear seat. The silly thing's in a snit.

It's scarcely midnight when Otto throws the car around in a turn so sharp we tilt up on two wheels. He turns us down some stately gravel lane. Tiny, wee nuthatches sleep in the briars, each with its head tucked beneath a frail wing. Slate roofs and thatched roofs. Pastures and woodlots stream by outside our windows, until a grand iron gate looms up in the dark.

We two tykes exit the car to rattle the closed gates. Quite formidable they look, wrought iron hammered to look like pikes and spears.

"Locked," says the tutor from the rear seat. "*Nunc si tam benignus eris ut me domum recipias, magister Otto.*"

The tutor with his delicate wrists and narrow hatchet face, he brings out the Welsh in Otto, who proposes we hurl the silly thing down on a blazing Regency settee or something and both have a go at him.

Otto says, "Not so fast," and he nods for me to shuffle around the gateway. I find a rubber welcome mat and lift one edge, and underneath is a ring of various keys just as Grandfather had promised. One key does the trick, and I swing aside the shuddering iron gates, and Otto guns the engine of the Rolls and pulls the car forward.

The doomed manse rises against the starry sky, pockmarked with windows and ragged with towers and chimneys. It looks terrified to see us arrive. A noble house that's withstood attack from Luddites and the Swing Riots and the keelmen riots, and now it's to fall to a pair of prancing ponces. Its executioners, we are. Haughty old house, helpless old house. The tutor still hasn't the foggiest. He expects we're here for a late-night romp through history.

Grandfather's firm has arranged that the place should be fully vacated for tonight. Nothing so much as a dog or cat should be in residence. Otto skids the Rolls to the front doors, and he and I leave our seats to mount the front steps. The tutor hangs back, cowed by the vast pathetic beast of a house, the straining statues of stone muscle propping up arches and lintels. The stiff columns about to lose their centuries-long battle against gravity.

When finally the tutor emerges from the car, a look gets on his face like when Otto stumbled across Mummy kissing the butler hardly a year after Daddy had gone missing in the ghost forest. The look on Mummy's face, a rapt look of rapture as if this old freckled, lanky old Scotsman she was snogging was some marvelous new flavor of ice cream. Mummy and the butler had been squirreled away behind the Domaine Leroy Chambertin Grand Cru 1990 in the wine cellar. Not to mince words, but when someone's acting so wishy-washy and reverent of all this sculpted history . . . why, this same rapt look gets on the tutor's face.

When that look happens, Otto wants nothing more than to shove the boy spinster facedown across a medieval trestle table and yank at his pants and have a go. If only because this stupid, twee, would-be Jesuit seems so lacking in any agency. One might as well do him in and have it done and cop a mite of pleasure in the process.

Another key opens the manor house doors and we three venture within. Inside, the tutor staggers about, saucer-eyed and ogling the grandeur of plasterwork everything and gesso and oil paintings of battle scenes. And you can see Otto's bilious gorge rising, this palpable sense of mounting disgust for the tutor man. And because the boy spinster clearly has no sense of self-worth, to assault him would be to injure nothing, not compared to, say, wielding a heavy silver cigarette lighter lifted from some Elizabethan sideboard and flicking the flint to produce a flame and putting that tiny flame to the tasseled fringe of some velvet swag to make a bigger flame that wicks upward to an embroidered valance to make an even larger flame that licks across the domed-and-frescoed ceiling, to consume chariots and cherubs depicted in the style of Constable. All of this Capability Brown. All of this pompous tapestry horsehair.

Here our learned tutor skitters about as if he's also ablaze. The boy spinster pulls at fire alarms, but nothing rings. He holds his wee telephone aloft but can't catch a signal. "Master Otto, you mustn't," he says, and stands as if to block passage into the next chamber. He shouts, "It's a national treasure, it is!"

Otto smiles and says, "Cecil and I are the nation's treasure." By this he means that no country is worth more than its present generations. Otto says the reason so few people balk at the pulling down of bronze statues and the crashing of ancient Buddhas is that history needs a bit of thinning every now and again, and people get sick of living in the long shadow of the past, and liveried palaces like Buckinghamshire Hall are monuments to people who've had their day, and the very same barbarians who laid claim to this title and lands would applaud Otto and me as we fan the pages of oversized encyclopedias and set the costly colorplates alight.

There's no sport in cobbling together a great and mighty empire, Otto says, unless you can also pull it down. To simply maintain the gilt residue of the glorious past is tedium. Our crude ancestors want to see us seize the reins of power. We're bright young things, and no bright young thing wants to squander his life as a custodian to the dead.

All about us silken wallpapers curl and fall in fiery shreds. Glazed porcelains crack in the growing heat. Before long the inferno will burst through the roof and we'd best be gone by the time the fire brigade arrives too late to save anything. The smoke reeks something dreadful as the frantic tutor races in tears, trying to stem the destruction.

The sight of our blubbing boy spinster so excites Otto that he chases after him with a flaming bit of encyclopedia page. Otto sets the man's jacket afire, and the tutor sheds the burning article of clothing. Here, Otto waves his flaming page and sets the man's trousers alight, forcing the tutor to abandon his shoes and socks and burning trousers in a heap. As if wielding a magic wand, Otto ignites the silly man's vest and underpants and in short order the sanctimonious fop is bollocks-out starkers, dashing about trying to hide his shame, and lithe as a baby gazelle he is.

Far be it from Otto to be wrong. The spry thing is fit. Trim as Pericles or Agamemnon. He bounds round the flaming rooms as Otto and I give chase. It's quite exciting, it is, to find oneself a predator in hot pursuit of such pale, milky prey. Why every muscle fiber of the panicked thing fairly stands out in high relief. His skin is the silky, soft skin that one usually finds only on the inside of most people.

Ours is a mad, giggling chase through smoldering bedchambers and smoke-choked passageways. And here a look gets on Otto's face like got on the faces of those barbarians who laid claim to this land before it was a palace, when it was only blood and dirt, as red as the red mud of Australia.

Otto runs as if on the pitch at Sandhurst and the goal is to tackle the best, most fresh baby peccary and have at its innocent, tender everything, and to spoil the baby for every yob and hoodlum who'll have a go at it in the dismal future. When at long last Otto's hands find purchase, he throws the boy spinster, weeping tutor, wailing tutor, Otto flings him down on a burning Regency settee and offers a choice.

"Submit," Otto says, "or you'll be pinched by the coppers." Otto says, "Cecil and I will testify that you went bonkers, tore off your grotty clothing, and turned firebug."

You see, this is the leverage Otto's been angling for.

The courts always back wealthy, tiny boys against naked, daft tutors. The boy spinster will be convicted, he will, and shipped straightaway to Australia where he'll be had at and gone over by myriad miscreants and criminals against nature, and when those sloppy yobs do him to death, the boy spinster won't go to heaven. Perish the thought. No, God doesn't associate with damaged goods. And yes, the silly thing will be damaged beyond all repair so he'll be dispatched to live forever in Hades where all deviants will have all eternity to play Winnie-the-Pooh on him.

"Or," Otto offers, "you can let me have a quick go." He says, "I won't tell the Jesuits. And I won't tell God. And we'll, the three of us, share the nursery and live happily ever after."

Here, Otto tosses the electric car key to me and commands me to start the Rolls and be ready to escape in an instant. Already the wail of a siren is coming across the nighttime moors.

The blubbing tutor curls into a ball to cover his nakedness on the settee. Even as flames eat at the room around us. Even as Otto wets two fingers in his own mouth and spits into his palm and says, "God needn't ever know." And Otto pulls the boy spinster's ankles wide apart like in Lady-in-the-Lake. Otto leans forward to have a quick go. And what with the trembling, twee thing naked and blubbing—for real or for pretend—whatever the case, it's all too exciting for Otto to hold off, and even before I take leave Otto is bang—Bob's your uncle—done.

In closing, Otto backhands the busted specs off the tutor's face. Once more they break apart, but now the eyeglasses also burn, so that's the end of them. And Otto laughs at what he sees, for to judge from the mess, the would-be man of God has also had it off. Despite all his convictions, the boy spinster's had a right messy go on the Regency settee. He's forever spoilt a national treasure with something leaked from every orifice.

Conflicted tutor, compromised tutor. And now he's stopped weeping and cups both hands over his face in quiet self-recrimination.

## 27

I ASK NANNY IF SHE'S EVER DONE SOMEONE IN. SHE'S GIVING ME MY BATH,
and a look gets on her weathered face like when we all heard Otto call
out, "Shadle, old boy, may I see you in the morning room for a moment?" Old nanny had popped her head in first and found Otto standing at the top of a tall stepladder near the chandelier. When he saw
her, Otto said, "I don't want you, old girl, I want the butler, don't I?"

The nanny had scurried back belowstairs, but not before hearing the butler say, "You rang, Master Otto?" And Otto's voice had
responded, "Closer, Shadle, I want you should see this one particular
light bulb." Then had followed the crash that shook the house from
the Domaine Leroy Chambertin Grand Cru 1990 in the wine cellar to
the weathercock at the peak of our roof.

You see, here, when we'd all rushed into the morning room, Otto
still stood atop his ladder. In his arms he held the handles of a long
pair of bolt cutters. A tool that Grandfather had only the day prior
brought round to gift Otto as a present. Like a giant scissors, it was.
The chain for the chandelier had broken, broken or been snipped,
glittering chandelier, dear chandelier, and an ethereal thing that
seemed composed of only sparkle and light had plummeted to the
carpet with the weight of a hundred kangaroos jumping smack on
the same tiny joey, and it's only then that we paused and took note
of the butler pulverized by lead crystals, bits and bobs of crystal, so
freshly mashed to hash that it took another clock tick before his
blood began to seep out, and Mummy rushed to kiss his red hand,
the lanky old Scotsman.

The look on nanny's face when she spied Otto atop that ladder,
that same look gets on her face now as she shaves carefully around

my nipples. Doing so she says the tutor has all the downstairs at sixes and sevens, he does. There isn't a footman or scullery girl who hasn't fought the randy thing off. No one's getting their household duties accomplished, not with that young letch trying to have a go while working folks' hands are full with the tea tray or washing the pans.

And here I say I'll set things right, I will. The solution is obvious.

After I'm clean and smooth and Otto has slapped me all over with witch hazel, he and I trot out to collect a late-model Land Rover Range Rover no one loves any longer. Well into nighttime we are, and we go round to a luxury flat somewhere and locate the correct unlocked door and rummage through a steamer trunk to make off with a voluptuous plastic blonde, a classic pert-nosed English rose some rich playboy wants to be rid of. Next we motor round to a townhouse, and try the windows that open on the mews off the back, to find one that's unbolted, where we come across the next perfect plastic lover sat in a chair as if watching old Benny Hills to await us. This second doll is a right strapping footballer. Some of the lovely latex unloved-ones are the most beautiful men. They are hale fellows well met, the great healthy rough-and-tumble sort who'd go in for rugby and run the ball down the pitch at Sandhurst to the thunderous cheering of crowds, if not for the fact their he-male muscles are molded from pink rubber.

This second one's a handsome ginger bloke with a roguish smile. Both he and the voluptuous blonde are destined for the secret lake, to settle into the depths of the secret lake with the Land Rover Range Rover, but I ask Otto to wait. I tell him about nanny's dilemma.

Otto seconds my proposal, so we ferry the dolls home, where we deliver them both to the randy tutor. Like feeding time at the zoo, it is, and Otto whispers in a Richard Attenborough pillow-talk voice, "Let's watch as the bloodthirsty python attacks these two innocent pink plastic love dolls."

The boy spinster tucks himself into a love sandwich between the blonde English rose and the ginger footballer, and for the moment it seems we've solved the problem and the household can get back on an even keel. At that we're off to sink the Land Rover Range Rover into the secret lake.

# 28

TO OTTO'S HORROR OUR TUTOR HAS CONVERTED BODY AND SOUL TO OUR corrupt faith. It's something of an embarrassment to see the thing swanning about in a dressing gown, usually Otto's dressing gown, and apropos of nothing allowing the gown to drop from his body, only to reveal himself fully unclothed to one and all and full-on excited. And you've never seen anyone so quick to ditch his old life of William of Malmesbury and Ovid.

Yes, it's one thing to stalk the baby peccary to its hidden burrow in some stinking train-station loo. It's quite another to have the wee peccary always doggedly demanding to be eaten, night and day. It's quite tedious, if you must know.

As Otto's fond of saying, "No piece of ass never gets old."

He's done more than simply warm to the idea of being a deviant, our tutor. He's recast himself as a full-fledged zealot to the ways of having it off, always pestering Otto to have a go. A baby wallaby who can't get eaten enough, he is. All quite tiresome. And when the ravenous thing can't have it off with us, he's stalking the small army of nameless footmen belowstairs, and stalking the poor rag boy who blacks the boots, not to leave out the old coalman who drops round to fill our bin in the basement.

There's no keeping a secret, not when the tutor's private bits are always black with coal dust.

These honest tradesmen trying to do their jobs, now they've got to contend with this predatory tutor trying to nab them bang in the butler's pantry. And it's no wonder the greengrocer won't come round, nor the butcher make deliveries to our house. It's our tutor, now the randy ghost who haunts this house.

In order to evade the clutches of this newly aroused puma, Otto takes extra assignments from Grandfather so to be gone great swaths of the night and day. As for me, I do my level best to redirect the puma's passions to Euripides and the House of Plantagenet and his former gods, but to little avail. The engorged thing is always pawing to have a go. And not one clock tick after having it off, he's pawing to go again.

It goes without saying how the nursery reeks worse than ever.

For Otto and me, our rescue comes in the form of Grandfather, dear Grandfather, wise Grandfather, who chimes a tiny letter on Otto's wee phone: Otto's first mission to do away with someone. Not any famous person. A Miss Sunny Delight, she is, per the tiny letter. Grandfather gives Otto a Walther P38 and says where to find Miss Delight, and to merely press the muzzle to the side of her head and be done with it. Nothing fancy. And Otto says I can accompany him. I'm to apprentice to the apprentice.

Gracious Grandfather, grateful Grandfather says we did a bloody bang-up job in getting rid of Buckinghamshire Hall. And now we're on to bigger missions.

It strikes me that I ought to tell our tutor about Otto's secret lake. There he can dive down, dive down, dive down and have it off until he never comes back up for air. Let him haunt the beautiful rubber dolls with all the other randy ghosts. But for now I'm happy to escape, and the tutor can stay home and abuse random footmen.

Otto and I are off to collect a BMW Nazca C2 someone no longer loves, and to put an end to Miss Sunny Delight.

## 29

IN THE EVENT YOU REMAIN UNCONVINCED, OTTO IS A MOST CLEVER BOY. AS he'd be the first to tell you.

You see, Otto says that when a person dies it's the same as opening a bottle of fizzy water. When you place the muzzle of a gun smack against a person's forehead and pull the trigger, it is. When you approach a person on the street at night and ask their name and place the muzzle just so.

The person's spirit bubbles up and evaporates the same as infinite wee bubbles rise and vanish from a bottle of soda. Odorless and colorless. This takes ever so long because, according to Otto, clever Otto, apprentice Otto, every human cell holds its own tiny bubble of spirit. Given time, the whole of the person's soul boils away. To leave the body just a vessel of flat tonic, wholly unpotable.

It's as simple as that, Otto says. Once the top is off a person.

The nursery continues to be uninhabitable, what with the tutor dissecting the plastic unloved-ones down to their articulated aluminum skeletons. Looking spot-on the crazed madman, he's eyeing the servants for his new collection. The way our perfect specimens must look posed at the bottom of the secret lake, the way they must resemble the stuffed antelopes and jaguars in our library, it's how the tutor must be acting on this same impulse. To have his cake and eat it, too. To kill a thing yet to always have its beauty with you. Beauty being crucial.

## PART 3

# THE SUNNY DELIGHT JOB

## 30

**IT'S ONE THING TO OFF A SERVANT. TO RUB ONE OUT. IT'S ALTOGETHER**
another to off a stranger who hasn't burnt your toast too many times
or done you with her ugly mouth. Here, Otto's of two minds about
our next mission. The Sunny Delight Job. No doubt a Page Three
Girl, what with a name like that. Miss Sunny Delight.

Here a look gets on Otto's face the same as what got on Mummy's
face. At the butler's funeral, it was. At the time, Otto whispered that
Mummy would need to go to hospital and have something out. Just a
bit of her wet insides was all. You see Mummy was going to have a joey
even if Daddy hadn't been round for a year or more. Otto had been
sniffing at keyholes, he had. Otto had sussed them out.

At the butler's funeral Otto had whispered, "A Scottish joey." He
whispered, "So she needs be having the thing out." She's got to flick
it away like so much nasty snot off her forepaw. You see, Mummy was
in great demand those days. She's had such grand goings on. Her
dresses were far too fitted to accommodate carrying a wee unborn
bairn of some dead Scottish butler.

Villagers haven't anything better to bang on about, says Otto, other
than Mummy not having a proper decent English baby. Anything's
fair game as far as the tales Catholics will carry.

As for Miss Sunny Delight, Grandfather says we're not to do anything with the body, the corpse of Miss Delight. We're merely to let
it lie there where we've shot her. There being a farm off the Purcell
Road. A modest nothing of a place in the countryside, where Grandfather guarantees no one else will be home on the night in question.
Otto would rather we sink Miss Delight in the secret lake. It seems
odd not to. We could shut her inside a Maserati and sing "Nearer, My

God, to Thee," the both of us in our high, twee, angelic voices. The two of us angels singing as Miss Delight settles to the bottom to be well received by the ranks of the dead Navy divers, well-muscled Adonis types waiting to welcome her to their afterlife to have it off.

Why, just the idea makes Otto and me want to jump in and dive down to join the snogging party.

The divers' weight belts keep them under. As does the weight of their empty tanks. Not to mention how they don't want to surface, randy ghosts, wicked ghosts, they don't want to be put to eternal rest. Not while Otto and I keep procuring them pretty brunettes and slender supermodels each week. By now they've not unlikely moved on to having a go at each other. A vast, lightless, deep pit full of fit dead people having it off with each other and with lovely rubber toys. Depending on your frame of mind that's either the best or the worst place to wait out eternity.

All that lovely dark, free from high-minded speech about fair-trade sustainably harvested rot. Oh, just to be tucked under that deep water with all the goes you'd ever want. It's rather like the idea of paradise with a phalanx of spot-on virgins. Grandfather has it on good authority that too many divers have disappeared and that soon the military will cordon off the lake with razor-wire fencing. Not to worry, Grandfather assures us that England boasts a great many deep lakes.

Once those are full up, there's Scotland. And wouldn't it tickle the Loch Ness Monster. For Nessie to find her realm tucked in with a bevy of lovely lads and lassies, that lovely loch made over into a bustling Playboy mansion for randy ghosts and the sexy toys that rich bastards want thrown out on some tip.

We're, Otto and I, motoring down the Purcell Road. Otto takes charge of the Walther P38 given to us by Grandfather. Otto repeats how it's no great offense to put such people out of their misery. Grandfather says that old worn-out horses like Marilyn Monroe and Kurt Cobain are only too grateful to be done in, if done properly. In his role, Otto's rather a doctor delivering the ultimate cure for what ails them, isn't he?

We've no snapshot of Miss Delight, have we? But she's to be the only one home hereabouts, in a bedroom at the back of the house. She won't give us any grief, says Grandfather. We're simply to put the gun barrel to her head and fire the one bullet, then to leave her be to bleed out.

By now we've arrived at the house, we have. The abode of Miss Delight. It's easy to hate someone ugly, you've only got to look at them and know you've wasted a look-see to want them dead. Why the tutor is example enough. Fit tutor, trim tutor, now he's a right monster by the look of him. You see, having it off with the English rose and the ginger footballer wasn't go enough for him. Now he's gone to the potting shed for snips and pruning hooks and bolt cutters to dismember and disembowel all the plastic insides of the unloved-ones. The thing is with such beautiful dollies you'd expect them to be plastic through and through, but the last I'd looked the ravenous tutor had taken them apart and was trying to eat their hearts and brains. You'd never guess such beauties had a brain or heart. Of course the brains and hearts are rubber, but rendered in such fine detail!

The creator needn't have bothered, but he did. It rather dampens the desire to have a go, to see the tutor up in our nursery having at the fake albeit beautifully detailed pyloric valves and bronchial tubes. He looks quite the savage maniac without a thought of Thomas Aquinas in his head. To see him fallen asleep in his heaped nest of plastic bowels and glands isn't a ringing endorsement for his good character.

In his nest of entrails, the tutor, that monster we've wrought, Otto and I, the tutor is chewing on something tucked inside one cheek. He spits this something, pink and oval, into the palm of his hand. "It's an ovary," he tells us. "When I chew, the blastocysts erupt just like in Dioscorides and release eensy plastic eggs." It's rather a popping, foaming sensation within his mouth. To demonstrate he spits a host of plastic pellets into his hand. He says, "They ought to get down one of the plastic fallopian tubes." He says, "But seeing how it's all in pieces now there's no future for them."

Here the tutor pinches up a squiggle of plastic tubing and puts one end to his lips and blows it full of air as if it were a party favor, and as a result a mess of weensy plastic sperms ejaculate out of the tube's other end. A doll's vas deferens.

"Wonderful craftsmanship, eh wot?" says the tutor. "Top drawer, what? It's a wonder God makes us so realistic, don't you think? We needn't be."

I want to tell him some slave laborer in a factory in China made those sperm in the palm of his hand, but even I'm put off by the sight of the tutor grabbing up a lovely plastic pancreas and giving it a nibble.

The thing about the internal organs of beautiful folk is that the organs themselves are quite strikingly attractive. It's true: a lovely face reflects a lovely kidney. To see beauty only from the outside is to miss the better parts.

Should she stumble in, Mummy would be appalled. Just now, Mummy would regard this untidy melee of eyeballs and ducts and want it all gone into the dustbin. Some of the vitals the tutor has already gnawed beyond recognition. Now he most certainly can't be trusted alone with any footman, and I resolve to deliver a new plastic beauty queen or bodybuilder to him every few days.

In regard to beauty, crucial beauty, here we come across Miss Sunny Delight in her bedroom. In her bed, our Miss Delight is Athena, Venus, Aphrodite, is she not? Sound asleep, likely drugged to make our task the easier. Doped by whoever no longer loves her. A lovely thing she is, with a face quite impossible to hate. It must be her, Miss Delight, because she's the only one about.

And while she's beautiful, she won't be if Otto does his job. And it's not so much killing that offends Otto as it is the destruction of such beauty.

At first Otto won't. He knocks one hip against a table and topples a vase of flowers as if to make noise enough to wake her, so to make her jump from her little bed and give us a fright so we'd retreat and tell Grandfather we'd no chance. We're sorry, we'd say, but she'd got up, hadn't she, and odds were she'd bite us so we'd fled.

It goes without saying that Grandfather would lecture us. He'd say a boy who can't put an end to some obscure Miss Sunny Delight, such a weak-willed, flighty, thin-blooded boy would never be given the big-big mission to do away with the likes of an Amy Winehouse or a Meat Loaf.

No sound stirs Miss Delight, who only slumbers there in dream-less repose, breathing with only a soft rise and fall of her chest. Here I don't envy Otto his duty. But such deeds are the stuff Empire is built upon. Grandfather would say as much. In lieu of such talk I take Otto's free hand in my hand and knit his fingers between my own, to make the both of us making this kill.

Otto whispers, "Thank you, Cecil," and buoyed by my gesture he leans forward and places the muzzle of the gun smack against the side of Miss Delight's head.

And Grandfather and the blokes as work for him at the family firm, if we don't kill Miss Sunny Delight, Otto and I, we might as well do ourselves in. Stern Grandfather, staunch Grandfather, he doesn't go in for half measures.

Bang.

## 31

IT WAS A TERRIBLE, NO-GOOD EVENING THE NIGHT WE NICKED A LAMBORGHINI Urus and drove through Buckinghamshire proper. Sadly, Otto's life has not been limited to the eating of jellied eels. He's got blood on his hands, he has. And this is an episode I haven't told you of, because I'd rather you embrace Otto as a winning boy.

But if it matters to you, Otto will meet a terrible end. You can mark my words.

Here at last we unveil our masterpiece. Our Tyger. You see, we nicked the Lamborghini Urus and drove the quiet streets well into the night's second half. An unremarkable night but for one pajamaed man standing curbside in front of a large, lovely house. A man just set there like a rubbish bin awaiting collection. The night, a blustery night with on-and-off gusts to tumble the wrappers and paper nappies along the gutter. A great moon soaking up all the light in the sky.

Wrapped in a dressing gown he was, the man, the belt knotted round his waist and slippers on his feet. Two houses farther along, another man stood curbside like rubbish, smoking a cigarette in his pajamas as if awaiting an omnibus or whatnot at this wee hour. In the next block of houses a number of men and women stood a distance apart from one another, all in their nightclothes, all facing the street. Each watched as we drove past.

Only their eyes moved, as if they were playing opossum and feared drawing our focus. This, what we saw, was called Tyger, a service Otto had pitched to Grandfather, saying how humans remained prey animals at heart despite eons of civilization. The project spearheaded by darling Felix.

You see, well, to be forthright, Otto's not got much of a head for devices and matters numerical. Lovely Felix, brilliant Felix, he can hack voting machines and get the most absurd persons elected to high office. Why he's half the profiles on social media and those dating apps where common folk have it off. Clever Felix. He runs the entire operation from a dank cell in Holme House, a not-lovely prison in County Durham. It bears repeating that Felix is quite besotted with Otto.

On the next nighttime block a young woman stood curbside wearing a modest, long dressing gown, her hair hanging in a long braid down her back. A knackered car had pulled up near her, and music thumped from its stereo. A crew of yobs climbed out, leaving the car doors open, the music thumping, as they wandered over to the girl. Of the yobs, some stripped off their pullovers and started to flex on her. Others stepped close and behind, all surrounding her, and began to pet her hair and touch her nightgown. As Otto and I watched, they talked to her in low voices about getting into their car and going to a party, they did. A textbook pack of predators, they asked her reason for being outside at this hour.

Otto and I parked up the block, and he got out of the car with the gun, as if to rescue her. To drive off the hyenas and save her from being eaten. Fey, twee coward that I am, I hung back and watched. The yobs clocked Otto coming and shifted their attention to him.

They were calling him *white knight* and *Sir Galahad*, the yobs were, and moving to heckle him, but heckle from a distance due to the gun, and Otto stepped up to the girl and asked, "Are you Amanda Chapman-Morgan?"

The young woman nodded. A pretty young woman.

A yob shouted, "We saw her first, mate!" They hung back, the pack, wary of the P38 but still pawing to have a go with their prey. And it was here the expression got on Otto's face as he raised the gun and the hyena pack ducked and scattered. Otto put the muzzle against the side of Amanda Chapman-Morgan's head and pulled the trigger, and she crumpled up dead on the sidewalk.

The yobs sprinted in every direction, leaving behind their noisome car. The other men and women standing curbside, they'd watched the murder unfold, they'd watched with flat, stoic eyes. Then they'd turned and each stepped to the door of a house, each to his own door, and were gone inside. Otto returned to our car and we drove away without the least hurry from the dead body of Amanda Chapman-Morgan.

Tyger is called Tyger, it is, because to Otto's way of thinking people need a circuit breaker. In particular clever people who deal in numbers and words, they forget they're always waiting for a lion or tiger to devour them. It's in our genes it is. That ancestral terror builds up, and they call it anxiety or depression. Tyger is merely a way for people to *not* die. Subscribers go to the street on a designated date and time. A random name is chosen by computer, and Otto or some other henchman does the person in.

It's a strange lottery, it is, in that each subscriber pays a fee and the winner as it were is awarded—her family is or her friends are—a surreptitious sum in the millions of quid. This payment plus the winner's complicity plus the desire of all the subscribers to continue the process, this prevents any inquest from delving too deep. Tyger takes a winner every month, and the act of facing death, of going to the curb late at night and expecting to die yet usually not dying, this does wonders for the mental health of physicians and solicitors and architects. In that way, Tyger bolsters the sanity of a great many among the professional classes.

Our Felix ought to be proud.

Tyger, Grandfather thinks, is brilliant. All pipe smoke and colonel's jawline. Grandfather took notice with raised eyebrows and said, "That boy had only to find his footing. He'll be a credit to the Empire yet, he will!"

As for Otto, he will pay for his misdeeds. He will be made to suffer terribly. You can take that to the bank.

# 32

NOT ON CHRISTMAS BUT ON MERELY ANOTHER MUDDY, DULLISH DAY, OTTO and I took Grandfather by both hands and tugged him to his chair by the library fire. Otto lit his pipe. I poured him a dram of brandy, and we both settled ourselves on the carpet at his feet.

Here Otto delivered his larger abstract on Tyger. You see, with Tyger Otto means to capture the carriage trade in free-floating angst, he does.

"It's all in Darwin," said Otto. The inescapable condition of our evolution, he means. My brother contends that we're all born with an innate terror of being chomped upon and gobbled down. "On some Stone Age level we're just monkeys dashing across the Pangaean veldt." Otto said, "Tool-using and scone-buttering monkeys, but monkeys no less."

Recalcitrant Grandfather, taciturn Grandfather, he looked not averse to hearing us out.

As Otto put it laborers and servants and the like can chalk it up to spooks, that ancient fear. It's the suburban classes who truly suffer. They fancy themselves too rational to put any faith in ghosts. These chartered public accountants and stockjobbers. So they're left with no resolution except to medicate. Otto said, "They find themselves in an awful predicament."

The professional classes would never admit to being descended from hairless kangaroo babies shivering and quivering as they await some kiwi bird to eat them. "We're all evolved from prey animals," said Otto. Even the Queen has the instincts of a prey animal coursing through her veins. On some cellular level even she awaits some saw-toothed carnivore to snatch her out of her majestic burrow.

"In particular the Queen," said Otto in a thrilling growl. "Alone in her apartments at Balmoral with no one to look in on her, and all of those hungry corgi dogs just awaiting their chance!"

The image sent a shudder through me from stem to stern.

It was a hairy business, this selling Grandfather on Otto's plan. He gave no quarter to the half-baked.

On occasion, Otto said, science gives this generalized terror a name. Gypsy moths, say, or ozone depletion. Middle-class strictures doom us to these periodic panics, be they Africanized "killer" honey bees or spontaneous hive collapse. Peak oil or spiraling frog populations. None of the learned can admit they're simply hardwired to expect a violent death. Instead, they call it the Harmonic Convergence of 1987 or the Nibiru meteor of 1995.

"They call it SARS," said Otto, "or the Y2K bug."

The tabloids have caught on and regularly serve up new panics such as swine flu, acid rain, the Zika virus, the West Nile virus, the gypsy moth, the 2012 Mayan Day of Annihilation, and electromagnetic radiation from cell phones.

Of course, Grandfather will have complete oversight of the entire Tyger enterprise.

At this Otto's tiny phone chimed with a letter from Felix, who wrote, *01000011 01100001 01101110 00100000 01111001 01101111 01110101 00100000 01100111 01100101 01110100 00100000 01110101 01110011 00100000 01100001 00100000 01101110 01110101 01100011 01101100 01100101 01100001 01110010 00100000 01100010 01101111 01101101 01100010 00101100 00100000 01101100 01101111 01110110 01100101 00111111?*

In response, Otto typed, *77 121 32 108 111 118 101 108 121 44 32 73 32 99 97 110 32 103 101 116 32 121 111 117 32 97 108 108 32 111 102 32 116 104 101 109 33!*

Here Grandfather puffed his pipe. Dour Grandfather, severe Grandfather.

"It's not fair," Otto pressed his case. "Why should only failing celebrities enjoy a lovely exit strategy. A properly done rubbing out. Why shouldn't the middle classes also have the benefit of a professionally done doing in?"

At this, perhaps we had the old warhorse. Grandfather plucked the pipe stem from between his teeth and pointed it at Otto. "Mind you," said Grandfather, "we're to have no useful persons hurt!" By this he means no hod carriers or porters or washerwomen. In addition, he said, "My boys, sign me up! Add my name to the rolls!"

And by way of reply Otto took the index finger of one frail, febrile hand and drew a cross over his own heart.

**33**

PLEASE BEAR WITH ME. WE MUST ALWAYS BE RUSHED INTO THE NEXT MOMENT, by our duties and by our servants, if not by the clock or calendar.

In short order Otto has been well versed in Grandfather's teachings: human beings were but filters full of asbestos and dioxins and had best be put to rest in sealed vaults like nuclear sludge. By now Tyger has proved a grand success. Scads of subscribers are made to feel ecstatically alive each month while the beneficiaries of one subscriber are made well-off. It goes without saying Otto ventures out monthly with a computer-generated name. Efficient to the bone, Felix is.

As Otto is fond of saying, "70 101 108 105 120 32 105 115 32 115 111 32 99 108 101 118 101 114 33."

More often than not the Tyger winner is some stodgy man, a jaded barrister or journo. A number are women. It makes no never mind to Otto. Using Grandfather's reach-me-down ethos Otto never hesitates to stalk and award a winner.

On the night in question we nick a Koenigsegg Gemera, a car I hadn't known existed until I'd set inside that one. A lovely car. We motor the M5 to the M42 and then motor the M56 to the M60, don't we? We're off the motorways, here, into the suburban districts lined with subscribers. A warm night it is, buzzing with insects. The bright open doors of public houses with goers spilling out, hands full of pints and ciggies, saucer-eyed as Otto and I roar past.

We follow satellite nav, Otto and I, to find a Miss Pamela Flora Birdsong, a pleasant-enough-sounding person at any rate. Our night's winner as it were. We're up and down mews, roads, and market streets, passages, and backways to no avail. All these byways are lined with men and women standing curbside, eyes front, some smoking, others texting tiny letters on their wee telephones.

In hindsight it seems less a coincidence what occurred. It's more the case Grandfather pulled strings to put Otto to this most awful test.

In short order, there she is: Miss Pamela Flora Birdsong, a baby peccary who until now had had no name. Not to us at least. We park and Otto says, "I can't. Oh, Cecil, don't make me."

We look at her, and she surely knows she is the winner to judge by how she begins to tremble and how the fingers of her hand rise to touch her throat, and her lips move in silent prayer:

*Be to us, O Lord,*

*A support in our setting out,*

*A comfort by the way . . .*

Church of England, she is, every inch of her.

Whether he could or couldn't, Otto climbed out of the car. The house in back of her, her natural habitat, a shack done up with lace curtains in the front window, it was. An attached house in a long row of the same.

Her lips shaped the words:

*A protection in adversity,*

*And a port in shipwreck.*

Here a look gets on his face like when he'd done the yard boy, and Otto walks the short way and lifts the P38 to the head of Miss Birdsong, who has a proper name now.

Her lips shape the words:

*And at length we may return again to our home in safety.*

Otto shoots away a good portion of her head. All the spirit boils out of her. Even as the street's accountants and professors are retreating back into their homes, Otto stands over the body.

Our governess was all she was. Not the one with the goiter, but the governess whom Otto had so loved. The one he'd shooed away with his wretched poem. And now he's done what he'd tried to avoid all along, hasn't he? And with that bullet all the goodness was gone out of Otto, and Grandfather had won. And when Otto walked back to the Koenigsegg Gemera nothing was beyond his doing now, was it?

## 34

**HOUSEFLIES PLAGUE THE NURSERY. GREAT BUZZING DROVES OF THEM.**
A trend that does not bode well as they've nothing to feed upon. The plastic abattoir should offer them no sustenance, not unless one of the unloved-ones is of flesh and blood. Heaped like cordwood, it's hard to discern if one among them might be real, an actual victim, no less. More of a mystery is how such a corpse might come to decompose in our lovely nursery.

Otto and I decamp to the dog house. Literally hiding, we are, in Daisybelle's old house. I hunt up the wet nurse, who kneels in the doorway of the dog house and undoes the laces of her bodice, but Otto waves her away. I plead that Otto must eat something.

He responds by shaking his head. "Cecil, I'm sure it's of no use." So we continue to camp out here in the red dust of the dog house on a nest of Daisybelle's old blankets. A look gets on Otto's face like when we went with Mummy to have it out at hospital. Just a spiffy mop-up procedure after which we'd get ice creams. Strawberry for me since I'm the fainting, frail type. The more racy orange sherbet for Otto seeing how he's been to manly Sandhurst.

As Mummy was escorted back and her insides were sorted through and the bairn problem routed out, a look had got on Otto's face. Paging through an issue of *Hello* magazine he was, when he said it. Without meeting my gaze he said, "Cecil, seeing how we're not to have another dog, I don't think it's fair Mummy should ever have another baby."

I said it wasn't exactly the same thing, was it?

To which Otto responded, "It is exactly the same." Otto said, "That was my motive for cutting down the chandelier. I only wish Mummy had also stood below it."

Left unsaid was our hope that between the rusted National Health machines and the rough handling, Mummy would be left unable to get up the duff from thence forward. It takes only a look to see that her track record at raising children is hardly spotless. If she's set in her ways to have a go with our Scottish butler and not to avail herself of birth control, it's best she relinquishes her most womanly bits of the sort gnawed upon by the tutor.

Here in the dog house a look gets on Otto's face the same as got on him in hospital, and Otto says, "What if Grandfather should get underneath the morning-room chandelier?" Otto says, "Cecil, would you help me?"

You see, a tiny letter had come over Otto's wee telephone. A text, as common people call such a letter. Grandfather wrote to ask, *Otto my boy, which of your fingers do you consider your pussy finger?* His intentions crystalline.

Grandfather's not happy. The same sun that dawns on us also rises on Miss Sunny Delight, who's no doubt scampering about a back meadow as befits a Kerry blue terrier, practicing her gait for the next National Kennel Club dog show. Exhibiting the attitude of alert determination and disciplined gameness such a lovely terrier is prized for. Blue-ribbon Miss Sunny Delight, best-in-show Miss Sunny Delight. A morning similar to her every morning because Miss Delight happens to be a show dog, doesn't she? A purebred bitch whose winning days are almost behind her but who can't carry a litter so she's massively insured. A great piggy bank, so to speak, but the money can't be got at until someone breaks her open.

None of this did Grandfather inform us of. And it's one thing to do in an old mare like Marilyn Monroe, who's profoundly unhappy and suffering no end of bad marriages and whom even Arthur Miller can't make happy but instead he roasts her alive, the legacy of her, in a famous play for all the world to have a laugh at, but it's another thing to shoot a lovely terrier in the head. A dog with such lovely brown fur and eyes, who'd race you around the garden the way our spotted pony once would. That night as Otto had drawn a bead on Miss Delight a look got on his face like got on his face when what happened to our spotted pony happened, oh, ever so long ago it was.

The long and short of it is Otto didn't put an end to Miss Delight. Instead he shot a bullet—bang—into the ceiling of the bedroom. So the sunrise finds us in a law-of-the-jungle situation. Somewhere, Grandfather is weighing the idea of offing Otto. Likewise, Otto is pre-plotting to do away with Grandfather, thus allowing the family firm to pass into our tiny, twee hands as sole and exclusive heirs and proprietors. And it's all quite Shakespearean, it is.

Even being mulled over in the red dust of a bunker at the bottom of the garden near where the spotted pony was laid to rest, it's Shakespearean. I ask Otto if he wants to play Winnie-the-Pooh and he says no. I ask, does he want Lady-in-the-Lake, and he does not. Undaunted, I spin the idea we should make off with all Mummy's cosmetics and hairpieces and clever outfits and go on the stage as a sister act and flirt with stage-door johnnies and be sugarbabies to boatloads of old rich men too old to have it off, but who expire quickly and bequest to us, why, great pots of money and jewels, and we can retire in America where simply knowing a heap of words puts one in the upper crust of society, such as it is. Perhaps Felix could even work his voting-machine magic and get Otto elected to the American presidency? What's more, Grandfather would never sniff us out.

Otto gives me a look. "Cecil, America sounds ghastly."

I suggest Canada instead. To raise Otto's spirits I begin to sing the "Chica, Chica, Boom, Chic" song and cast about for all the chewed-on dog toys I can pile atop my head, but I stop when Otto looks about to cry.

On the bright side, Miss Sunny Delight's most likely trotting about in a field of clover. On the brighter side, Mummy and her Bavarian ruffian have yet to put in an appearance hereabouts. Otto still looks to be in a muddle.

It's been lovely to be fey, girly boys always having things done for us and things done to us. But now comes the time we must do for ourselves, and yes, it's sad to be always growing up and sprouting more Welsh hair.

Stymied, I reach into a coat pocket and fetch out a small something dusted with lint. It's a cashew nut, it is. As is our practice, I stick the small end of the nut in my ear hole and lodge it there to make a fake, pink plastic hearing aid. I fake Grandfather's plummy, to-the-manor-born voice and ask, "Miss Garland, you're friends with Tommy Manville, are you not?"

Here Otto looks up with a tearful, frightened Judy Garland face. Otto's fear and sorrow are no longer his own. He can place his worries on Miss Garland's boney shoulders and let her carry the burden. At that he goes to script, the script we both know by heart. Otto smirks Judy Garland's face and says, "Tommy Manville? The asbestos playboy? Who doesn't know Tommy?"

Pretend Grandfather touches the hearing aid in his ear and says, "And you've met Doris Duke, have you?"

Pretend Judy Garland, Judy in the dog house puffs on her invisible cigarette and says, "The William Morris heiress? That Doris Duke?"

Pretend Grandfather gently corrects her. "The Philip Morris heiress." Even our errors are locked into our ancient script.

Mischievous Judy Garland, elfin Judy Garland, she cups one hand around her mouth and whisper-shouts, "Call for Philip Morris!" That 22 June 1969 Judy Garland says, "Doris is a lovely woman! Her *and* her money!"

Fake Grandfather, skinny young Grandfather tells her, "Their money won't last much longer."

Pretend Miss Garland tucks her chin down and pokes a dimple into one gaunt cheek with her skeleton's finger. She asks, "How's that? They're both loaded," in her slightly pissed voice.

Our sunny day is short lived as raindrops begin to stampede on the dog-house roof. Snug inside, crouched here, pretend Grandfather says, "Do you know the term *mesothelioma*, do you not?"

Pretend Judy stubs out her pretend ciggie on the ground, the dirt where our spotted pony lies buried, and she says, "I don't believe I do."

Here pretend Grandfather says, "That's neither here nor there. What matters is that a class-action lawsuit is going to hit the asbestos playboy and after it does he won't have a pot to piss in."

Pretend Judy pretends to look taken aback by such coarse talk.

"And your Doris Duke," pretend Grandfather thumps on, "a similar slew of legal actions will soon destroy her fortune." He asks, "Do you follow?" The patter of rain makes the little house feel like home. The smell of Daisybelle and her blankets and old chew toys. The hollow in the dirt floor where she'd curl into a wreath to fall asleep.

Pretend Judy fakes a head-scratching exasperated look here. "I still don't see why I have to die!"

"Because," says fake Grandfather, lowering his voice lest a pretend Mickey Deans asleep in the adjoining bedroom overhears, "unless your death catalyzes a world revolution among the fey, wispy, lisping hordes, those same deviants will join forces on legal grounds to destroy the entire world economy."

Here the cashew nut drops out my ear. It lands in the red dust and old shed dog fur. Nasty thing. It lies there like a doomed, pink baby joey, but I eat it anyway. Like a brash dingo would. It's how Australia works.

Down the Purcell Road, Miss Sunny Delight chases cats and buries bones, not knowing how close she came to Kerry-blue-terrier heaven.

And here a look gets on Judy Garland's face like when she found her spotted pony dead, and she breaks character. Frightfully bad form, that. She casts aside the script to say, "Cecil, what do you suppose ever became of poor Evelyn?"

## 35

AS A MOTHER, MUMMY HASN'T MADE ANY GREAT SUCCESS. BUT AS A WEE
slip of a girl she once went skiing and steered a washed-up singer and
would-be presidential candidate bang into a tree. Just as Grandfather
had taught her. That had been near her first job, the Sonny Bono Job,
and she took to the work with great relish. A great killer, yes she is, but
as for being a mother, she's left much to be desired.

She used to tell Otto and me, as she tucked us in at night she'd say,
"My lovely boys, my sweet innocents, why when I was your age I'd already drowned Natalie Wood, hadn't I? And I'd smacked on the head
William Holden, I had." Goodness knows she could set up a patsy like
that Mark David Chapman person. A rube to pick up the slack during
a busy season. She'd tell us, "I could wind that Hinckley person round
my little finger, couldn't I?"

Grandfather used to call them *temps*, these young men and
women who might be hired on for a single job. They were never very
bright. No bright stars, they. Why, they could scarcely shoot a Kennedy before getting pinched. Mummy had only to meet such men
before she could suss out the ones with killer instincts. It's how she
met Daddy, it is. "My darling boys, your father had such aspirations."
She'd lean over the crib, the jewels and the perfumed scent of her.
"Your father hadn't any people to speak of, but he'd possessed an
animal charm."

Here she'd stop talking and a look would get on her face, a look
like got on her face when that deranged woman flung herself on the
windscreen of our Bentley as we were driving on holiday. This same
look as got on Otto's face a time back when he took me to visit the
Buckinghamshire Asylum for the Homicidally Insane. Oh, this was

nannies and nannies ago, soon after Daddy's vanishing. Far too many nannies back to count.

The asylum looked a fortress stacked out of great grey stones, it did. All the windows iron-barred with the pale hands of lunatics clutching the bars from the inside. Picture spidery-thin fingers wound round the iron like insane vines, they were. And pallid faces framed between the bars. Leering, toothsome, hollow-eyed. Haggard, gimlet-eyed, caved-in faces. Stammering mouths. A whole façade of such faces waited to greet us upon our approach by the Pembroke Road.

You see, Daddy had only weeks prior gone missing at the beach, and Otto had questions he wanted answered, so he marched me to the stout door of that murmuring, stuttering bedlam and rang the bell, and told them who our Mummy was and her place among the county families, and who Grandfather was, and the old rector who ran the unhappy enterprise asked us in to tea: a miserable assortment of tinned biscuits and bilge presented to us with lofty formality and *papier serviettes* by a hunched housekeeper who seemed not one degree above being an inmate herself. The asylum keeper asked our business, and Otto told about the madwoman who called Daddy by his Christian name. Daddy had put his head together with a local constable and had a brief exchange, and the woman in question had been trundled off to this asylum for observation. Otto had said, "It was for her own well-being." He'd said, "It's why we have the National Health, isn't it?"

Here the keeper had paused, his knees tucked together and a cup and saucer balanced upon one. He blinked in deep reflection. "Why," he'd asked, "you don't mean Evelyn, do you?"

Otto had told the man, "We needn't name names." We hadn't come to learn the woman's name. Our only question was, why had she tried to spoil our holiday? Here Otto picked at the crease in one leg of his trousers. In doing so he lifted the trouser cuff to reveal his chubby pink ankle. The argyle sock had fallen whorishly against his shoe to show this bare expanse of fleshy ankle, suggestive ankle, and at the sight of that pink skin it became obvious the asylum keeper could deny Otto nothing.

Not taking his eyes off the plump ankle, the keeper asked, "Would you like to speak with her?" He added, "I must warn you . . . she's not well, not well at all."

We three set aside our cups and dry, tasteless biscuits and journeyed into the stone bowels of the place. In one hand the keeper carried a great loop from which dangled keys as large as cutlery. Heavy, rusted skeleton keys these were. To judge by the ragged din behind each door, every cell held the nightmare of an unbalanced mind. Otto and I took hold of each other round the waist as if we might be set upon at any step. The howls of a nighttime jungle are as nothing compared to these wards and dayrooms. To blunt the stink of the place I ran my fingers through Otto's sweetly scented hair and held those fingers cupped over my nose and mouth.

Gates opened before us and locked behind us as we disappeared deeper into the warren of the place. Seldom had we felt so ready to be had a go at. So nakedly open to such a company of randy maniacs. One could only guess how many of Otto's pen pals sniffed the air at our passing and lustily abused themselves to the dream of having little Otto in endless brutal goes. Our pen pals lived thick within these walls and the faint chorus of our names, Otto and Cecil, seemed more than a fantasy song haunting the place.

In no short order we arrived at a numbered door. The keeper selected a key and it rasped in the disused lock. He whispered, "Evelyn, are you decent?" He whispered, "It's the doctor. I've brought you two fine young gentlemen as guests." Standing so as to block our view into the fetid cell, the keeper said, "My lads, please do not overtax her with your questioning." His voice quelled to a whisper, he said, "You'll see that she's not herself."

Here he stepped aside and gave way for us to enter. Here was nothing I could recall of the woman who flung herself upon our bonnet. The eyes that met ours hardly seemed human. "It's the orders," said the keeper, "they came from rather high up." He regarded the patient in question. "She's been infused with a cocktail of sedatives and whatnot." The chemical effects of which had reduced her to a jumble of limbs propped heavily against a stained wall. A chain trailed from a manacle around one leg to a hasp set in the stone.

She still had a breath of youth about her, but one could see the Bertha Mason overtaking that.

The dull-eyed woman squinted at Otto. "You're him," she said, "the tyke from the car. Why you're almost growed-up, you are. I almost took you for your father, I did!" Her hands roamed the small mound of her belly, and she said, "Feel." She said, "I can feel it coming."

In hindsight, this scene was, oh, footmen and footmen ago.

Otto made no movement toward her but said, "You have life inside you?"

She caressed herself and said, "He'll be your half brother, he will."

A look got on Otto's face same as when he crushed the chauffeur's skull, and he said, "Do you know where he's gone, my father?"

She shook her matted head and said, "Where has James got to?"

Here Otto saw the impossibility. Poor Evelyn was bonkers. He asked, "Might I write to you?" He turned to the keeper and asked, "Might I write to her? Can she read?"

The keeper snorted. "She's only expecting a bairn, sir. She's not a full-on illiterate."

At this, those vacant eyes came to settle upon me. "He's your brother, Cecil, isn't he?" With stained fingers, she bid me come forward, saying, "Do you know how handsome your father told me you were?" She smiled and said, "Why you're twice that."

Her gaze shifted, and she said, "So you must be Otto." She beamed. "Do you know how proud your father is of the both of you?"

Here it was a look got on Otto's face, the same look as got on Grandfather's face when Grandfather dialed the telephone and ordered the Phil Silvers Job. Stiffly, Otto told the keeper, "You've been most kind to give us tea. Will you see us out?"

And with that the keeper shut and locked the cell door, casting its occupant back into our history.

The keeper prattled on. "Your grandfather has been kind enough to provide for her upkeep." He'd shepherded us from the dismal cell and closed the door with no further word from the inmate. He'd led us on a reverse journey, back through gates and doors, saying, "Rest assured, she's to remain in our care at least until her child is born."

Otto, in a dispassionate Richard Attenborough voice, as if he were merely watching a tiger eviscerate a weeping dik-dik, said, "Have you placed the child? Will it be adopted?"

To this the keeper would only reply, "I'm not at liberty to say."

Otto pressed his point. "Is my grandfather to adopt it?"

And the keeper repeated, "Sir, I'm not at liberty."

As we took leave of the asylum, Otto told me not to look back. We mustn't look because that lunatic woman would be in her window, and in all likelihood she'd be spouting her gibberish about how Daddy loved us and how Daddy was immensely proud of us. When in fact we were despicable, detestable, dainty things despised by all good people. Otto told me, "That only goes to show how mad she is." He took my hand and fairly towed me down the Pembroke Road. "You know how the world hates our sort," he told me. "Why, the world would just as soon see us herded into railway cars and carted off to some isolated camp to be burned to cinders in some furnace and those cinders cast to the wind." Here Otto dashed fresh tears from his eyes and said, "Daddy loathed you and me. It's crucial you accept that."

And to leaven his glowering mood I suggested we strip down to the altogether. Once we got home, we two should tart ourselves up in a lot of Mummy's old nighties and bed jackets and try to flag down rides along empty, dark reaches of the motorway.

Normally Otto would jump at the chance to flag down goes and to allow some sadistic wretch to imagine he could wring our necks and bury our twee bodies in a shallow grave before we'd flash a knife and hold the sadist hostage and make him weep for his life and spring out for some nice fish and chips and take us dancing down the public house, lest we shoot him dead, the poor tosser.

And just this once, Otto said, "No, Cecil, not tonight."

## 36

OUR DAY IS SATURATED WITH PEA-SOUP FOG SO DENSE YOU'D BE HARD-
pressed to point out the sun's position in the sky. Still, weather is the
least of our worries, isn't it?

One can't fault the footmen for failing to carry the tea tray into the
nursery, for it's become a chamber of horrors. The smells. The scads
of houseflies. Our own Madame Tussauds. It's the lair of our very
own plastic Jack the Ripper. Using the unloved-ones we've brought
him, the tutor carves them to pieces and glues together the innards
and the outward features to create the carnal fantasies he makes and
remakes on a whim.

Done with worshipping God, now he plays god, pasting together
male and female to create unspeakable monsters he then has it off
with. He'll slice bits off an Olympic shot putter and combine them with
parts from a ballerina and a burly hooligan. The nursery, littered with
plastic gutted carcasses and aluminum skulls.

From would-be Jesuit to criminal against nature, he's gone. A Dr.
Frankenstein using rubber cement. He's collaged together a Prince
Charming with two anuses where the eyes should be. Then a lithe
figure skater with eight breasts. Then a blond lumberjack with five
penises on each hand in place of fingers. And once the glue has set
he'll have a go before taking the thing back to pieces and building
anew something the likes of which creation has never seen. With each
corrupt evolution he's got myriad new ways to have a go. Our tutor,
reinventing himself as the next Charles Darwin. The survival of the
fetishist.

The situation with Grandfather remains at an impasse, with Otto
continuing to dispose of Porsches and Jaguars, but hauling home the

unloved-ones to keep our tutor occupied. Elsewhere, Miss Sunny Delight continues to thrive. Otto kites hither and yon. The tutor, distracted. I seek refuge in the basement with nanny. As she shaves away, nanny gives me an earful of the latest gossip. Word has gotten round the village about the tutor's collection of monstrosities, and no one will deliver to us for love or ready money.

What's more, nanny is quite beside herself with fretting. Nothing less than a body has turned up hereabouts. Two dead bodies! A pair of randy punters, they were. Old nanny says, "Master Cecil, it's murder most foul, innit?" As she works the razor over my sensitive, stunted pre-male bits, she says, "Done like kippers, they was. Opened from bottom to top, each man was, with his innards got out."

I tell her to mind her shaving, or she'll have me butchered in no short order.

Here she helps me from the tub and begins to blot me dry with a lovely, soft towel. Doing so, she says, "Why it fairly makes my flesh crawl, don't it?" She helps me into my dressing gown, still prattling on. "Master Cecil, folks as say all the blood was got out. Both fine, strong men, too!"

I tell her to hush and quit carrying tales.

As for me, I busy myself with correspondence. No one is as needy as the sexually predatory locked up for multiple life sentences. But when it comes to spinning yarns I've not got Otto's flair. Truth be told, I've soured a little on scribbling love notes heavy with cutesy pillow-talk about having it off in the bath or how I sleep in the raw and suffer the most enticing dreams of brusque sex killers climbing in through the nursery window and wrapping me all in plumber's tape and . . . well, it's all rather lost its charm without Otto. Off on various missions as he is.

I've the house to myself, haven't I? With the servants belowstairs I wander to Mummy's room, to her dressing room, and push the hangers this way and that as I sniff out the gowns and cloaks that carry her scent. The headiest aroma clings to a simple black dress, cut snug with a high hemline and a mandarin collar. Sleeveless. All the better to show my spindly, pale arms to their best advantage. It takes not a moment to have the thing out of the closet and on my back. It zips up the side so that's no great effort.

It's nothing nanny need know, but, in a pinch, I *can* work a zipper.

If you ask me, Mummy's brand of appeal is a tad bit too over reliant on foundation garments. An illusion impossible to maintain beyond a certain point in courtship. On my lithe hips, however, the frock fits like a dream.

What's needed now are the right stockings and shoes and in short order I'm sat at the vanity table applying contour powder to make the bridge of my nose appear thinner. I rouge up. Do my eyes the way Otto showed me. Clever Otto. Thanks to him, I've lovely eyes. I dust my bare shoulders with talcum to look every inch the porcelain doll.

Only then do I hear it. A great bellowing voice booms up the stairs. A roaring, howling, full-throated animal call that bellows, "Urethra!"

As Otto once seduced a previous ogre, I set my cap to charm this most recent escapee from some maximum-security penitentiary.

I descend toward the entry hall to find a footman has unsuccessfully barred the front door to a hulking ogre only partially clad in a torn, blood-spattered prison jumpsuit. His ogre eyes find me poised midway down the steps, and his tone softens, "Urethra?" Soft now with admiration and wonder. As if he were addressing a Greek goddess.

A look gets on the ogre's face like got on Daddy's face as he watched Mummy's homecoming at Heathrow after she'd done the Phil Hartman Job. The same look as got on Otto's face as he watched the yard boy soap himself in the shower.

I wave off the footman, who sprints a retreat, no doubt quitting his position in this bonkers household. Standing a few steps above the stranger I offer a slim hand, my fingers glinting with bejeweled rings. As Urethra, Lady Urethra, I ask to whom I have the pleasure of speaking. Should this barbarous ogre suspect he's being made a fool of, he'd batter me to a pulp.

He falls to his knees. Kissing my hand, he moans, "Urethra! My queen. Urethra, my only!" He says, "It's your devoted Digby, I is!"

I ring for the chauffeur to bring the car round. As the crazed stranger's chapped lips plant kisses higher along my thin arm, I suggest we two take a romantic stroll on a sandy ocean beach.

We make the journey to the sea in an ecstasy of thrilling, dangerous kisses and embraces. This crazed Digby, he takes the liberty of squeezing my tiny chest with his calloused mitts while slobbering sweet nothings in my ear. Bracing it feels, to be mouthed by a sex criminal, me a wee baby quoll ready to be torn limb from limb should the mood shift.

What I do here I do in the spirit of a Richard Attenborough, I suppose. My glamorous outward appearance belies the fact that I am a naturalist, a scientist keen to conduct an experiment. This calls for leading my test subject, slobbering ogre, staggering ogre, into the driftwood towers of the ghost forest. My mind is awash in violins as I step from the car and place a dainty foot in the sand. We're to play a round of What's the Time Mr. Wolf? And if I'm captured we'll move on to play Winnie-the-Pooh and Lady-in-the-Lake.

The ogre, the crushing weight of the man, sinks his steps deep in the loose sand. The day's mist has dampened a thin crust over the beach. And as fleet as a gazelle, light as a tern, I'm able to skitter along this crust without falling through.

Bogging down, my ogre plods along, his legs plunging knee deep with every stride. Still, I lure him into the forest with winks and blown kisses. Owing to the pea-soup fog we've soon lost our way among the ghostly trees. Such effort to move leaves him winded, this Digby, too breathless to more than whisper, "Urethra." A whisper as soft as the fog. Fog that drifts about to hide us from one another for moments at a time.

The honest part of me would rather be seized and had a go with and strangled. This seems preferable to my predator losing interest and seeing I'm not worth the trouble. That I'm not appealing enough to pursue. To that end I slow my steps and bat my eyelashes and even weep quietly as if in mortal terror.

I'd rather die than know I'm not worth the killing. I'd rather be eaten than know I'm not worthy food.

And here my ogre gives forth a great shout of, "Urethra!" He shouts, "Help me, my lady! I'm caught, I is!"

I turn to find him sunk up to his waist in the sand and continuing to slip lower. He looks as if he's going down on a tiny elevator like the Wicked Witch of Oz did when she was melting. Or he's dropping through some secret trapdoor. Up to his waist in sand, then he's up to his chest. He spreads his arms and holds himself there for a moment, buried to the armpits, saying, "Urethra, please." Asking, "Urethra, what's happening?"

I go back, but not so close he might grab me and pull me down into the ground along with him.

The sand is at his chin now, and as he opens his mouth to say, "I love you," loose grains pour over his lips and down his throat, and he chokes and coughs up sand. His head sinks under. A flood of sand covers the top of his sinking scalp. Now only one of his trembling hands still sprouts from the ground.

Was this how Daddy had vanished? And the old duffer whom Otto had lured here?

Against my better judgment I step forward and take the stranger's hand. I haven't the strength to save him, but I can give comfort until he's smothered and suffocated. This act of charity will be my undoing.

His grip crushes my fingers, the grip of a drowning man, and he drags my hand down, then my slender arm. In a clock tick my hand will be under the sand, then my arm, then my head, and I'll be dragged headfirst down to hell by this sex killer.

The dying weight of this ogre is pulling me into a living grave.

To make a big starfish of myself, I spread my legs and free arm. This leaves only my mouth to save me, my wee nibbling plant-eater's mouth, and I bite deep into the monster's calloused hand. Bite until my teeth meet bone, the cartilage joints between the knuckles, and I taste blood, choking on blood, inhaling and drinking blood as it erupts in pulses from that buried-alive, frenzied heart.

My herbivore's tiny jaws clamp tight, and I shake my head to sever tendons and rip apart muscle from the hand. Blood and sand mix to make the gritty red mud of Australia in my mouth, the mouth of a baby joey determined not to die here. Determined to live. If not forever, but for now.

Facedown in the red filth I chew and swallow mouthfuls of flesh until the hand gripping mine is a skeleton's hand. Me now a meat eater. Not unlike the tutor with his practice of nibbling on plastic gallbladders. Me making the grip greased with blood. Until the skeleton's grip gives way. And here I'm safe as my attacker is sucked down, with his final breath a scream muffled through the sand as he shouts, "Urethra!"

Likewise, I'm also suffocating, unable to breathe. I gag at something blocking my throat. I vomit the something into my bloody hand and find the object is a finger. Not unlike the fingers displayed in our library vitrine. Still warm. Not yet the blue of death. This I hide inside my closed fist. My first trophy. And I lick at the blood cooling sticky around my lips.

Here I return to the waiting car, stepping lightly and with care around the invisible buried pockets of hell waiting ready to swallow me whole.

## 37

**I'M NOT TWO STEPS IN THE DOOR BEFORE NANNY SEES ME AND ASKS WHY**
I'm red all over. She asks, "Has Master Otto been going at you again?"
She whispers, "A filthy business, what goes on in that nursery."

Here a look gets on nanny's face like the time she went to the
kitchen window. At dusk, it was. She stood on tiptoe to look out across
the darkening yard to where a figure moved in the shadows. The figure itsy-bitsy-spidered down the ivy below the nursery window. A horror, it was. Starkers, with a dozen legs and a different set of genitalia
between each pair. A number of heads sprouted from its neck, blond,
brunette, and ginger, and its naked torso was spotted with numer-
ous nipples. The monster crept out the nursery window and climbed
down the ivy, then edged along the shadows and made toward the
gate at the bottom of the garden, and beyond that the back lane that
led down to the village.

Now it's not just the ghosts, is it? Our lovely manor house is hatch-
ing all sort of abominations to menace the poor villagers. Not only
do our servants meet no limit of bad ends, now there's a shambling
monster on the prowl, no doubt pawing to have it off with the toughs
and roughs, those poor sots who get shut out of the Crested Eagle at
closing and will have a go with anything for a quid in a dustbin. All
that, and to top it off there's whispered talk about a deadly lake, a lake
pretty to look at but deadly to anyone who breaks the surface.

Under nanny's watchful eye, the monster, jiggling with extra limbs
and breasts and peckers, it had roamed through the gate and disappeared with the last light of day into the woods.

At the memory, the same look gets on nanny's face and she crosses
herself. She reaches toward me to have off my jumper so's she can

bathe me, but I step back and say that just this one time I'd like to try to bathe myself. My hands and face, crusted with dried sex-killer blood. Heaven forbid the old crone discover the finger.

You see, the finger is still in my pocket. The Digby pussy finger. I dare not let her find it lest I be forced to tell how I'd chewed it off the dying hand of a sex killer buried alive in the ghost forest.

The nanny leans close and whispers, "Master Cecil, a word to the wise is sufficient . . . your mother is home with her hulking German."

At long last I can set Mummy's heart at ease. Such joy, such glee. I've formed some rough idea about Daddy's vanishing, I have, and it wasn't angels or space aliens lifting him into the sky. However, before I can make my case I'll need a few hours among the books in our library.

Thanks to Grandfather we've no end of books about geological goings on. There can be nothing in our world that the ancients haven't plumbed to the core. One book in particular, titled *The Erosion Process and Behavior of Resultant Sedimentary Materials*, looks to be especially slow going. It concerns itself with the degradation of rock into grains of sand and how such grains are displaced by wind and water. Being about glaciers and whatnot, it's hardly a page turner. Impatient pea brain, antsy pea brain that I am, I'm hardly into the Mesozoic Period before my interest wanes.

It's here something catches my eye. The corner of a page, someone has folded it down. To mark a topic some reader has found notable. This subsection of the book is titled "The Chimney Effect." The chimney effect. The article's abstract, every line of it is highlighted with yellow pen. As per these highlighted words, when a dune engulfs a forest the trees die. The portion of each tree still rising above the sand, it bleaches and falls to bits. The buried portion of each trunk rots, but as it does it leaves an underground cavity as deep as the tree was tall.

A *chimney*, it's called, this vertical pit in the sand. It's as big around as the tree was. Typically a layer of windblown sand seals the top. One step on this thin trapdoor will send a person plunging to the bottom of the pit. Even as the fragile shaft collapses inward to bury the victim. Beneath this cave-in, under tons of damp sand the victim simply disappears.

The collapsed chimney leaves no trace. Only a set of footprints lead up to the spot. And unlike a snow avalanche there's little or no air under sand as deep as a telephone pole is tall. You can't carve a breathing space like you could in snow, and wait for a rescue. You're crushed and smothered and your back's broken by the fall and the weight of it all upon you. If not forever, you're alive, but not for long.

All of this is highlighted, and written in the page margin is the word *Possible?*

Here, of course here, Mummy steps into the library to reshelve a Pearl S. Buck novel. Mummy's timing is impeccable. She sees me holding this book of all the books. She crosses this room cluttered with stuffed jaguars and panthers, walking past the vitrine, and she bestows a kiss on my cheek. "Cecil," she says, seeing me see her see me holding the book open to "The Chimney Effect." That horrible result of something rotted out at the center.

As for me, I close the book. I kiss her cheek in return and ask how Switzerland was. The Digby pussy finger sits in my pocket, the pocket of my jumper.

"Lovely," Mummy says. She makes no mention of the blood dried around my mouth, nor of the sand in my hair. That sex-killer blood, a little of it, is now smudged on her cheek.

I make ready to slot the book back among its fellows on the shelf.

Mummy asks, "What are you reading, Cecil?" and reaches for it.

It's about sand, I tell her.

She takes the book from my hand, saying, "Sand, Cecil, is very deadly." She opens the book to exactly the passage on chimneys. Her eyes merely scanning the page, she says, "Fungi devours the dead tree, and it's the roots of this fungi that hold the shape of the pit. Like the thinnest layer of cement, the dead fungi become."

Here her eyes say she did it. She killed Daddy on account of Evelyn. And her eyes say she knows I know. "Cecil, you ought not take sand for granted." With that, she claps the book shut and reshelves it.

# 38

TONIGHT'S NOT GOING TO BE A REPEAT OF MISS SUNNY DELIGHT, HER WITH her brass name tag and winsome terrier ways. Why Otto would no more shoot a dog as emigrate to Australia, especially not once Miss Delight had sensed the gun next to her furry head and opened her bright, button eyes and gave a pink lick to Otto's hand.

No, tonight we're on a mission to locate and do away with a Mr. Pleshy Tibbets. The blushing, baby-talk, twee two of us, Otto and I, speeding along in a nicked Bugatti Royale, we're determined to make good by Grandfather. You see, Grandfather assures us that it's no great tragedy when a person dies.

The village is in a terrible state. People round these parts spook easily, don't they? Among them's a gamekeeper who reports down the pub he'd run across a monster out along Tishingbeck, even got off a shot that spoiled one of the beast's several heads, but clearly not the important head seeing as how the thing loped away and escaped. A demon from outer space, common folk call it. Hightailing it over hill and dale every night. Folks claim to see it climb out the Crossroads well. And there's folks who claim to have found their livestock interfered with, all worried, like, around every hole. Cattle and sheep alike.

Round the village square the building walls are posted with handbills. Each displays its own version of the great beast, some shaggy with teats and scrotums. Others crowded all over with limbs, while a third version seems quilted together from a bevy of faces. Perhaps this last version looks the most unsettling: a walking carpet of nothing but smiling beauties and smirking chaps.

None other than our own tiny footman tells how the demon haunts our grounds and garden, from gloaming until near dawn, no doubt after a night of peeping Tomming and having it off with inebriates collapsed and incoherent in flooded wayside ditches and under mossy bridges. Tales to chill the blood, these are. A beast fringed with willies and pimpled with erect nipples.

Folks hereabout tell as how it's a selkie or a troll or some unholy offspring of the two. While others have seen it leave a hundred footprints with each passing, like a centipede, as it crosses a fresh-plowed field. Others, they swear it's the fallout from Windscale and the radiation what leaked from the plutonium and meltdown of the nuclear reactor, and it's an escaped circus sideshow dosed with that radiation. That's spurred it to sprout all manner of extra appendages. A thing shaggy with tumors, it is, and any tosspot who's had a midnight go with the beast isn't quick to tell about it.

For the moment Otto's home. Home from Tyger or whatnot. Otto says, "Cecil, we're to keep our eyes peeled for the beast."

Otto says, "Consumption," paraphrasing Grandfather, "is the purpose of mankind." And in no way a negative one. It only makes sense. The tuna fish simply weren't eating enough mercury, were they? Nor were the snowy egrets breathing in sufficient asbestos and heavy metals. If Mother Nature was to be saved, humans would need be take action.

According to Grandfather the population explosion was planned. World leaders needed more humans to constantly vacuum clean the environment. No species is as efficient as the human, with his liver and kidneys, at filtering out the filth. That's why it's essential that individuals gobble up as much muck as possible. In this way the noxious bilge can be landfilled for centuries. Otto says, "Humans are terrible at disposing of everything except themselves." So it only makes sense that we become repositories for all the dioxins and whatnot before we go each into our lead-lined casket and concrete vaults, where our remains won't leak our corruption back into the soil.

Otto says, "Grandfather has looked into these matters, and lesser humans also act as traps to collect and store really harmful germs and viruses such as HIV and hepatitis, thus making those bugs less of a threat to better humans. In effect, lesser people are sponges, always sopping up the most dangerous of biological hazards."

Not an ignoble purpose, is it? Otto says, "If they shouldn't be lapping up the germs and viruses, then the rest of us would be in greater danger, would we not?"

According to Grandfather, common people can't help themselves. It's best they be allowed to suck up all the filth and corruption and leave the world a fitter place for their betters. And for the future.

You see, for most of human history common people made things, didn't they? For example, shoes and pots and other people. But now the purpose of most people is to mop up the unclean world. All that air and water and everything solid must pass through the filter that is our lungs and fatty tissues and livers. In effect, people are a trap for toxins, aren't they?

Grandfather is oh so clever. As is Otto.

As Grandfather always says, "The common folk *are* Australia, aren't they?" Stuffed to the gills with all the microplastics and asbestos and phytoestrogens and polychlorinated biphenyls that people in power won't suffer.

"Grandfather calls it terraforming," Otto says and he steers the Bugatti down a lonely nighttime lane. "Grandfather says modern humans are nothing better than roving mops and vacuums, so it's no real tragedy to kill a person. Just so long as someone disposes of the mess properly."

Otto is only being Otto, he is. We're off in our nicked Bugatti to snuff out Mr. Tibbets, so it only goes to follow that Otto's outlook is bleak. If he sees this doomed person as a vacuum bag, filled with dioxins, well, it's no great crime to kill him, is it?

Here it is our headlamps sweep over something in the roadway. A figure from a nightmare. It stumbles into the right-of-way and freezes, blinded by our glare. It seems supported by a dozen legs, slender legs as well as the hairy gams of burly footballers. Crowded betwixt these legs are all sort of dangly bits and quims galore. A multitude of arms flail from the torso, and no fewer than four heads top the shoulders. What's more, the all of it is pasted with nipples, wee pink ones as well as the brown, hairy type.

Otto brakes the car to a tyre-skidding halt. We two stare in open-mouthed terror as the beast speaks. Only one of its heads speaks, a man's head, a familiar face, but not in this context. In a voice known to us, the creature says, "Master Otto, Master Cecil, can you give me a lift into the village?"

It's our tutor. The boy spinster, all got up in fancy dress glued together from chopped bits of the unloved-ones. A mess of pasted-together dismembered and remembered limbs and whatnot, fashioned into this late-night, lane-going sex demon. A sight to compete with any duck-billed platypus or dodo in the Outback.

Otto waves for the tutor-thing to climb into our rear seat.

"Just as far as the Crested Eagle," it says.

## 39

**THE TUTOR STAGGERS BACK EVERY MORNING BRIMMING WITH CASH FROM**
having it off with potted tossers, toughs and roughs who've given him
a go in a dustbin for a quid. Tweaking his twenty nipples and having it
off in his rectal eye sockets. The rubber thing's a great favorite among
the hooligans who've only ever been to Amsterdam to have a bit of
the rough.

To enter the nursery is to walk into a mass grave. Houseflies continue to reproduce on some hidden decay. Slain athletes are layered
with dead lingerie models, all tangled in the anonymity of their nakedness. With somewhere in this morass the naked tutor, pale and still
as death after a nighttime of carnal carousing. He's shed his rubber
hide from the prior night. This sexual carapace is worse for the wear.
Pulled. Tweaked. Violated and impregnated in countless plastic loca-
tions. It's cast aside, ready to be butchered and remade as the next ab-
horrent fantasy. A jumble of fake flesh shifts to reveal the least robust
arm. The only sallow thigh twitches, and a snore rattles forth from
a face carved and sunken with exhaustion. No more a chaste bookworm, our classics scholar, he mutters in his sleep, "Είμαι ο βασιλιάς
της σαύρας."

Breakfast finds Otto and me coming to table with Mummy and her
paramour. As the parlor-floor maid sets out things on the sideboard,
here Mummy says, "Otto? Cecil? There's someone special I'd like you
to meet."

Standing beside her is a martial sort of blond Hun, the heel-
clicking sort, complete with waxed mustache and a dueling scar running across one cheek, one of those ragged scars German college
boys carve into their own faces. They cut themselves and pack the

wound with horsehair to keep it from closing properly, they do, so our strange stepfather isn't fooling anyone. There's something more the headwaiter than the field marshal about the man's military stance.

Otto points out that Mummy has gone back to wearing black. In particular, black blouses. Not out of mourning mind you, black signifies she's embroiled in a *délire amoureux* or erotomania. You see Mummy always goes in for a bit of rough handling, she does. That's the Welsh in her. In particular, Mummy demands her nipples be gone over, you see, at times manhandled to the extent that wearing a white blouse is out of the question. It's to hide that possible tiny bit of blood, the black is. Not an approved look among Mummy's social set, even tiny, leaked-out spots of blood.

Mummy with her newlywed glow, her honeymoon glow, she's mutton dressed as lamb, she is. I've yet to tell Otto. About the chimneys, I mean. About how Mummy most likely plotted to bury Daddy for revenge. For mad Evelyn being up the duff.

Upon meeting the German, a look gets on Otto's face like when he read the latest batch of pen-pal letters. Among them, a letter from the Buckinghamshire Asylum. The crazy woman has come back into our lives. Oh, it's been just nannies and nannies, and a half hundred governesses since we paid her that first visit. Servants truly are our only means of marking time. The nameless footmen and butlers that trickle through our lives serve as the grains of sand in an hourglass.

That's not to say Evelyn isn't still chained to a stone wall, but yes, she's long since birthed her baby and christened it James Jr., and the baby was seized by the National Health or some such outfit. Per her letter, her raving, grand plan is to rally her fellow lunatics. To stage an uprising, no less. To muster an army of the violently demented, and to roam the countryside in search of her spawn.

That same look gets on Otto's face now as he and I turn languid, bird-voiced, cooing, and we each take one of the Hun's massive hands. We cling and drape ourselves against him. We busy our hands inside his bathrobe, feeling for delicious treats. The Hun recoils. Of course the Hun recoils, as any manly predator would cringe from our unhealthy touch. His impulse is the same reflex what keeps a coyote from eating a diseased rabbit. It's clear from our slinky, sex-kitten manner that Otto and I are the repository for broken chromosomes and bioaccumulating industrial solvents. We're the legacy of fireproofed pajamas and nonstick cookware. We're the product of off-gassing carpets and aluminum salts used by ancestors long before our conception.

We're everything infectious, looking to jump ship to a new host.

We're wee baby guppies swarming now to eat our parent guppy. And now we're a family, aren't we?

As plates are passed, a look gets on Mummy's face like when Otto was in the changing rooms at Sandhurst and some prankster made off with his linen so he was compelled to go raw under his kilt what with final examinations that day and the Commandant's Parade. Otto suffered no end of ribbings on account of word getting around that he'd no linens. A conspiracy, it was. Meaning his fellows could all walk close behind him in passageways and use their ceremonial swords to lift the hem of his kilt until Otto was quite scarlet and vexed by no end of exposures, even before the ordeal of the parade ground when Otto's pipe-and-drum regiment formed up and passed the review stands and a stiff wind was his undoing. Burdened as he was by the bagpipes and him the lead piper, he'd no chance when the gust first fluttered, then raised his kilt full to waist height with Mummy in the review stands, not to mention the Queen, Her Royal Highness, in attendance with all the Sandhurst parents and alumni now privy to Otto's freshly shaven bits and a prominent bite mark, each tooth mark brazenly clear against one ivory buttock, and not the bite radius of another wee boy but the bite mark of a great toothy groundskeeper or a bricklayer or such, with Otto just piping away in lockstep, oblivious to the stir he'd raised among the dons, and poor Mummy torn between sympathy and disgust, and onlookers cadging field glasses from each other to better spy a closer look at that, that bite mark on the wistful, winsome, twee buttocks of Otto, who later spilled to me that he'd done it himself, not the bite mark per se, but he'd flushed his own linen down the changing-room crapper and complained loudly so one and all would know he'd no option save to get on with it and take his exams with his raw bits spilling against each cold seat and then to shoulder his bagpipe and form up in the ranks to be paraded in the wind.

As for the bite mark, a barman had done it, hadn't he? Some tattooed, punk rocker skinhead, he was. He'd let Otto in after the lock-in and used his black-painted fingernails to make the scratch marks hardly noticeable next to that livid bite mark. Like a shark, it was. Like a regular Jaws. Otto had only to say the same culprits as made off with his linen, they'd also sunk their predatory teeth into him during the confusion. As stunts like this were always pulled off in the changing rooms. The result being to cast Otto as a fully sympathetic figure. An involuntary harlot. Just the perfect mix of innocent victim and road-tested gutter tramp. A favored status Mummy had yet to grasp as she watched the Queen watch Otto's bloody, bite-marked buttocks march bang up and down the field. A sight of such animal appeal that even the Queen was made to wipe her mouth with the back of one gloved, royal hand. Her corgis, panting.

Much later, Otto would tell me it felt thrilling: to be both pitied and desired. And to be chased about naked by every hungry eye. To play the part of both the pathetic victim and the delicious prey.

This is the exact look that gets on Mummy's face now as she watches Otto rub his youthful body fully up and down the long legs of the Hun.

We're bait, Otto and I, dripping with poison. We pet the massive hands and give them kisses, wetting our lips for best effect. We knit our tiny fingers between the Hun's large ones as Otto says, "Cecil, why this one's a giant, isn't he?"

It's only the most diseased rabbit that can eat clover within full view of hawks and foxes and feel no fear. We're the rabbits the wolves run away from. Here a look gets on Otto's face like last night when we found Mr. Pleshy Tibbets asleep and Otto put the muzzle of the P38 smack against his head. And it wasn't even much noise, Otto said, because the brains absorbed the sound, didn't they? Neither was the mess much bother because it sprayed out the other side, at least according to Otto.

Did I mention yet that Mr. Tibbets was a horse? A lovely horse. Not a man at all. A thoroughbred trotter, he was, who needed permanent putting out to pasture. Another piggy bank of insurance money to be broke into. The poor sweet old gelding. Otto had murmured Richard Attenborough pillow-talk to this horse, stalled alone, late at night in an otherwise empty farm. Otto had whispered, "Let's watch now as the apex predatory tiger cubs shoot to death this innocent horse no one loves."

Not that I watched. I couldn't watch. If you must know, I stepped back to the car and got in, and clamped my hands over my ears, and Otto pulled the trigger.

At breakfast Otto takes the Hun's massive hand and rubs it against his own cheek as if the hand were a flannel. "Do you skin dive?" Otto asks. Adding, *"Ich kenne einen schönen See voller Schätze."*

The bell rings, the bell for the front doors. It rings again, and the footman it seems is in no great hurry to respond.

No doubt Daddy's long-ago internet tot has roped in another randy pervert, drawn here with beer and condoms to have a go with Otto.

Here I excuse myself from table to walk the distance down the passageway to the front hall. The bell rings once more as I reach up to throw the bolt and tug aside one of the heavy carved doors to re-veal a man. A man standing at our threshold. Quite posh, he is. Not a prole, by the look of him. To judge by the gentleman's bearing and Sandhurst parade-rest stance, he's my equal. This stranger looks down upon me and says, "Cecil, my darling boy, is that you?"

You see, I'm of two minds at the moment. Half of me would shut the door in the man's face, while my other half would throw myself into his arms. This man, glowing and sporty with all of lovely England behind him, all the dovecotes and gothic tracery and half-timbered whatnot.

Before I'm to do either, footsteps sound in the passageway be-hind me. A melodious female voice trills, "Cecil, who's there?" Not a clock tick later, the same voice says, "It can't be." Arriving at my side, Mummy, her voice shrill, her face gone quite pale, she says, "James?" She asks, "After all these years, can it be you?"

## 40

**MUMMY, IT WOULD SEEM, IS A BIGAMIST. DADDY IS DELIVERED SAFELY TO US.** Young Daddy, shining and brilliant Daddy. Not a day older than he was in the ghost forest all those years and years ago, the great fleshy veins worming on either side of his forehead.

The house is at sixes and sevens with everyone rushing at once to resurrect Daddy's old slippers and smoking jacket and take his coat and usher him to the dining room for his tea. Mummy's reverted to her pill-popping ways and at this writing she remains supine on the morning-room settee balancing a cold compress on her lovely forehead. Otto stands at the ready to jab her with a hypodermic should she need further sedation.

Our German kneels next to the settee and massages Mummy's lovely feet. Their language barrier at present works in his great good favor.

## 41

**I STAND CORRECTED. MUMMY, IT WOULD SEEM, IS NOT A BIGAMIST.**

Daddy is not Daddy. He's the bairn of that lunatic, Evelyn. Despite all of our lovely clocks going unwound and our calendar being untouched, somehow decades have passed!

Decades, mind you! Not just a parade of nameless servants, but vital years have gone by! Our cooks alone are beyond number!

Without a single birthday in our lives, not one inflamed cake or piñata, the wee baby born in the lunatic asylum has grown into the man newly received into our household. His paternity goes without saying. The very picture of our father, he is. Here is James Jr., the pretender to Daddy's throne. The usurper.

Curious it is, how we can simply live our lives while decades pass in a clock tick. Otto, me, Mummy, we're all ages older than we'd ever let on.

## PART 4

# MILFOIL

## 42

ACCORDING TO MUMMY, THE LATE DUKE AND DUCHESS OF WINDSOR NEVER wanted to appear less than vivacious in public. So even when they'd no conversation, nothing to share with one another after decades of marriage, they'd sit at their prominent table in some posh restaurant and simply repeat the alphabet to each other in various melodic patterns.

I suppose Otto and I replay Judy Garland's last night for much the same reason. For comfort, that's a given. And out of familiarity.

Tonight finds us reduced to the dog house, again. A damp, drippy night in the dog house. The two of us make for a cramped fit, what with the tea tray and cups and scones and the sterling service. We've the books we could salvage from the hellish nursery. And a candle, we've a single candle as our only source of light. Nonetheless we've room to sit on a pretend 22 June 1969 windowsill and toilet, Otto and I respectively.

Otto produces a cashew nut from his pocket and dusts it free of lint. He places the small end into his ear and lodges the nut like a pink plastic hearing aid. In his pretend Grandfather voice he says, "All successful civilizations have relied on a slave class."

He says that until recently that class had been imported into an empire from conquered lands. In much of the world those slaves were castrated to keep them docile and to prevent their breeding. It's only since the middle of the last century that a really ripping science-based solution presented itself. You see, the birthrate for fey, feeble, polyurethane-defected things had taken a jump. A great demographic bubble of the nasty, xenoestrogen-stunted pre-males were born. As fake Grandfather, Otto says, "First we thought to blame the mothers.

Oh, the mothers felt just awful." He says, "But we knew better." He says, "We called it *toxic emasculation*."

My fake Judy Garland says, "Toxic emasculation?" She taps the ash from her pretend cigarette. "Why's it always the mother they blame when a kid's queer?"

But it wasn't the mothers, not really. As pretend Grandfather explains, skinny Grandfather, 1969 Grandfather, it was the mid-century explosion of styrene and isoprene and vinyl chloride. Or as pretend Grandfather puts it, "$CH_2=CHC_6H_5$ and $CH_2=CH-C(CH_3)=CH_2$ and $CH_2=CHCl$." He says, "We made it the mothers' fault so it wouldn't look like the doing of Dow Chemical or Monsanto or DuPont."

Just as World War II had given us the ballpoint pen, the plastics revolution had given us a new class of slaves. This was the hormonally disrupted crowd. The tight-pants pre-males who flocked to hear Miss Garland and bought her records and would soon wait on line to view her dead body. They looked to be the perfect slave class. Some of them quite clever, but doomed to being drones who'd work and work and die. They'd accrue wealth with no offspring.

Instead they'd engage in wanton acts of sexual deproduction. Chavtastic sexually deproductive acts.

Pretend Grandfather leans forward to light his make-believe cigarette from our very real candle flame. Rain patters on the dog-house roof. "Thanks to environmental pollution, a great legion of PCB-poisoned pre-males was being born. Precisely the slave class needed by Western nations," he said in his rich, Richard Attenborough tones. "Trouble was, we couldn't keep blaming the mothers forever."

Science had solved the slave shortage by creating this plastics-infused population of eunuchs whose only drive would be to have a worthless go with other pre-males. Shame would keep them in place. Shaming the mothers as well as shaming the slaves themselves for their deviant plastics-inspired impulses, but that wouldn't last forever.

"No," pretend Grandfather said, "we needed to change up our strategy."

God forbid the slaves grasp the nature of their situation. Here they'd been engineered in greater and greater numbers, and they'd been denied access to traditional means of advancement through the military and through marriage. And in being denied those paths they'd been denied financing for education and property ownership. And if this ever-growing class of bred-to-die drones ever glimpsed the big picture, why, everything would collapse, wouldn't it?

As per the script, here my fake Judy Garland will toss back the rest of her invisible drink, then extend the glass for a refill from fake Grandfather's make-believe enema bag. Another cocktail of champagne and phenobarbital, I suppose.

"No," Otto's Grandfather says, "should the cutesy, coy, polycarbonate-poisoned pre-males catch on . . . well, we'd be out our slaves, wouldn't we?" He says, "And the class-action lawyers would get into the act . . . just as with asbestos and tobacco and opioids, and the whole of the Western synthetics industry would be made bankrupt."

On cue, my Judy Garland asks, "So that's how come I have to die? Tonight?"

"Exactly tonight," says Otto's Grandfather. "It's a very precise operation, this keeping of slaves."

Cutthroats and mercenaries were waiting to play their roles. In one night, the ruling class had to shift the narrative. From shame to pride. Judy Garland would die, and all her adherents would come to embrace their engineered disabilities as badges of honor. On the night of her funeral, the gay pride movement would be born.

"If only," pretend Grandfather says, "we'd worked this trick with asbestos! If we'd made mesothelioma a high-status indicator . . . then the Manville fortune would still be intact!" Young Grandfather shrugged. "If we'd spun birth defects as a bold new fashion, then Thalidomide would still be raking in the bucks."

My Judy Garland weighs the idea of calling for her pretend husband. Of screaming. Or doing anything, not just to save her own life but to thwart this tragic shift in history.

Through the doorway of the dog house, I can see a new monster, a quivering mass of breasts and genitals, itsy-bitsy-spidering down the ivy below the nursery window. The plodding horror drags a dozen rubber scrotums in the mud as it slouches toward the sleeping village in the distance.

Fake Grandfather adjusts the cashew nut in his ear. "First we controlled them with shame," he says, "then we controlled them with pride." Otto perfect-laughs his pretend Grandfather laugh. "It worked for Hitler, eh wot!"

The Stonewall incident—staged and cast and phony—would mark the shift.

Here in the dim crouched interior of the dog house, in the light of a single candle, a look gets on Otto's face like this afternoon, just today, when we'd journeyed back along the Pembroke Road back to the Buckinghamshire Asylum and took tea with the keeper, him with his grotty tinned biscuits and candied ginger, and we'd requested another audience with Evelyn, venturing through locked gates and heavy doors, back to that numbered cell.

There, the keeper had knocked. The room's occupant made no answer, so he unlocked the door and peered within. The person we'd found was hardly recognizable as a person, much less the attractive woman who'd shouted through our windscreen. The figure curled in a nest of soiled rags, one thin limb looped by a manacle and linked to the wall by a length of rusted chain. Time had stood still for her, poor Evelyn, shut away from sunlight, and some steady diet of millet porridge had given her the slender figure of a mummy dredged from an Irish peat bog. How I envied her her tiny, leathery waist!

When her eyes fixed on Otto, the woman cried, "We must find your father!" She winced as if the words had burned in her throat. "Your father will help us find James Jr."

As for Otto and me, our ruse had been well rehearsed. To waylay the keeper, I was to suffer a fainting spell, so here I'd stepped close to the man and collapsed bodily against him. The keeper's withered arms arrested my fall.

Otto had insisted, "My brother needs fresh air. Please help him into the passageway and loosen his clothing."

As I was lugged from the room, and the keeper rid me of my jumper, my shoes, my stockings, my trousers, linens, and began groping my nakedness as if checking for a broken pelvis or hernias, but in secret having a go with my helpless, inert form, as this cruel having-it-off took place, Otto would make his move. To the desperate Evelyn he'd whisper, "Your child is held hostage at 1057 Briar Hill Lane."

He'd tell her not to count on Daddy, that Daddy was in kangaroo heaven eating cherry tarts and pineapple ices. Otto would put a finger to Evelyn's cracked lips to silence her, and in that last possible moment he'd slip the Walther P38 from his pocket and present it to her to hide.

It's that same look what gets on pretend Grandfather as he watches the tutor's latest sex monster disappear into the rainy night.

## 43

TONIGHT OUR MISSION IS TO COLLECT A VINTAGE CHRYSLER IMPERIAL AND
bash it about, ramming traffic dividers and sideswiping Neolithic
standing stones, and in general getting full revenge on a lovely car
that had failed to make some rich nob happy. A usual night of joyrid-
ing before the Chrysler takes a final plunge into the car park at the
bottom of the secret lake.

Only tonight Otto proposes that he and I play the sporty, robust
types and drive our posh car around in search of shy, blushing, effete
types we can coerce into giving a ride, then use those lads as baby peccaries for our own benefit. Pre-male yard boys and the like. Not forever, but for now. Nothing lasting, granted, we'll just flush out some
low, commonplace peccaries, the bank-clerk type, or shop assistant,
and have a rough, messy go, and then toss them aside.

We'll hunt out the rude, coarse kind of pre-male with greased hair,
to whom having it off in a posh car with a couple toffs is a great lark.
Even if those two fine gentlemen give you fake names and a made-up
phone number, and they wipe themselves on your shirt, your best
shirt, like it's a rag, and they don't even offer to ride you home, but
only pull up to the next corner without so much as parking the transmission, but only leave the engine run as they say for you to climb out
and they tear away into the night.

Otto and I look for those walking-home types you can give a lift to.
Those types, they bang on about going to some nothing trade school,
and their bright future, but you get their naff clothes off and see them
as all they are, merely a pretty piece of trash to be worthless in another
year's time, and that's the predatory mindset Otto votes we adopt. At
least for tonight. To hunt down barmen and the like.

Tonight it is, we drive past a figure. By a bus stop, he is. Standing smack under the one light on the entire street. Like meat in a butcher's window, he is. Halfway between haircuts, he looks. A shaggy, leggy lad clean-shaven, he wears a hoodie. Trainers and jeans. Good for a go, he looks. Nobody's Pericles or Agamemnon.

As Otto wheels the car around for another look, he says, "That one fairly stinks of loneliness, don't he?" As we make our second pass, the lad steps to the curb. He looks to have no people and no education. He's the type who hasn't much, and in a year's time he'll lose his good skin and hair and have nothing. And Otto's right, the loneliness comes off him as thick as smoke.

Otto wheels around for a last pass, saying, "Why, he stinks of needing it."

The lad looks to be so alone that he'll do human toilet and tell himself this was love, why, he'll do anything we ask just so long as he's not ignored and left to stand there alone. He's a baby animal so unwanted he'll do rusty trombone and risk his life—risk catching hepatitis and AIDS—to ward off another moment of being some pre-male nobody set under a bus-stop light in the middle of cold nowhere.

Otto pulls to the curb but leaves the engine go. He puts his window down and says, "You had your dinner yet?"

The lad shakes his head.

Otto revs the engine and says, "Get in. Our treat."

The rear door is knackered since we sideswiped a phone box, and it takes the lad a good pull to get it open. "Shame about your car," he says. "It's a beauty." He scrambles a bit, only halfway in before Otto gets moving.

Otto sideswipes a utility pole. He says, "My name's Christopher." He nods my way, "And this is Cyril." Otto eyes the bloke in the rear-view mirror. "What do people call you?"

The lad looks at the town going by faster and faster outside the windows. He says, "People what like me, they call me Digby."

And here a chill goes through me. What they say about a goose walking over your grave, it is. You see, I've yet to tell Otto about the sex killer I chewed the hand off, the other Digby, and here's another. Still, it's a commonplace name. This signifies nothing.

A sneer gets on Otto's face, and he asks, "Can we like you, Digby?" The lad says, "I suppose."

Otto throws me a look, and asks the rearview mirror, "Can we both like you, Digby?" Like a cat he's being, with a working-class, uneducated mouse with no prospects trapped in the rear seat Otto can tease.

The lad says, "There's a chip shop still open, if you go left at this next corner." As if all he's after is his haddock and mushy peas. He leans forward to tap Otto on the shoulder, and the lad points out the way to go.

Otto makes the turn, too fast, skidding a great, noisy scream of rubber as our rear tyres fishtail, find purchase, then throw us in this new direction. Otto asks, "Cyril and I would both like to like you at least a couple times. Each." There's no overlooking his intentions. "You up for that, Digby?"

We jet past the lights of a chip shop, still open in an otherwise dark stretch of buildings. Our Digby cranes his neck to watch the shop disappear in our wake. He says, "They have skate." He says, "It's cod you get, but you can get skate if you don't mind splashing out a bit." By now he's turned full round, and he's watching the chip-shop lights vanish behind us.

"Digby?" Otto throws his words at the rearview mirror. "You do rusty trombone, do you?"

Sunk into himself, the lad says, "I don't know what that is, now do I?"

Otto says, "But you'll do it, won't you? For a mess of chips and an extra piece of tilapia, you'll do rusty trombone?"

"No," the lad says, shaking his head. "They no have tilapia there. It's not that nice a place."

Otto asks, "How hungry are you, Digby?"

In almost a whisper, the parabens-arrested lad says, "They'll be shut in a bit."

It's here Otto pulls the emergency brake and spins us a rubber-stinking doughnut in the road, bang in front of CCTV cameras. We motor back toward the shop lights. We park.

A look gets on the lad's face, our lad, like it's Christmas morning, and he's Tiny Tim delighted to find a plum in his filthy stocking. He muscles open his knackered car door and waves us toward the lights and the stink of grease. "They have kebab, too. You'll like it."

I get out to join him, but when I walk round to Otto's door, Otto says, "In a minute."

The lad stands, holding open the shop's door, as if by doing so he can keep them from closing up for the night. He calls, "Can we have skate?" He says, "It's worth it, if you've the extra quid."

In the driver's seat, Otto has out his wee telephone and appears to be reading a text letter from Grandfather. He waves me off.

I go with the lad, if only to suffer the moment Otto couldn't bear. At the greasy pass-through window, a counterman writes up our order: Six batches of fish and chips, each with a side of mushy peas. The lad lifts a hand to hide his mouth, and behind his hand he whispers to me, "They have this mayonnaise, curry mixed with mayonnaise." He whispers, "It's better than the tartar sauce, but it costs extra. Can we have it?"

I say, yes, of course.

"You heard the gentleman," our lad tells the counterman. Busting with happiness he says, "Don't bother with the vinegar, because we'll have double extra curry with everything."

I pay. A man shoves a mop around the floor, pushing around the stink of bleach. Our Digby leads me to a table to wait for our food. He pulls out a chair for me. He seats himself, only backward on his chair, his legs splayed, and he leans his arms and chin along the top of the chair's back. Here it is, what Otto didn't want to see. In the oily yellow light of the place, our lad looks to be the old pre-male troll he'll someday become. Panting and pawing for extra fish and so happy to get curry that he can't sit still. His legs bounce at the knee, and he keeps looking up to see if the food's ready. He's a little tyke and an old codger at the same time, with scabbed knuckles, and spots on his chin. Out of nowhere he asks, "How long does it take to save up for a motorcycle?"

With that, all the fun's got out of tonight.

So happy to get fed, our lad bangs on about applying to some trade school. He's set to apprentice to a painter if he gets in. Then he'll be set for life, he will. "They make pots of money, housepainters do," he says. He looks to the pass-through window. "Come back in another couple years," he says, "and I'll buy your dinner."

And with that I'm not even hungry. The lad's got a name, now, and a botched family life with a drunk mum and no dad to speak of. A pre-male to the bone. And he's always pictured something like tonight, some fine gentleman seeing the potential in him and giving him a chance, this Digby, and with that kind of a leg-up he'll for sure get his full measure and make his mark. And won't folks on his street be knocked back when they see him pull up in a fine car like ours, and see he's got fine friends, friends with standing and education, who believe in him and see past all the rough and shabby to see he's born for great things?

And he's ever so grateful to Christopher and me, he says.

Our lad's talked himself into a bright future by now. A captain of industry. A politician, could be. His hoodie's coming through at the elbows, and his trainers are run down at the heels. We could feed him, and he's in such a state that he'd let us have a go in frenzied acts of sexual deproduction. And he'd be such a good doggie he'd let us have it off any nasty way we wanted, we could even let the tutor have a messy go, but then what?

It's no fun to drag a wee pre-male peccary from its slumbering life, only to hear its hopes and dreams and all its starry-eyed aspirations, and then to tear it to bits and stuff those bloody bits back down in the hole from whence they came.

What's important is the meal's paid for.

As our lad bangs on about what great friends we'll be, lifelong companions and all . . . I interrupt. If he'll excuse me, I've got to go tell Otto something.

He asks, "Who's Otto?"

Christopher, I say. I'd meant to say Christopher. I'll only be a moment. As I exit the shop, a voice shouts, "Order up!" I step around

160

the car and get in the front seat beside Otto and tell him to drive. Just drive away now. Drive.

Our lad leans out the shop doorway. He's holding a paper bag and says, "Christopher, wait until you tuck into this!"

Otto starts the engine, hits the accelerator, and peels out. Neither of us look back. As we leave the chip shop behind, the bright lights wink out. It's being shut up. If our lad is still standing at the curb with his arms full of skate and curried mayonnaise and mushy peas, he's lost in the dark.

Otto asks, "What scotched it?"

I tell him the lad had hepatitis. He confided in me he had hepatitis and HIV and all sort of warts, but he was still eager to have a go. I say the lad quite fancied Otto.

Otto shakes his head. "Poisoned bait." He says, "That was a close call, wasn't it?" And he brings the car around, heads us out the long ways toward the secret lake.

## 44

**THIS DOESN'T BODE WELL, I TELL OTTO. LAST NIGHT. IT ONLY GOES TO SHOW** we don't have it in us to be predators. Why, we're worse than the boy spinster. Had we got that lad, Digby, up to the nursery last night, the tutor would've had his hide off in a twinkling and be wearing it down round the Crested Eagle the next dusk.

Tonight, our mission is to collect an unloved team captain and a rubber prom queen. Our first order of business is to collect an Audi A8. We've all night, haven't we? Once we get the car, Otto says, we'll have another go at spotting some wee dik-dik to prey upon. Tonight, he says, won't be another repeat of failure. Just to play it safe, he brings along condoms and beer. "In the event the bait's poisoned," he says.

Otto's set his cap to meet some pre-male Billy No-Mates and offer the lad a beer and to doctor the beer with the pills the strung-out governess left us. Toward that end, he's got a beer open and dropped in the pills. He rides us around on the lookout for lonely punters. The night's raw and wet, with a cold wind that'll work in our favor. Otto's not had it off in a fortnight, and he's pawing for some idiot lad who takes a posh car for high-minded respectability and gets in. That's a lad who doesn't know pish, and who'll take a beer and be a fallen-asleep baby panda bear while Otto has it off every which way.

The cold makes for slim pickings, with most tossers off the street. We go round the train station and the transit hub. Down one way is a lad, walking with his shoulders hunched against the wind, walking fast with his head down. He's not much, but he's what he is. Short-legged.

Shaved head. A little Nazi in his boots laced up with red laces, he is. A nose as poxy as a whore's knees and his neck all tattooed. Just the opposite of last night's sad go. No, this one's hardly a wee, weak peccary to terrorize. Here's a brash hooligan grizzly bear, and the prospect of having a go on this scarred beast and leaving him to wake up starkers in some trash heap, why, the idea's got Otto stirred up no end.

Steroid yob that he is, his scalp and the back of his thick neck are all over pimples. Nothing like having a go with some big steroid yob and biting his nipple in the dark and having the nipple explode in your mouth because it's more to reality a pimple.

Otto pulls the car alongside and matches the beast's pace. He puts down his window and says, "Mate? You fancy a beer?"

His boots clomping along, not breaking stride, the yob says, "Fuck off."

Otto waves an unopened bottle out the window. "Here," he says. "Take it."

The yob looks over and says, "How am I the fuck to open it?"

Here in the dim of the car, Otto pops the cap of the beer. To make that hissing sound. The sound of a soul escaping. But instead, he hands out the beer he's mixed pills in. "Here," he says, "it's open."

All this shows a masterful feat of driving: Otto managing to stay alongside the walking yob, while opening the decoy beer, and handing over the doctored beer.

The yob takes the bottle without thanks and tips it back, still walking. He takes a breath between swallows and says, "I'm not getting in any posh car with a couple queers, if that's what you have in mind." He pulls another long swallow on the bottle. Still striding along, shoulders bunched against the rain, he shakes the bottle as if hearing how much is left. He drains it. "Now you can sod off," he says, and pitches the bottle, smash, against the side of our nice car. He turns on his heel and starts down a side alley.

Otto doesn't follow, but only cruises forward, picking up speed. He offers me the decoy beer, and I take it. The satellite nav on the dashboard shows this street curves around, eventually to bring us to the far end of the alley down which the yob disappeared. We'll head him off. We're like cheetahs, we are, waiting for our prey to tire out. "We'll get a taste for it," says Otto, meaning we'll get the hang of being predators. We won't always be aging pre-male bunny types who sit and wait for some not-choosey old dingo to give us a go.

Otto means to have it off in the yob's every hollow. To turn the beast faceup and have it off, then facedown, then to repeat the process. Then maybe to cart the yob home to the nursery where the tutor can glue some extra parts on him. And finally to leave him sprawled in some market square, bollocks-out starkers except for the extra tits and peckers stuck all over his shaved head.

I can't say I fancy peeling the kit off that beast. The army-surplus cargo trousers and camo jacket and whatnot. Much less doing so without his help, seeing how he'll be an inert lump blacked out on pills and nothing but deadweight when it comes to getting his gear down and off his legs and tugging his tattooed arms out the sleeves of his jacket. It looks to me like more trouble than it's worth, but Otto says we must or else we'll just be a couple of left-behind peccaries having it off with Sir Richard and nature films from here on out.

"It's growing up, is what it's called," Otto says, and he brings us within sight of the alleyway where the yob should appear.

Nobody steps out of the shadows. Our headlamps frame the alleyway. Our windscreen wipers push the rain back and forth. Nobody appears. Otto says, "Go and have a look, Cecil."

Otto wets two fingers in his mouth and spits in his hand and makes ready to have a rough, messy go. In his pillow-talk Richard Attenborough voice, Otto says, "Let's watch as these two twee little hamsters have multiple goes on this great sleeping rhinoceros."

He means for me to go into the dark. I drink the decoy beer so to wait out the clock. I drink until it's gone, and then I get out of the car. Beastly night, blasted night. Like a cave, the alley looks. Like an animal's lair.

Frankly, the point of one being a predator is to have it off with prey one finds attractive. A hulking, rain-sodden oaf of marginal hygiene collapsed in a drugged stupor hardly sounds like anyone's delicious baby peccary. Not even Sir Richard could be hard up enough to have it off with this one.

The headlamps throw my shadow out ahead of me, but not far into the alley. Despite the rain it stinks of piss. Busted glass crunches under my every step, and I'm wishing I'd worn the carved-out rubber skin of some unloved-one. The picture of me, skulking down a dark alley, all extra peckers and nipples, that would give the skinhead a start, wouldn't it? If nothing else, it would keep the rain off me. I'm beyond the headlamps' reach when I stumble. My feet trip over something. Boots laced with red laces. It's our skinhead, it is, laid out on the pavement, facedown and nose busted, and the blood not running.

I put two fingers against the tattooed side of his neck, smack against a swastika that marks his carotid artery. And where I ought to feel a marching beat, I pick up nothing. I turn his head faceup and his open, glassy eyes flood to overflowing with raindrops. And he's heavy he is, soaked and heavy, deadweight not worth the struggle to get his pants off. And whether it was the pills or the fall against a brick wall or the pavement that cracked his head, it's anyone's best guess. His pants are crotched with piss by the smell of them, and I've no intention of getting him naked much less dragging this great inert yob back to our nice Audi.

Here the Nazi moans. He's not dead, is he? Only knocked cold.

If Otto wants to have him, Otto can well come out the car and have it off here.

In the strictest sense, as predators I think we've done our worst.

I leave him lie in his rain and piss and step double-time back to the car. There, Otto puts down his window and asks, "You have it off, Cecil?" He hands out a beer, and I take it.

I have a go on the beer, a good long swallow, and gasp for breath. He's dead, I say.

Still behind the wheel, Otto says, "Fuck all." He says, "What do you mean he's dead?"

I drain the bottle and smash it on the road.

Otto says, "Get in." He revs the engine and drops the car into gear. In a clock tick he'll pop the clutch and leave me.

I dash round and climb in the shotgun seat, even as the car lurches forward. The rear tyres fishtail on the wet roadway, squealing up smoke and steam for a side-to-side moment before they find purchase and we roar off into the night.

# 45

**MUMMY SAYS WE MUST DISMISS THE TUTOR AT THE EARLIEST POSSIBLE** opportunity. She seats Otto and me in the library beside the fireplace and pours the tea and passes the cups and cress sandwiches. Here a look gets on her face like this afternoon when the Hun fell off our north tower, a drop of five floors that might've only fully paralyzed the poor man had not a moment later a massive carved granite gargoyle got dislodged from the tower parapet and come plunging down to crush the newly paralyzed Hun to a bloody pulp. A tragedy made all the more tragic owing to how only an hour before Mummy had taken the tea tray up to the nursery. She was well aware the room had become an abattoir for butchered dolls, but she'd steeled herself, she had, and arranged an array of marmalade tarts and cups and clotted cream and candied rose petals and had carried the tray upstairs as a surprise. She hadn't a free hand to knock when she found the door a wee bit ajar, so she'd hipped it open. Just an ever-so-quiet bump of her hip. Here she'd stepped through the doorway with the heavy tray in her arms and the teapot under its quilted cozy and the cream pitcher and candied dates, so many delightful surprises, and in place of Otto and me she'd found a great knotted mass of arms and legs having it off, all manner of hands and feet all lumped into a heaving pile in the center of the nursery floor with its usual not-good smell, and rubber glands and plastic intestines strewn about for good measure.

Mummy, you see, isn't easily put off, is she? She set aside the tray and set about filling cups and asked, "Milk or sugar?"

At that the heaving pile heaved its last, and having had it off, the pile untangled itself to become our tutor, the boy spinster, all got up in one of his rubber suits that look like all manner of carnally conjoined unloved-ones all glued together in a frenzy. The smaller portion of the pile stepped aside to resolve itself as the Hun. Her new husband. And since he'd no English and she'd no Swabian there was no telling what had gotten into the man's mind. He'd clearly had a go with the boy spinster in the guise of a plastic orgy, Mummy could see that much.

Not one to mince words, she'd excused herself and exited the room. No custard heart had she. Mummy had done the Lady Di Job, had she not? Hastily dressing himself, the Hun followed in yammering pursuit.

Mummy, silent Mummy, sullen Mummy, she ascended the stairs to the roof of the north tower where a panoramic view of all Buckinghamshire could be had. The rolling fields of rye and the damp hedgerows twittering with sparrows, the hayricks and stiles and all such pastoral goings on of the fecund county. And set against that green and pleasant landscape, Mummy and her Hun had a meeting of the minds, a great clearing of the air, until quite by accident the Hun flew over the parapet wall and plunged the five floors to the forecourt pavement, screaming a German-accented shriek as he flashed past the nursery window where the sweaty tutor was gorging himself on marmalade tarts.

The Hun landed with much the same flesh-pounding-stone thud as our governess had made. There he groaned softly in German, not dead, but unable to move even as the massive carved gargoyle sprang free of its rooftop niche and came hurtling straight down at his terrified Hun face, doing even more damage to our poor, battered forecourt and spattering the outsides of the library windows with pulverized massage therapist.

Mummy had forced herself to watch all this unfold, finding herself once more a widow. Undeterred, she set the parlor-floor maid to scraping the gore from the library windows.

The police held an inquest, but nothing came of it. Mummy replenished the tea tray and had it brought to the library fireside where she summoned Otto and me to join her, and even now the village curate is taking away the Hun's shattered corpse, and the maid is soaping the panes.

Mummy passes the candied rose petals and marmalade tarts. Buttery tarts, tangy tarts. That look from before gets on her face, and she turns to me. "Cecil," she says, "I'd be deeply in your debt if you'd do me the most disagreeable favor . . ."

To look at her now, distressed Mummy, downcast Mummy, it rends my heart. She's only to ask, I say, and I'd be privileged to move the moon and stars for her.

Mummy reaches to take my hand in hers. Her choice of husbands aside, she's thoroughly clever and lovely. She squeezes my small hand and says, "Cecil, would you be Mummy's big, brave boy and sack the tutor?"

And there it is. The Hun is got out of the picture, and the tutor's to be sacked.

Here Mummy smiles upon me. I smile in return. Otto takes my free hand and holds it, and he smiles at the both of us. We're all so happy, we are. It's just the three of us, and there's still the frosted sandwich cake with raspberry filling to be cut into.

## 46

MR. PLESHY TIBBETS HAS WON THE ROYAL ASCOT. IT'S IN THE DAY'S NEWS-paper, isn't it? The horse Otto was to have done in, for a princely sum paid by some other horse owner to eliminate the competition. Otto's faked the job, and Grandfather isn't pleased, not in the least. Some client has splashed out millions of pounds to have a competitor's horse—bang—done in, and that client's not happy, so Grandfather's not happy, and he's sending text letters to Otto's tiny telephone by the minute.

Not that Otto is perturbed. Otto is so clever. It's clear he hadn't the heart to shoot a lovely horse. He'd instead sent me to wait in the car with my ears stopped up, while he'd fired a bullet into the ceiling or whatnot. Not killing a wee Kerry blue terrier is one thing, but failing to off a Royal Ascot–winning gelding is a declaration of war, at least as far as Grandfather sees it.

Otto says, "The damage is done." As he sees it, "It's not as if Mr. Pleshy Tibbets can un-win the Royal Ascot." Moreover, Otto and I still find ourselves as baby joeys stuck in their mummy's fur coat, unable to climb back into her bottom or to reach the pouch where milk and warmth will make us adults.

Rumblings come to us over Otto's little telephone. In wee text letters Grandfather castigates Otto for his lack of mettle. But shame is of little use against us flighty, feeble, endocrine-defected pre-things who've lived our entire pre-male lives as disappointments. Honor and Empire have never been our top priority. Instead, Otto is planning a safari into London, into the dark heart of Mayfair, no less, there to prey upon the greatest predator known in the animal kingdom. It's no use, us stalking hopeless lads on the dole, and drugging hostile

Nazi types. Otto says we'll be good for nothing in life unless we slay the apex predator and assume his place. Such is the Law of the Jungle.

When Otto pontificates like this he's impossible to resist. I for one would follow him to the ends of the earth. With that, Otto is off to plan his expedition.

In short order Grandfather arrives at the house and throws his overcoat at the footman and asks that I be sent to the library to discuss the whole sordid business. I've yet to sack the tutor and now I'm drawn into this battle betwixt Otto and Grandfather, and the Hun not even planted in the churchyard. I need more hours in my day, don't I?

Among the stuffed jaguars and panthers, Grandfather takes Daddy's old chair. He calls me on the carpet and says, "Cecil, my boy, you're our last hope." Vexed, he seems, his fingers worry at his watch fob. Grandfather fishes the pipe from his pocket and packs it with tobacco and lights the pipe. He's hardly taken a puff before he exhales the smoke, puffing quick puffs. He's like a locomotive pulling on an uphill grade.

Grandfather says, "Perhaps Otto hasn't enough Welsh in him to make a proper horse killer." He says, "The boy's got too much of his father." He says that it's all excellent practice and great fun, this killing of household servants. But unless those skills translate to the real world, of what use are they? It's a nasty business, he says, this torching of National Trust properties and killing Kerry blue terriers and racehorses, but it's an important service to humanity.

Grandfather says, "Where would we be if the present were always saddled with the past?" And, no, he's not happy with Otto as his heir apparent. Here a look gets on his Grandfather face like when he speaks before Parliament. "It's our duty to the future to prune away the dead wood and allow the sunlight of opportunity to grow new fruit."

He tells me, "Our family is no more or less than the nation's army, but whereas the army shoots for quantity our goal is quality."

As for Daddy, Grandfather airs no end of gripes, in particular about how Daddy botched the simple job of dropping Building Seven of the World Trade Center, a job any intern could've pulled off, but

Daddy had miswired his blasting caps, hadn't he, and when it became clear that Building Seven wasn't going to topple itself, Grandfather had to put Mummy aboard the Concorde and smuggle her to the site so she could sort out all of Daddy's squibs and finally bring the building down hours and hours behind schedule.

"Making bricks without straw," says Grandfather, "that's what it was to work with your father."

Here Grandfather sinks deeper in his chair, depleted, and a look gets on his face like when he recalls the Lady Di Job and how it was light duty, it was, and all Daddy needed to do was flash a bright strobe light in the Pont de l'Alma tunnel to blind the driver of the Mercedes and send the car crashing, only Daddy being Daddy and not Welsh, he'd brought the wrong adaptor for power outlets on the continent, Daddy had, so he was useless until Mommy arrived with the correct adaptor and flashed the strobe, and the rest is history.

It was she who sprinted to the wrecked car and retrieved the trophy finger that sits in the vitrine near us. Now Grandfather rises and steps over to examine the various fingers. His brow furrows as he puzzles over something, most likely the newest addition, a thick, roguish finger labeled *Digby's Pussy Finger* in my own childish scrawl. He looks from it to me, his Grandfather eyebrows raised in surprise and respect.

"Your father was neither use nor ornament," says Grandfather. Here he shoves his hand deep into one pocket and brings forth something as small as a playing card and as thin as toast. He hands it over to me: my very own wee telephone.

He says, puffing away, "Cecil my boy, our people have done this line of work going back to the Gunpowder Plot." He plucks the pipe from his mouth and points the stem at me. "Our dynasty is at stake." Here he raises both arms wide as if to encompass the totality of our lovely crenellated manse, the gardens, the fields, the tenants and woodlands. "All of this will be lost in a generation if I've no suitable successor."

James Jr., Grandfather says, has not a drop of Welsh. It would be wholly unsuitable for him to succeed as patriarch.

As for our tutor, corrupt tutor, craven tutor, I hold out no hope the Jesuits will have the pre-male back, nor will any household employ him. Not after what he's become, the perverted wearer of monstrous costumes, who haunts the village all night and panics drivers along the high road. He's even unfit for heaven. Damaged goods.

It's fallen to me to find the boy spinster a new paradise where he'll enjoy having a go with endless partners for all eternity. A corporeal paradise now that he's unfit for any spiritual one. At present, the tutor is sequestered in the nursery with his toys and his ostracization.

The tiny footman enters the library to announce that luncheon is being served. I ask Grandfather if he'd like to join us, but he declines my invitation. "I couldn't bear to look upon your brother," he says, as I help him into his overcoat. He leans into the fireplace and empties his pipe by knocking it against the firedogs. His car is waiting at the door, and in a clock tick he's off.

As for luncheon, cook gets high marks. She's given us deviled kidneys and jellied eels with black peas, and stargazy pie and forcemeat faggots and potted shrimps. Mummy tucks in, as does Otto and James Jr. A tray is sent upstairs to the nursery. Mummy won't abide the tutor at table.

As the footman brings the Eton mess into the dining room my new telephone chimes. Only Otto makes note of it. My first mission has arrived as a tiny letter from Grandfather. And Grandfather can't be faulted for not asking Mummy to do this job, but it does leave me in a rather bad lie.

It says I'm to kill my brother.

## 47

**MUMMY WEDS JAMES JR. TODAY. IN A CATHOLIC CEREMONY, GOD HELP US,** the two of them stand smack where the yard boy's casket sat, they do. Horrid. Just horrid!

"Like an Alfred Hitchcock it is," Otto whispers to me. The church all got up in flowers, weeds really. A wedding feast of gooseberries and pickled tripe in the offing.

Dear Grandfather must walk Mummy down the altar as Otto and I stand in as groomsmen.

It seems James Jr. was brought up a Catholic, too. Born in a madhouse, too! To that end Mummy's looking to convert. Like a weathercock she is, flighty Mummy, duplicitous Mummy. They're pledging troths despite or perhaps because of his remarkable resemblance to young Daddy. Now that the Hun is out of the picture. They wed, perhaps out of Mummy's guilt. Whatever the motives, Mummy wears white, a strange choice seeing as how the two issues of her loins are standing within arm's length.

Only the silly tutor looks at home here. Banished to the back pews, as he is. Attired in his knackered duds, but dutifully cowed by the idols and incense, the great clouds of incense, and splashings of holy water upon those in attendance. The erratic ringing of small bells. The synchronized kneeling and standing. It's all a great mystery, this religious business.

Baby James being so fully formed and so manly a specimen, a great meaty specimen as to catch Mummy's eye, it reflects very badly on Otto and me. Dear Otto remains vexed. So rattled he is that he must swallow one of the many pills left by our governess, if only to steady himself for the ghastly nuptial ceremony.

Baby James standing here in a morning coat serves as proof that neither time nor tide has waited for us, and that Otto and I are what we fear most. We're as Digby looked in the chip shop: a mewling tot and a drooling codger at the same time. Not a good look.

Never a good look.

As we stand beside the altar Otto whispers, "Cecil, how could twenty-odd years fly by while we did little else but watch nature films and have it off in the nursery?" You see he'd always fancied that life would be endless, and goes would be likewise, and we'd exist as coddled babes amid servants and pleasures forever. Otto whispers, "That blasted pipe organ wants for tuning."

Here the priest pauses in his rote gibberish and tries to cut Otto dead with a cold look.

As rebuttal Otto pinches the crease in one of his own trouser legs and pulls it up to expose a margin of naked ankle. Great, fleshy ankle. Slatternly ankle. Otto, you see, has not deemed to wear stockings to the wedding. His own mother's wedding ceremony! And the pale, milky sight of such ankle skin, steamy and bare for all the world to desire, it spurs the priestly man to heavy breathing and the swallowing of excess saliva. The ankle is a sight so enticing that the priest is forced to tear his gaze away and continue reading aloud from his incantations.

Here Otto lets drop his trouser cuff and whispers, "You and I must seek revenge on those who've prompted us to squander our lives in pleasure!"

With Otto I always feel as if I'm disarming a nuclear bomb, and I tell him as much.

Hopped up on his pill popping, Otto snaps his fingers. The sound cuts through all the churchly piety. Otto says, "A nuclear bomb, oh, Cecil, you are brilliant!" He says, "We must need move from the seduction of distraction—nature films and the like," he says, "to the seduction of destruction."

Here Mummy gives us a harsh silencing look.

But rather than fall quiet, Otto pushes on. "We must get our hands on a nuclear bomb," he says, "and purify the world!"

Grandfather levels Otto a stern look.

Yet outrage has loosed Otto's tongue. He perseveres, saying, "I'll not waste another minute having it off." His words ring in the sanctuary. "Not until we retaliate against the animals in control of our lives!"

## 48

**WHAT'S TO BECOME OF THE BOY SPINSTER? TO RETURN TO HIS CARRELS AND** cloisters is out of the question. The tutor's cast out St. Thomas Aquinas and Erasmus and company, in exchange for unbridled sensuality. That leaves scant options, especially in regard to the afterlife. The matter is under discussion as Otto and I take the motorway toward London. As Otto sees it the boy spinster is damaged goods. A priapic glutton beyond redemption, he is.

As for whom we're calling upon in London, Otto won't say. When I press him, he pops a cashew nut into his ear. Otto plucks a cashew from his pocket and plugs the small end in his ear, and that turns us into pretend Grandfather and Judy Garland. End of discussion. This car, a Maybach Exelero, becomes the 22 June 1969 bathroom well past halfway through the night.

According to pretend Grandfather, the plastics people had been coming up with a whole mess of iconography to sell the new pride: pink triangles and rainbow flags and no end of plastic stuff.

In his pretend Grandfather voice, Otto says, "Why, they're a lost cause, aren't they?" Those fey, parabens-tainted pre-males. "They hadn't the foggiest notion what horrible acts to engage in so a lot of us robust, rough-and-tumble types had to take leave from our wives and families and church going to produce the equivalent of training films. We had to pioneer, did we not?" The scrawny, paltry types had hardly the pluck to ice a scone, so it fell to the burly, manly types to engineer all manner of nasty pastimes such as human toilet and double fisting and rusty trombones. All manky acts of sexual deproduction.

Pretend Grandfather touches his fake hearing aid and says, "You see, Miss Garland, it's like raping Africa of her diamonds and uranium: you can't leave the job to the people who live there." All the while, class-action lawyers were monitoring the anogenital distance and gynecomastia, just itching to file for damages on behalf of two, three, four generations of men with skyrocketing rates of testicular cancer and plummeting sperm counts. "Unless you die, here, tonight, Miss Garland, the result will be catastrophe."

The mincing, hormonally defected boys will catch wind of the harm done to them by bisphenol A. Why, the twee, nervous things are half plastic already. And DuPont and Monsanto and Dow Chemical have no intention of being sued into grinding peonage.

As pretend Judy Garland, I bide my time with bits of stage business. I mind the ash on my make-believe cigarette and sip at my invisible champagne cocktail.

Pretend Grandfather drones on. "So it's fallen to me and hairy he-men like myself to weaponize the pansies." To train them with blue movies, as it were. "We've even made plans for the first Pride Parade, we have." A lurid procession wherein unclad hired cutthroats will be pulled on flowered wagons through the streets, to model a reckless, brazen sensuality, and goad the shrinking violets to vent their hereto closet-contained go-havings.

He says, "In our next stage of the operation . . . well, I'm only telling you this because you won't carry tales." In the next phase, the same agitators who'd killed Miss Garland and invented a great gushing lifestyle for the heretofore wilting violets, these same soldiers of fortune would insinuate themselves in the cutesy, flitting ranks and disseminate a particularly noxious virus first invented in the Belgian Congo during research toward a failed vaccine.

"Putrid stuff," says pretend Grandfather, and here a look gets on his face like when he'd done what needed doing to the spotted pony who lived at the bottom of the garden. A dirty, heartrending task, but not so unlike his entire life's work. "You see, Miss Garland, when you vivisect a great mess of wild chimpanzees and get out their kidneys, and you've got just vats and vats of filthy chimpanzee kidneys, it only follows that one kidney is going to be foul, eh wot?" Here pretend

Grandfather shakes his invisible enema bag brimming with champagne and phenobarbital as he might a cocktail shaker.

My pretend Judy Garland listens to the fake sloshing and asks, "Is that thing really necessary?"

As the script requires, pretend Grandfather, skinny, young Grandfather produces a fresh martini glass, a stemmed, gleaming thing, and pours it full from the bag. He hands it across the small bathroom to where Miss Garland's spidery hand accepts it. Doing so, he says, "Since my dealings with Miss Monroe, this method has yielded the best results with the least unpleasant side effects." Those side effects being, oh, the ordeal of throttling a person and shoving pills down her slender throat, or jabbing her with gruesome, big syringes, or snaking a plastic tube down someone's esophagus. In the script, pretend Grandfather attempts to redirect to Miss Dorothy Kilgallen, but Miss Garland will have none of it.

My pretend Judy Garland sips her deadly cocktail. She asks, "So if you get the tight-pants crowd to hold their defects as a point of pride, the entire global plastics industry will be saved?"

Otto's pretend Grandfather leans forward to pour her glass full. "Not merely saved, my dear. The plastics industry can continue to pollute people's bodies unabated. The flowery, feeble, flimsy boys will be the canary in the coal mine, but no one will take heed."

As Grandfather always says, common people are just the sponges for sopping up. For example, there was no financially feasible way to rid the World Trade Towers of their millions of pounds of asbestos—except to explode them and allow millions of lungs to filter the muck from the air. Pretend Grandfather shrugs and says, "A simple act of *force majeure.*"

As for plastics, microplastics go into the fish. The fish go into people. People are disposed of with great care. That same process is always straining the toxins of the world through the kidneys, lungs, livers, spleens, and fatty tissues of the proles. It's the wonderful little secret built into consumer materialism. The consumers pay for the privilege of collecting chemical agents and germs and viruses. Then all of it, the asbestos and dioxins and germs, goes into a nice casket and gets entombed in a lovely vault, end of story.

Here Otto falls silent. We've reached the edge of London, and he's looking for the slip road off the dual carriageway. He pulls us into a lay-by as he punches buttons on the satellite nav. London is chaos, he says. Just all of it bollards and roundabouts and pelican crossings. No end of flyovers and trunk roads. He still won't say where we're going, who the predator is that we're to prey upon, but he pops open the glove box and takes something out.

It's a Walther P38. In answer to my unasked question, he says, "It's Mummy's."

You see, he'd handed over Grandfather's gun to that crazed Evelyn woman, hadn't he?

It's dangerous business nicking Mummy's gun. She's fine with us wearing her clothes and makeup, but making off with her gun is crossing the Rubicon. Otto stashes the gun in his jacket pocket and makes a hook turn onto a connecting byway.

He picks the cashew nut from his ear and eats the nut without further comment, except to wince at the bitter taste of earwax. Here a look gets on Otto's face like got on the tutor's face the last time the tutor and I spoke.

That last time we were in the nursery, the tutor was sorting through a heap of rubber phalluses and orifices, all of them quite grotty with old lubricants and dried-on dust. And Hamlet-style, he held a cut-out vagina at arm's length and said, "Cecil, I've stopped trusting in the natural anything of anything. I feel I must control it all, and that leaves me with only the small outcome of what I want. That's versus the infinite outcome of what creation and destiny want for me."

We were, the tutor and I, surrounded by his great collection of rubber people turned inside out. Plastic footballers and beauty queens thoroughly looted and ransacked of all their vital plastic organs. The hovering droves of black houseflies.

I was not without empathy here. We are all of us marooned in our permanent boydom. Chemically inhibited, phytoestrogen-intoxicated pre-males. We're not unlike Peter Pan and the Lost Boys, always having a go and having it off and lingering in long afternoon bubble baths and playing at games and eating iced coconut meringues.

Religion and medicine had failed him, the boy spinster said. He selected a plastic coil from the rubber offal, a stray superior vena cava perhaps, or a median cubital. He examined it and tossed it aside. "As a tutor," he said, "I've been something of a disappointment." He said, "It's simply that knowledge and faith are so . . . inexact."

He plucked a rubber bulbourethral gland from the rubbish. Regarding it, he said, "Are you aware, Cecil, that science is still undecided as to the exact purpose of the Cowper's gland?"

In contrast there's no arguing with pleasure. Pleasure and arousal carry their own authority. Neither needs external shoring up. Nor can they be argued away. A person might avoid pleasure and arousal, but he can't disprove them.

"One can't be argued into lust," said the tutor. "It occurs or it does not."

You desire. You are desired.

You consume. You are consumed.

"Instead of trying to know one God on ever-deeper levels," he said, "I've grown to know many, many people on a very immediate superficial level."

The trouble is that you drink and you're drunk and it always takes another drink to maintain that state. So it is with having it off, he says. Instead of banking on some inevitable permanent paradise, having a go is seeking out a short-term pleasure. He said, "I've stopped trusting in some unseen, gradual process. I'm forcing every process to a premature outcome."

It boils down to a lack of patience, doesn't it?

This BPA-poisoned pre-male. This hormonally disrupted pre-male. The tutor gestured to the dolls around us, gutted and discarded. Plastic things found to contain no magic. "You see, Cecil," he said, "I want proof. Faith won't suffice. I want to cut open a person and find a soul spurting out, but it's always something else, isn't it?"

It's a liquid. It's always only some form of liquid jetting out of everyone.

He said, "And after that I must try again with a new stranger."

It's a dangerous business, calling out tutors as possible serial killers, but I asked if he'd killed anyone. Had he been killing random villagers?

Here the boy spinster didn't answer, but by not denying it he'd more or less admitted to the act. He said, "Cecil, I've lost my trust in everything. It's all I can do now to cling to the instant joy of breaking things."

He swung his foot, kicking up a great jumble of pancreases and thyroids that bounced around the nursery. He said, "I've lost my ability to build up anything over the long term. At best, I can only look at what others have created, and the more beautifully made it is the more joy I find in destroying it."

At this, this robust kick exposed an unwelcome sight. Interred among the unloved-ones an actual body presented itself. The corpse of our coalmonger or the gamekeeper, the face now dark with lividity. The belly swollen and traversed by houseflies. The reeking source of the nursery's greater-than-usual stench.

One needn't be a Miss Marple to see what's gone on as of late.

Here a look had gotten on the tutor's face like had gotten on Otto's face when he darted around and torched Buckinghamshire Hall. It's the same look as got on Otto's face when he'd dropped the chandelier on the butler.

To placate the bereft tutor, I told him that nanny must give him a bath in the zinc tub, and a full shave. Head to toe. Front and back. To be all clean and hairless, that would set his world to rights. But my advice was of no use.

Here the boy spinster looked near to tears. He'd found a plastic heart amid the rubble and now clasped the heart to his chest as he said, "Cecil, I know I'm the tutor, and that I ought to be instructing you, but can you help me?" Base tutor, wicked tutor, he asked, "How am I to be redeemed?"

## 49

**AND THIS IS WHAT I HAVEN'T TOLD YOU, HAVE I? IT'S NOT THE SORT OF THING** people want to hear about. Not bang up front. The truth is someone's been going about nights and conking old potters and tossers on the noggin and having it off with them and then splitting them from stem to stern and rifling through their insides as if in search of something.

To date, the reason I haven't brought this up is my fear that the splitter-opener was Otto, and I'd like you to like Otto inasmuch as Otto is likable. My fear has been that my brother was popping out nights and doing these violent deeds, slaughtering drunken toughs and roughs put out of the Crested Eagle after hours. I also didn't tell you because I worried you'd jump to the conclusion that the killer was me.

You see, I've downplayed my part here. It only seems expected that I was hiding something story-wise, in particular that I was hiding the fact I'm a serial killer of drunken tosspots, and that I didn't tell it here because I wanted to be liked.

We all want to be liked. Even pre-males, especially pre-males. We all hide the parts of ourselves that reflect on us badly.

Only now I'm off the hook, and Otto's off the hook, because it would appear the tutor's been doing to soused derelicts what he's been doing to the unloved-ones. Nonetheless, it does leave us with a problem larger than simply sacking some ineffectual classics scholar.

# 50

OTTO DRIVES US ALONG THE M40 TO THE M25 WHERE WE TAKE THE LONDON
Orbital Motorway clockwise to skirt Watford and Enfield to the M11
at Ilford through to Woodford from where we bother over to the un-
knowable reaches of Redbridge from where we skip to the A12, skirt-
ing the uncharted wastelands of Eton Manor and cut along to blaze
a path through a mishmash of streets to Hackney where we find ourselves giving a wide berth to Fitzrovia, dodging St. Pancras, from there
we stumble upon Paddington and must double back to Marble Arch
and around Hyde Park to land smack in the dark heart of Mayfair.

Otto brings us to the stoop of an imposing Regency townhouse.
We leave the car, mount the steps, and ring the bell. It's not a clock
tick before dawn, and the street is silent and inky with wisps of tulle
fog. One could not ask for a better setting to pay our call.

To say we're nervous is an understatement. Here we are about to
meet someone who'd given us the world. Who'd brought us deserts
and oceans, and who'd introduced us to all the animals in creation.
He'd shown us how the all of Australia worked, from fish to birds.

To stand in his presence, why, it makes for wobbly knees and rubber chinning. This house stands for a big world, a world larger even
than Grandfather's. The man who dwells within is the Lord of the
Jungle and the King of the Beasts. At this threshold, Otto and I shrink
down to baby joeys sooty with Australian dust. Pre-pre-male nobodies.
Our shy eyes downcast, we hold hands, each feeling the moist palm
of the other.

Otto says, "We must present our case, and if he fails to take heed
we must have a go at him and do him in." He pats the gun in his
pocket. Otto's always so clever.

A footman comes to answer the door and inquire about the nature of our call. Otto gives Grandfather's full name with all its titles and honorariums, and the footman bows us inside and seats us before an impressive fire. He rings for coffee, then goes to alert the master of the house. All of this rush and bustle is owing to Grandfather's position. Lofty Grandfather, lordly Grandfather, he's quite the personage, as are we by association. A general hubbub sounds from the hallway outside, and at that a door opens. In walks a great hairy bastard. The most apex of all apex predators.

Mummy's Walther P38 remains scarcely hidden in Otto's pocket.

The master predator speaks to us in the pillow-talk whisper we've heard so many times before. His face has always been off camera, but his is a most famous face, and now a look gets on it like the look that got on the tutor's face the very last time I saw it.

## 51

THERE EXISTS A HEAVEN FOR THE CARNAL. A PARADISE FOR THOSE CON-
stantly having it off, the wanted and the wanting. It's where everyone remains a stranger known only for short-term pleasure. Where
all inmates are desirous and desired, and steamy desire itself is never
quenched.

On our final day together, the tutor and I stuffed the gutted dolls
and coalmongers into bin liners. Sorting out the nursery, we were.
We'd opened the nursery window for air, to air out the stench, and
once the bin liners were filled we'd put them out the window to land
in the forecourt below.

A low ceiling of clouds rested on the peaks of the roof, and the
grey daylight changed little from dawn to dusk. I'd telephoned Grandfather to send a lorry, and in short order the stuffed bin liners were
loaded aboard and being trucked off to the Buckinghamshire sanitary
solid-waste internment site.

All day I'd regaled the tutor with visions of a place always busy with
lavish automobiles arriving and beautiful girls and manly lads aplenty.
A secret world, I'd promised him, where a BPA-poisoned, hormonally
disrupted pre-male such as himself would be a great favorite and free
to have it off for all eternity.

After we'd returned the nursery to its natural unnatural state, we
watched a nature film and waited for nightfall. I asked if the tutor had
any people I should be in touch with.

He'd said, "No one." In a voice without rancor, he said, "No one
who'd have me now, not the way I am now."

It had struck me that I hadn't asked his name. Persons like nanny
and cook and the chauffeur must have Christian names, but they

move through our lives and are gone so quickly, it hardly justifies the effort to ask. To do so would be like naming a pigeon on the lawn or a glass of milk.

On the nature film the usual horrors had unfolded. From off-screen Sir Richard whispered, "Let's watch as this pack of wild hyenas feast on a terrified baby hippopotamus." And by the time the baby hippo was chewed to bits it was dark outside. I rang for the car but dismissed the driver. I would drive us.

The boy spinster had asked, "Where to, Master Cecil?"

From the seduction of distraction . . . to the seduction of destruction.

Heaven, I'd told him. He was going to heaven. Not kangaroo heaven with rum trifle and lemon syllabub, but a better heaven tailored specifically for him.

We'd motored along rutted lanes and down cow paths. From coppice to coppice beside still waters and fields of dozing sheep, I drove us across the nighttime landscape. The weather held dismal without moon or stars to be seen. As on so many nights, I'd taken us down a dirt backroad to Otto's secret lake. An ordinary lake past midnight with milfoil and a concrete boat ramp that slanted steep into deep water.

I'd revved the engine at the top of the boat ramp and told the tutor to get out.

He'd done so without pause. He might not be happy here, but he'd be too busy to take note of his unhappiness. It was a busy place below those cold waters, and once he arrived there, he'd keep no memory of our world.

As I'd sat behind the steering wheel, he'd walked down the ramp to the edge of the black tarn. My headlamps threw his shadow out far ahead of him on the water, stretching him to reach the very center, the very deepest point. He'd stepped out of his shoes. He'd slipped off his socks and stuffed each into a shoe. He'd shrugged off his coat and folded it and had laid the folded coat atop the shoes. As if the ghosts were calling him, he waded in. As if he'd someday be coming back.

Here I'd almost gone with him. He seemed that much at peace.

In the headlamps, the water shimmered around his legs, then around his waist. He'd stopped, the water lapping around his armpits as the sand had held the sex killer, Digby. But as Digby had screamed in terror, the tutor turned back to smile into the glare.

A look got on the tutor's face like the look that had gotten on the lad's face at the chip shop: bliss. The second Digby, the poor lad who dreamed of painting houses. As if it were Christmas morning, and he were Tiny Tim delighted to find a plum in his stocking. A smile busting with happiness. As if he'd always pictured something like tonight, someone fine seeing the goodness in him and giving him a chance. As if the boy spinster had always dreamt of being found worthy and delivered to this cold destiny with Pericles and Agamemnon. He'd waved one arm raised above his head. He called, "You ever wonder why God makes us so realistic on the inside?" He called, "Why he goes to the bother?"

In response, I asked him his name. After all of this: What was his name?

And he'd shouted in response, "My name? Digby!" To make a third Digby to pass through our lives to date. He shouted, "*Eo nunc inter deos vivere!*"

With that he'd pitched forward and begun to swim toward his shadow, and he'd swum as far as the lights from the headlamps could reach. The Australian crawl. There he'd gone under. If bubbles rose, they'd stopped. The water went flat under the stretch of the headlamps.

When he'd failed to surface I'd left the car and walked to the edge of the lake.

There, where his shoes waited with his coat, I'd seen the others. All along the shore sat all manner of black leather oxfords and two-tone spectators as well as full brogues in brown calfskin and loafers and trainers—dozens of pairs of trainers—and Doc Martens laced with red laces and deck shoes and sandals and boots, from duck boots and packer boots to jodhpurs. Some sodden and filled with rain. A generation of footwear, all of them pointed toward the water as if waiting for their owners to return.

Without divers' weight belts or air tanks, perhaps they'd all surface someday, bloat and float to the surface of the water. Or perhaps the deep cold would keep them intact, and they'd remain on the lake bed, impaled or impaling, for the rest of time. At peace or at play . . . the next best thing.

**52**

THE LOOK THAT GOT ON MY FACE WHEN I SAW THOSE ABANDONED SHOES, that's the same look that gets on Sir Richard's face. The Right Honorable Lord Attenborough. The predator's predator, who's made us watch as every helpless, twee baby was snatched from its bed and eaten alive. Sir Richard, who couldn't be bothered to pluck a tiny joey from a mummy's fur and stuff it into a pouch, or shoo away a pack of hyenas trying to gobble down a skinny baby giraffe. Here in the drawing room of his London townhouse.

A man, Otto once called him, not innocent of anything. This morning he sees his chickens come home to roost.

The footman serves coffee. The fire blazes on the hearth. Otto sets aside his cup and saucer. "No offense, Sir Richard, but we've not motored all this way to drink your coffee." We want to know, we want Sir Richard to tell us why he's created a world of vicious predators and tormented wee babies? Why has he frightened and sickened us going back to our first brush with the televized natural world? Otto says, "You stole our innocence, and you were paid handsomely to do so."

Here a look gets on Sir Richard's face like gets on Grandfather's when he talks about Marilyn Monroe. In the kindest tones he says, "I show you the world as it is, my boys. If the baby peccary isn't killed, then the baby cheetah should need be starve."

Otto says, "Bollocks." Otto can have quite the mouth on him. He says, "Look at you! You're Sir Richard! You could feed those cheetahs your nice boxed lunch from the caterers, no, but that wouldn't make for a thrilling program, would it?"

A look gets on Otto like when he found the pony and demanded the nanny make it alive again. He says, "With all your rubbishy fortune you could make Africa a bloody great blasted picnic with all the elephants dining on green salads and the lions supping on tomato aspic, but you don't, do you?"

Sir Richard pinches the watch from his vest pocket and looks at the time.

Otto says, "Look what you do." He waves a hand to throw our gaze around the great room with its books and hangings of rich stuff. "You could but snap your fingers and all the suffering in the animal kingdom would be resolved."

Sir Richard exchanges a look with the footman standing by.

"To make a start," says Otto, "you must recant. You must denounce yourself and all of your horrid ideas about the animal kingdom being all violence." His face fierce, Otto shouts, "It's not violent. It's just not!" He says, "Animals are people, too, but by labeling them as *animals* you're othering them and marginalizing them." Otto stands now. "It's you who's made them animals so you can feel superior to them!"

Sir Richard sighs and examines the contents of his cup.

Otto bangs on, "You colonize their home and enslave them and murder them," he says, "and spout all this Kipling about the Law of the Jungle and Survival of the Fittest."

You see, here Otto loses ground. Where he'd expected a fight, one is not forthcoming. Sir Richard merely nods for the footman to refresh everyone's coffee and pass a plate of the most lovely almond biscuits, the most yummy, crisp biscuits. Let them evict us. Let them try. The gun fairly bulges in Otto's pocket. By now I'd expected he'd have had a go on the hairy old predator and have done him in. Instead, Otto flings his arm in a fast arc and dashes his china cup and saucer to smithereens in the fireplace. A bit of noisy punctuation, it is, but that's all.

In broken sobs, Otto says, "Why do you accept such cruelty in the world?" He demands, "Why don't you do something?" Get out of the big, bloody jetliners, he means. Or give the tigers and leopards a delicious plant-based meat substitute. And little bits of the same could be placed in the webs of spiders, and all the food chain could be transformed into Winnie-the-Pooh.

So lovely is the vision Otto sets forth that salty tears roll down his face. The same goes for Sir Richard and the footman. Tears roll down all of our faces. And so lovely is Otto's vision, I'd no idea. It's rather like Ireland when only a wee patch of tomatoes, prior to the great tomato famine, when a kitchen garden could feed everyone, and one and all lived in a great relaxed leisure with nothing more taxing to do than milk a cow that wanted milking, and everyone got to have it off and have a go and sing haunting Irish ballads and ditties.

Otto says, "It's the soybean is the key. We've only all to eat tempeh and tofu and walnuts and such. And to get the predators to be eating them, also." He says how we'll be wee lovely baby things and play at games and be tucked into nice beds each night. We won't any of us grow old or die, but we'll just go into a lovely eternal babyhood.

Otto's talked himself into a smile. Here he's so enveloped by his vision that he scarcely takes note of the new footmen who arrive and escort us toward the street door. With bright, brimming eyes, Otto says, "Sir Richard, you will think about it, won't you?" Even as we're put out on the street, Otto shouts, "Awfully sorry about your cup, sir!"

And here we find ourselves standing on a street in Mayfair beside the Maybach Exelero, and our grand audience with the world is at an end. London's quite the watering hole with roaming herds of animals from all places and Hyde Park and London planetrees all mobbed together and milling about. Predator and prey alike, having it off.

Here Otto holds open the driver's door and tells me I must take the wheel. He climbs into the seat beside me. I touch the gas, and we're away.

## 53

LONDON IN THE RAIN HAS EVERY FOOTFALL A SPLASH, AND TYRES SLASHING up great waves from every puddle. Here no one gives a tinker's damn if you're a twee, pre-male Tiny Tim and you take a fall and do injury to your lame leg. Otto says we must make people care. To care at least about us.

To date he's overlooked a third option. Besides being either a predator or prey, we might instead become house pets. Much the same as the Queen's corgis, we'll be. Her Majesty is the apex-apex predator, and we must place ourselves in her care. For a sentence to be served at the Queen's pleasure.

"Oh, Cecil," Otto says, "we must land in prison. We simply must!"

It's here Otto rolls down his car window and levels the barrel of the P38 at a cockney flower vendor and shoots, but I jerk the wheel to waylay his aim, and the round merely blasts a hole in the man's woven straw hat and prompts him to look about with pie-eyed horror.

We leave behind Sir Richard with his almond biscuits paid for with the blood money from baby wallabies. As Otto sees it, we must trade freedom for a lifetime of being nursemaided and properly looked after.

Otto says you can be a horrid little pelican baby in prison and still notch plenty of goes. Thanks to Otto's pen pals we already have scads of suitors in various prisons and jailhouses, and if they're not going to break out to visit us we might as well go to live with them. Otto says that prisons have lovely, open-plan shower baths where the burliest types can soap you up and have a vigorous go. Here he levels the gun barrel at a lad selling the *Guardian* on a street corner. He says, "They're all prey, Cecil."

Again, I jerk the wheel to spoil his kill.

To Otto we're not just a pair of estrogen-poisoned pre-males on a killing spree. We're big-game hunters on safari in the Mayfair Outback. As the herds scatter, he shouts, "Hold still, all of you!" The problem is he keeps missing. "How else am I to kill you?" He says, "Cecil, you must drive more steadily. I've not shot a single one, have I?"

As for me, I'm not so awfully clever, but I expect a gun only holds a number of bullets. I jerk the wheel to put a stop to Otto putting a stop to a chimney sweep atop a house.

As he takes fresh aim, Otto says that convicted prisoners and lunatics are the new aristocracy. They're looked after like wee tykes and are fed and allowed to have it off with each other all they desire. In a prison or an asylum we'll be looked after and coddled. Not in Australia, perish the thought, we won't go there. But in prison there live great tattooed he-men who're always up to have a go. Now that Otto has failed to attack the great Sir Richard, now he must do away with a great many bunnies and kittens and crossing guards and coppers and countesses before he'll be granted eternal status as a wee pre-male prey in some locked box of go-getters.

Heaven, at least until death. Not forever, but for now.

Otto squeezes off a shot that almost hits a barrister. He says, "If we can't break the system, Cecil, then we must force the system to carry us!"

Kill no one, Otto says, and the nation ignores you and wants you to keep yourself and bathe yourself and zip your own zippers. But if you kill a great whopping number of people the entire nation wants to house you and feed you and mind your health, and you're never lonely or wanting for affection, and you're hemmed in by randy roughs and toughs pawing to have at you. The kangaroo's hairy pouch, it is.

London is chaos with omnibuses and pigeons and zebra crossings and bothersome people rushing about to avoid Otto's scattershot firings. Here a fishmonger falls into Otto's crosshairs, and I jerk the wheel to make the bullet strike Nelson's Column in Trafalgar Square instead. In the next clock tick Otto takes aim at a suet peddler and I jerk the wheel to make the shot strike the British Museum. By accident, Otto shoots the Albert Hall. Next, the London Eye. The magazine of his gun must be bottomless.

Left unsaid is that there's no great need to wound or kill anyone. We've been CCTV'd enough to get pinched a million times over. All we need do is chuck the gun with Otto's fingerprints, then return to Mummy's house and await our apprehension.

Still, Otto blasts away at shop clerks and bicycling rat catchers and dukes in the hope that the nation will adopt us.

PART 5

# *NOT FOREVER, BUT FOR NOW*

## 54

**THE POLICE HOLD AN INQUEST, AND FOR ONCE SOMETHING COMES OF IT.**
Inside of a week Otto and I are pinched, and made to face a high court, and sent down despite the pleadings of Grandfather's best solicitors. Multiple charges of attempted murder, or some such. Inside of a month, we're clapped in leg irons and dispatched to Holme House with haste. It's Otto's plan to a T.

He is elated, Otto is, and here an expression gets on his face like got on Mummy's when she was interviewing for new butlers and that lanky, snogging Scottish interloper came into our lives.

Otto you see adores wearing chains. Manacles excite him to no end, as do body cavity searches and the like. Glove-fingered strange men have a go at him from both ways as if he were a Chinese finger trap! He's everyone's little Welsh corgi, he is, made to sit and stay on command. The Queen will see to it that all of our needs are met, and Otto no longer prattles on about laying our hands upon a nuclear bomb.

Upon our arrival at Holme House, Otto's eyes fairly glaze over with nostalgia.

A special way that one has, Otto, my brother, the way he pauses mid-stride as we enter the cell block. His commodious prison-issue trousers creep by degrees down his legs. To reveal that scar, the great toothy bite mark of a Jaws, still livid on his milky skin. Sliding pantlegs, collapsing pantlegs, the cloth settles sluttishly around his ankles. The whole of my brother reduced to a trembling mass of shame and fear made flesh.

Such vulnerability, such weakness waiting to be destroyed, Otto, dear Otto, he is. A sight of such appeal that many among the attendant scofflaws fall to robustly abusing their tattooed selves.

You see Otto shall always be a moth drawn to the flame of male attention. Of masculine approval. Despite the fact that it will be his undoing.

He's once more the infant displayed at the Crested Eagle, only now a full-grown pre-male tyke basking bollocks-out starkers in that, that panopticon center of all those felonious eyes. That Otto, his hips begin to shimmy, a slow roll that turns the all of him in place, putting him on full display in slow rotation. Clever Otto. None can best his display of the enflamed harlot. The embodiment of carnal hullabaloo.

Charms to soothe the savage breast, and all that rot.

One thin shoulder lifts and rolls. Slow. The shabby prison tunic slips from his torso. Slow. Here Otto steps free of the heaped, grotty prison ensemble. Free of his shoes, he is. Even his stockings have melted away, and he stands before us in slow, undulating rotation.

Agile as a bat, Otto would appear to take flight here. In one heroic leap he launches his unclothed self at the wall of bars. That tier upon tier of bars that front the cells from this the stained concrete floor, rising to the rafters. Nimble as a spider, our Otto scuttles up the barred walls, always faster than the hands that snatch after him. A sight, a crime against gravity it is, the way Otto's toes and fingers propel him in every direction at once.

The catcalls and wolf whistles die down as many shy away from this thing. Part insect, part primate. This aggressive wall-crawling imp.

No flirtatious eye rolling. No "Chica, Chica, Boom, Chic" bump and grind. This Otto clings to the bars, jerking his weight from side to side until the wall of steel rings, bars connected to bars, walls connected to walls, all of everything rattling and ringing to the same vibration. Otto, little Otto, nothing anyone can catch, he's shaking to bring down the whole cage of this world around our ears.

## 55

ON THE CELLBLOCK EACH MORNING WE'RE GREETED BY LUSTY BELLOWS.
A rollicking company of whoremongers and housebreakers and pick-pockets and cutpurses and firebugs and highwaymen and rippers, they give us a roll and a toss and a merry good going over, they do. As for our victuals, the peeled grapes are not up to our usual high standards. Also, candied rose petals seem to be in short supply. Yes, the menu leaves much to be desired, but the fellowship of such robust comrades more than makes up for that hardship.

Otto is in his element, he is, and not even Grandfather can touch us here. We've the whole nation standing against us. What's lovely is how all the tradesmen and alewives must pitch in for our upkeep. Why, they labor to pay their taxes so that we might idle away. Otto fairly holds court, he does, to his coterie of preening babies and his privy council of pre-males. Others present themselves as strutting predators. Regardless of the pose, we're all royal house pets serving as coddled corgi dogs.

A plethora of our pen pals are co-incarcerated with us. And this makes for old home week, or May Week, or a gathering of the clan. With their serial-killing days behind them, these toughs keep occupied by filing legal appeals and pumping iron and having greedy, grasping goes with Otto and me.

In prison Otto is much in demand. He's got such grand goings on. Daily, he's to be found deep in the kangaroo's pouch, as it were. Such clumps of louts and bounders, the way they cluster amounts to a Christmas feast. It's like cook's Christmas specialty, where she stuffs oysters inside a squab, and stuffs the squab into a capon and *that* cook stuffs into a hare and the hare she stuffs into a goose, the goose into a shoat, the shoat into a lamb, the lamb into a boar, and the boar into a bullock until Otto hasn't the foggiest notion whose meat he's eating! Some days we grow a bit tired, what with being traded among the lions and tigers for the price of a few ciggies. "Still," Otto says, "it's no worse than Sandhurst when you think about it."

For his part Otto stages games. In pleasant weather we play What's the Time Mr. Wolf? in the exercise yard. In foul weather we play hide-and-go-seek, with inmates racing about between the cells. Here's where our real story begins. Otto says it's no good us not getting roast goose to eat and custard tarts on a regular basis. And he rallies the criminals against nature to riot. The firebugs blaze up mattresses, as do all and sundry make trouble for the guards.

Mummy mails us her cast-off gowns, and Otto dons them and mounts to the prison battlements like a vision. And here a look gets on Otto's face like got on Evelyn's face in the lunatic asylum when Otto passed her his gun and she vowed to bust out and reclaim her little James Jr.

Otto's scheme? To muster a spirited band of bloodthirsty pre-males and to storm forth from the prison and to raid the countryside. To loot and pillage and retreat back to use our lovely prison as our new castle. We'll be the new Saxon and Jute raiders charging out to maraud, then coming home to our snug fortress. We'll cart home a great treasure of lemon syllabub and candied rose petals and cress sandwiches.

"What's the worst that can happen, Cecil?" asks Otto. "They've not got the death penalty to throw at us." A real Stonewall to replace the one faked by Grandfather and his co-conspirators. Ours will be a savage end to endocrine disruptors and pseudo-estrogens in dental composite resins.

Otto's so clever. He paints such a picture of his wee, weak, pre-male army made powerful by sheer numbers. Paint our faces, we could, and ransack the really tony shoe stores.

With all of that in the offing, we are a jolly lot.

## 56

**WE'VE NOWHERE TO GO BUT FORWARD NOW.**

From prison Otto sounds a clarion call for recruits to swell our ranks. At first blush, he hadn't the foggiest notion how, but we've joined forces with Felix. Lovely Felix, the great lummox who'd sent us snaps of his stunted private bits. Why, he's none other than our favorite diagnosed sociopath, he is, the Felix we'd been pen palling around with for ever so long. As luck would have it Felix, unbalanced Felix, brilliant Felix, has access to social media. It's rather a low marvel, it is, and it allows all and sundry to have a go at one another, and just by pressing little keys clever Felix is able to issue messages the same way Daddy had once created his fake online boy. The boy what had brought the besotted pounces flocking to our house and given Otto no end of beer and condoms. The fake boy who'd saved our spotted pony, at least for the moment.

As Felix is fond of saying, "01010011 01101111 00100000 01101101 01100001 01101110 01111001 00100000 01101101 01100101 01101110 00100000 01110011 01101111 00100000 01101100 01101001 01110100 01110100 01101100 01100101 00100000 01110100 01101001 01101101 01100101 00100001."

Here it is Felix puts out our clarion call to all the pre-male nobodies. Our fellow specimens of toxic emasculation. Old, wrinkled, pre-male trolls and pink kangaroo babies alike. All the hormonally disrupted criminals against nature. As squirming bugs, Otto says we must see ourselves dead if we can't muster the strength to save ourselves. We must make a vast effort to rally and to climb to some form of adulthood. He says, "We're already in prison, aren't we? The most England can do is to put us back."

Here, a look gets on Otto's face. It's like when the fire in the nursery stove would blaze up, so bright that it made the rest of the room look dark by comparison. All the light in the nursery seemed to drain into Otto's eyes. A kind of fire, that if it ever got out it would burn all of us alive.

"We won't ever harm anyone," prisoner Otto says, "ever." He says we'll only make off with their raspberry jellies and buttered bread. We'll merely invade their homes and spirit away the jellied eels and whatnot, without the smallest amount of stabbing or bludgeoning. He says, "Not unless they put up a fuss will we hurt anyone." Here just one twitch of an old smile gets on Otto's face, and then it's gone.

Otto throws down the gauntlet. He challenges all the fey, feeble pre-males in the land to hold up chip shops and to monger whores. Not for the gains, no. Not successfully, but in order to be pinched and be sent down, and to find themselves imprisoned here with Otto and me and our company of aspiring marauders. Via social media, Otto calls for the firebugging of National Trust properties and the peeping of Toms, so that great hordes of pre-males with little education and no prospects will be dispatched to Holme House, they will, to become soldiers and lieutenants in Otto's grand army. And Felix, ever sociopathic Felix, disseminates the call worldwide with relish.

And here a look gets on Otto's face like got on my own face when I saw myself reflected in the surface of the secret lake, standing at the water's shimmering brink surrounded by the abandoned shoes and boots of all those who had given up and waded in and taken their final plunge and who'd spend eternity among the plastic and the dead, and who'd never rise above the red mud of Australia on the lake bed, where unloved-ones continue to pile up to this day. That same expression gets on Otto's face, and all I can recollect of Daddy is that same expression when he popped round the nursery to find Otto and me cutting out paper dolls of the royal family and having a giggle together. The same expression as got on Mummy's face when she had a glass of wine or a pill stashed in every corner of every room. That same expression had got on Daddy's face as got on mine reflected in the water as got on Otto's when he found the little spotted pony dead at the bottom of the garden.

People say, some people, that we live nothing after the age of, say, seven. After that we only relive the first time we fell in love. The first time we felt left behind. Or our first lovely pony getting her head stoved in with a brick by Daddy because he wanted his sons not to be always weak, twee, sentimental babies, but to face up to the grim realities of life and the cruelty of nature and the Great Barrier Reef, and to stop messing about with paper dolls and pots of glue, and we ran to nanny and begged her to make the pony alive again, the nanny who did it with her mouth, and she only told us how Daddy was full within his rights as a father and man of the house to stove in anyone's head he liked, and Otto had best learn a manly lesson before Daddy took a belt to him, and then this and that had happened, "Chica, Chica, Boom," until the sad accident when that same nanny had taken a tumble down the back stairs, and she'd got her head all twisted around, hadn't she?

Here Otto's look is the look of all our looks, and Felix nets the unhappy online pre-males by the lakeful. And here it's the way Otto always says, "There are only two types in the world: those who cry after having it off, versus those who laugh."

The way he says, "No one in hell suffers more than the Devil."

I ask Otto how long he intends to ravage the populace.

And Otto says, "Not forever, but for now."

And at that Otto says we should be the type who laugh.

# 57

ENGLAND HAD YET TO SEE SUCH A CRIME WAVE. OH, AN EPIC SPREE OF HOUSE-breakings and shopliftings and all of them botched, and all the would-be criminals pinched straightaway. What's more, the offenders were all of the pink, fetal, pre-male sort. A mess of bank clerks and tailors' assistants who'd up and stuck up a kebab stand. They'd nicked a Rolex watch, just strolled into Cartier and asked to see a Rolex Sky-Dweller, and walked out the door with it, they had. Easy to pinch, impossible to ignore. Nothing but bicycle messengers and bus boys, they'd popped round De Beers and set down to select a flawless, ten-carat, colorless diamond they'd promptly slipped into their mouths and swallowed. No end of these crimes took place. The twee robbers were flying in from the United States, even. From Spain and Brazil and even the Outback of Australia, without so much as a suitcase and no hotel reservations, but simply hailing a cab from Heathrow to Bond Street and getting pinched and sent down for trial and being convicted and bang they're trucked to Holme House where Otto and Felix await.

Felix proves himself to be a fine fellow as sociopaths go. He wrangles baby peccaries and tiny bunnies until the world must be emptied of floral designers and hairdressers. A merry immigration of Christopher Robins.

To a man, they're all the Digby sort. Criminals against nature. They come in with the same look that got on Digby's face when we ditched him at the chip shop. The moment the prison guards crowd these lads forward into the cellblock, an expression gets on each pre-male face same as got on Digby's when he got his mushy peas. They've come to find something bigger than pressing two toffs for curried mayonnaise and an extra piece of skate.

Here it is. A miracle among miracles, it is, for among the failed cutpurses and ruffians shipped here from all over the globe, here's Digby. Our chip-shop lad, no less. Our Digby, the fake-poisoned bait. The lad who'd touched our hearts so much I'd made believe he'd had AIDS and whatnot to leave him be.

That bus-stop lad fairly stinking of loneliness, here he is.

Otto looks at the chip-shop lad, and a look gets on Otto's face like when he'd look at the governess. The governess he'd written the poem for, vowing to dig out her eyes with a hatpin and have at her dead body, the poem he'd only got up to because he'd loved her so much that he'd wanted us to be rid of her. The governess he'd shot dead. Here that same look gets on Otto's face at the sight of our chips lad, and Otto says for no one to have it off with the lad because he's poisoned bait. A lie he suspicions, but a lie Otto wants to believe because he wants to keep just one thing pure in this world, so all the assembly of assembled go-getters pledge to leave the chips lad be.

And as this Digby shuffles off in leg irons, chip-shop Digby, curried-mayonnaise Digby, a look gets on Otto's face just like the look what got on Grandfather's face when he'd walked down to the bottom of the garden and seen what Daddy had done to the spotted pony. Stoic Grandfather, sorrowful Grandfather, he'd stood over the poor, knackered beast. He'd knelt in the wet grass and the blood, spoiling his wool trousers, and used one hand to pet the pony's soft side. He'd crooned the pony's name, too soft for anyone to hear, and told us that a good pony such as this one had no choice but to go bang to pony heaven where there were ever-so-many sweet carrots to nibble and ripe apples, where it never rained a drop so a pony need never stand sopping outdoors or have to be quartered in the stable.

Grandfather said that heaven is where an animal or a person is much happier than it's possible for them to ever be on earth. It was to this same happiness he'd delivered Judy Garland and Janis Joplin and Jim Morrison. In regard to those jobs, he'd said, "The only ones who fear death are those who've never lived."

As he'd stroked the pony's side, Grandfather had said that no life ought to be judged only by the final few clock ticks, and that our pony

207

had lived many fine and wonderful years with two just ripping young boys in a lovely garden. And here Grandfather had sought a shovel from the potting shed, and dug a hole, and placed the pony in the hole, covered with a favorite blanket, and filled the hole. The awful job of burying the dead.

So you see Grandfather wasn't altogether horrid.

All I recall about Daddy is that he'd taken his leave, so only Mummy and Otto and I stood as mourners. As Grandfather had fitted the sod back in place and tamped it down, he'd said, "Your James . . ." He'd said to Mummy, "He must be got rid of . . ." He'd said, "Or the next time this will be one of the boys, you hear?"

And here no look had gotten on Mummy's face, no look whatsoever. She'd told Otto and me to run gather a lot of roses and daisies for the grave. While she'd stood behind with Grandfather to discuss an important matter in private.

# 58

AND HERE IT IS, ANOTHER DETAIL I'VE YET TO TELL YOU. NOTHING SO GRUE-
some as the tutor splitting a sauced tosser from stem to stern, but this
involves Mummy, and through all of this Mummy's had a rather bad
go, hasn't she? Aside from wedding James Jr., that is. But overall, more
sinned-against than sinning. Any expression that gets on Mummy's
face is just like the expression that gets on Grandfather's face or the
expression that gets on Otto's, you see, because we're all cut from the
same Welsh cloth.

Despite the poor tutor being trapped forever among randy ghosts
at the bottom of the secret lake, those skint mugs and gits of the village still cross themselves and whisper tales of the High Street Monster to this very day.

Nonetheless, Mummy is not without blame, for she contacts
a prison smuggler and smuggles Otto her cast-aside frocks. Lovely
things strictly forbidden to inmates. This includes a simple black
dress, cut snug with a high hemline and a mandarin collar. Sleeveless,
it is. All the better to show Otto's spindly, pale arms to their best advantage. It takes not a moment to have the thing out of the parcel and
on his back. It zips up the side so that's no great effort.

Even without foundation garments, it's a look Otto readily pulls
off. So readily that the uniformed guard patrolling our tier stops quite
pie-eyed, and a look gets on his face just like the look that would get
on the pony's face when Otto gave it a ripe apple. Here a waiting
cadre of pre-males seize the guard and truss him with torn strips of
bedding. Trussed like a goose he is, and when the next guard comes
sniffing at keyholes and catches sight of Otto, he too is trussed and
set aside. Until all the prison staff are thus all set aside. And here the

whole of Holme House is brought to a full-on boil, it is. An effect really quite breathlessly done and something I've not steeled myself for, the impending pillaging of the surrounding countryside.

So here I pick through the parcel of what else Mummy has sent us, the various Aero chocolate bars and Curly Wurly bars and Yorkies and Starbars and Turkish Delights.

Among them I discover a wee slip of paper, with printed there a name. A disturbing name, it is, seeing how this person appears to be the next winner in Tyger. Yes, *that* Tyger.

And here my fingers sift through the candied rose petals and fragrant French-milled soaps until I locate a stray cashew nut. This I insert in my ear as a pretend pink plastic hearing aid, and as per all of our brotherly conventions, here Otto must fully consign himself to becoming Judy Garland for as long as I'm fake Grandfather, so all the great dirty machine of our pre-male revolution must also wait on tenterhooks while Otto's prison cell becomes a 22 June 1969 bathroom on Cadogan Lane.

## 59

**YOU SEE THIS SHOULD END HERE IN KANGAROO HEAVEN WITH ALL OF US TO** be house pets of the nation. Our own lovely secret lake where all are tucked in and having it off, but according to Otto we must convert the whole world to our faith, and this territorial expansion I fear will be our downfall.

When he sees me place the cashew nut in my ear, a look gets on Otto's face just like got on Daddy's face when we buried poor Daisybelle. Looking on, Daddy had said, "If you knew anything about animals you'd know Daisybelle hated you and hated her life here."

Otto had looked up from the little wreath of a dog lying in the hole. His eyes streaming.

Daddy had gone on, "She wanted you to be a virile man, Daisybelle did. She hated that you are such a measly, mincing thing. That dog wanted nothing more than that you should grow up and shoulder your burden as a soldier of the Empire."

Here that same look gets on Otto's face as if he still stood beside that open grave with Daisybelle curled at the bottom.

To break the spell of that moment I press on. I touch the pink plastic cashew aid in my ear and clear my throat as Grandfather would. Skinny Grandfather, young Grandfather, he says, "You had an older sister, Miss Garland, had you not?"

Here Otto is trapped. Even with his legions of pre-male cutthroats looking on, he must affect a fake cigarette between two fingers and pinch the stem of a make-believe martini glass brimming with champagne and phenobarbital. As fake Judy Garland he must sit at the edge of a pretend toilet and cross his legs at the knee and say, "You mean Suzanne? Suzanne's dead."

Ever solicitous, fake Grandfather must say, "May I inquire as to how your older sister met her end?"

Pretend Miss Garland shrugs one boney shoulder. "Pills. Pills and booze. Oh, I don't know." As per our script, she sips her pretend drink. "It was five years back." Otto grasps what I'm up to, but he must see it through to the end.

Pretend Grandfather asks, "Did you love her?"

Pretend Judy Garland says, "She was a pain."

Pretend Grandfather asks, "Do you miss her, your older sister?"

Pretend Judy Garland asks, "What do you think, bub?"

In our playacting, fake Grandfather checks the time on his watch. He lapses into rote, his little speech about how barbiturates will be absorbed by the lower intestine in a clock tick, leaving only a slight purple inflammation for the medical examiner to find. There will be nothing in terms of vomitus. It's a speech he'd recited to Miss Monroe and Miss Kilgallen among so many others.

Interrupting this, fake Judy Garland asks, "Aren't you afraid?"

Our fellow inmates look on, captivated by how we seem entranced in our passion play.

Pretend Grandfather asks, "Afraid of what, Miss Garland?"

"I don't know," she says. Her eyes dart around the pretend bathroom, the nighttime dark of this small room in Belgravia. She says, "What if this plastics deal—"

"Xenoestrogens," says pretend Grandfather.

Miss Garland nods. "You're only hiding the problem." She asks, "What if someday it touches someone you love?"

All of Holme House falls pin-drop silent as they listen and watch our performance.

Pretend full of himself, in make-believe full confidence and ersatz bravado our fake Grandfather spouts on about the glory of his lineage and his Empire, and how such works as the Suez Canal and the defeat of the Spanish Armada arose from the finest character of real men and eons of ancestral pluck and only the best traits of the finest warriors being brought into the fore. Fake Grandfather with his imitation certainty bangs on about his bloodline being descended from the kings of the earth. Pretend Grandfather with his sham courage says, "No child of any of my children will ever be any less than a great, daring, manly specimen!"

Here the little performance that is Grandfather, it begins to fray.

Fake Miss Garland has only to puff on her pretend ciggie and swirl the contents of her invisible glass as pretend Grandfather bangs on. His pretend words playacting brash, he says, "Our Empire is solid and will remain solid, the beacon of civility and steadfastness . . ." He falters. "The birthplace of great men whose legs stride . . ." He falters. "The very model of civilization for . . ." Those words that were so rock solid on 22 June 1969, they begin to crack and spall and crumble when spoken now. Until fake Grandfather heaves a bit with the effort to deliver his speech.

Such words as *Empire* and *sacrifice* and *perseverance* fail to boom, but instead get swallowed and choked back. And by the time my make-believe Grandfather is spouting his 1969 words about *legacy* and *heritage* in a nowadays prison cell of Holme House, it's hardly a rousing call to action.

Here my fake Grandfather falls to blubbing so hard that Otto's fake Judy Garland must cross the bathroom and take the invisible enema bag from him and say, "I'll give you a break, okay? If it'll make you happy, I'll do myself."

This she does. Otto performs this bit in pantomime, even as pretend Grandfather blubs on as real Grandfather eventually would about not knowing how plastics-based toxins would wreck the Empire. And how the ancient Romans found themselves in the same boat with their hubris. How they'd conquered the world, hadn't they, but then invented the metal lead and made it into plumbing and made leaden dishes and drinking vessels, and in the upper-crust households every luxury was lead, lead, lead, never guessing that exposure to lead was dumbing them down just as certainly as exposure to mercury drove hatters mad, not until they'd raised up a generation of crazy Caligulas. But by then the Roman Empire had begun to fall to pieces, hadn't it?

The damage had been done, so now we'd all have to suffer another Dark Ages, thanks to plastics. Lovely plastics. And here, Grandfather, real Grandfather would say, "You boys must forgive me." He'd say, "I've bequeathed to you status and titles and wealth, but in the process I've destroyed you."

Grandfather would sob, "Our stock once got satisfaction and elation from subjugating indigenous peoples and extracting natural resources, and now all that pleases people is OxyNorms and having it off!"

By now the pretend Miss Garland was fully expired, and you'd think such a stage play would take the starch out of any impending Viking raid upon the region. But no, Otto becomes Otto once more, who signals to his henchman Felix who signals to our chips-boy Digby, and the prison gates are thrown open, and our grand army of endocrine-disrupted, genetically dead-ended products of toxic emasculation commanded by Master Crybaby is loosed upon the land.

## 60

**AS THE BLOOD-DIMMED TIDE FINALLY RISES, OTTO AND I DO ONE LAST JOB.**
Our last expedition for Tyger.

From Holme House we hightail it in a nicked Bentley Bentayga along the A19 southward to the A66, cutting eastward to Middlesbrough to catch the A172 to Carlton-in-Cleveland where we make a misstep to Faceby but double back to Jeater Houses, followed by Borrowby further south, then South Kilvington to the A19 through Cross Lanes to Shipton by Beningbrough to the A1237 where I nod off not to awaken until we've reached Biggleswade with Otto routing us bang into Greater London by way of Spitalfields to the A40 west to the A4202 and bang we're into the black hole of Belgravia. Carnivorous Belgravia, eat-or-be-eaten Belgravia.

Since passing through Whitechapel I've been near to retching from feeling carsick, haven't I, yet here we are. Once more in the horrid, primal jungle heart of central London.

An icy, arctic night it is with veils of snow falling around each streetlight. And every dog's bark smothered to nothing by the white heaped atop everything. Badgers and bees alike sleep snug in their burrows and hives. And only old bankers and chartered accountants shuffle out to stand curbside in front of their posh homes. Tyger subscribers, all. We motor past the lot of them, standing in mukluks, shivering in lined anoraks shouldered over flannel pajamas.

Otto and I drive a prigged Bentley Brooklands Saloon as we fishtail along.

Our outing, as it were, is a lark. A nighttime jaunt to spy some prey animal—an aerospace engineer or Lord Chief Justice or tinned-herring importer—and snuff him out per our instructions from the

Tyger computer. We drive along reviewing the late-night ranks of Anglican licensed lay ministers and probate solicitors and professors emeritus, Otto trying to suss out an address.

Otto says we've come to settle a score. "Cecil, old boy, you'll never guess who the computer coughed out," he says and holds up the slip of paper with a name printed across it.

I look, but have read and reread already to make the name stick. I feel wobbly on my pins.

"As daunting as it seems," Otto says, "we must soldier on and put our shoulder to the task."

Halfway down some lane, here's a face we know by heart. Otto parks the transmission and lets the engine idle. He and I get out and plod over to the man on the sidewalk. A man with a patrician brow and a colonel's jawline, smoking his pipe, he is. A pink plastic hearing aid curled within one ear.

As per protocol, Otto reads from the slip of paper, "Are you Wystan Osbert Seaton?"

Just as so many of our nannies and chauffeurs have been offed by accident, here the computer has given us Grandfather's name. Wholly by accident. And whether his thumb was on the scale or Otto's was, who can say?

Here, Grandfather needs be trust the system. He is the system. As Judy Garland offered her neck so must he. As Marilyn Monroe threw in so must Grandfather. The authority of the cause, the decree of the computer holds sway. And the same Sword of Damocles that Tyger holds over others, it holds over Grandfather now.

## 61

**GRANDFATHER WITH THAT GREAT BLOCKY HEAD OF HIS, IT'S LIKE A FILE** cabinet with the bottommost drawer pulled out. Jutting jaw, colonel's jaw. The old boy pulls himself up to full height and says, "Otto, Cecil," in a Lord Richard pillow-talk voice. He steps close to a streetlight and inclines his head backward so the glare falls on his tilted face. Like so much a winter's spotlight, it is.

Poor Grandfather, dotty Grandfather, he asks, "Are you familiar with the term *nest spoiling*?" He explains that when a baby bird is about to fledge it defecates in the nest. It spoils the nest so soundly that it can never return. A great, heavy evacuation of its fledging bowels it leaves, so that it feels happy to be rid of the nasty place where it had felt such joy and safety for so long.

"Spoiling the nest," he calls this. Dear Grandfather, he tells us, "The world has fallen into such disrepair because the postwar generation wants to leave it a blasted mess." He says, "Oh, they'll never admit as much, especially to themselves. No, we've mucked about too much with nature and plastics and Empire."

Here he pauses as the snowflakes dissolve to shine on his face. Snowmelt fills the wrinkles of his skin and glazes over any liver spots. In a clock tick he's a young man, skinny Grandfather, 1969 Grandfather. He closes his eyes, he does, against the bright of the streetlight, and says, head back, face uplifted toward the night, he says, "My boys, your generation is the largest the world has ever seen. Your peers outnumber the stars, and when your time comes you will take the entire world down with you."

Grandfather, that stalwart doer of those who need done in. He says that no matter how much we profess to hunger for a better world, our every action makes living more of a misery.

"We must make the world a place we're happy to depart," he says. "As we die we must make ourselves the envy of the living." To this end Grandfather and his ilk have sown chaos, they have. So they might shuck their mortal coils with nary a look back. Battle-axe Grandfather, dreadnought Grandfather, if he's to be taken at his word, then the entire point of Western civilization has been to always sully the world. To soften the eventual blow of death. Compared to the mess they've made, death should look like a grand and glorious holiday.

Noble old warhorse that he is, he does bang on so. The snow bucketing down, a winter's night to last forever with the whole world reduced to this snowy row of houses on Belgravia Square.

Neither Otto nor I voice any objection. It seems fairly obvious what he's saying.

As Otto once described Sandhurst, at term's end all the boys were at one another's throats. It's easier to be with rage than to be with despair and loss. If things don't end badly, they'll never end, so all the Sandhurst chums who must part company need become mortal enemies.

Once we realize we must leave the garden there's little doubt we'll set about wrecking and soiling the place. We'll begrudge bequeathing an improved Eden to those who'll survive us. "It's nothing personal," says Grandfather. "It's what every generation must need do."

At this he's like Digby, he is. The Digby in the midnight chip shop. A twee waif and a frail old codger at the same time. The all-and-everything he was and ever will be, past and present, held together for a fleeting moment. Here stands the two most fragile parts of him, our Grandfather, dear Grandfather, and he's impossible not to love.

Grandfather forges on, "I only ask that you boys not be hypocrites. If you're to smash things up and thrash the place, it's best you do so sincerely. Once you render the earth a burnt-out, plastic-coated cinder, it shall be all the easier to walk away from."

He opens his eyes and gives the P38 a glance. "Best get on with it," he says. Still shining, young Grandfather, his shoulders dusted with snow, his eyes fall closed. Otto steps up.

As his gallows speech, Grandfather says, his lips whisper, lips wet with snowmelt, "Thank you two, my brave little boys. Thank you for putting a stop to this."

Here, Otto must pull the trigger. A look gets on Otto's face like the night when we found his beloved governess, Miss Pamela Flora Birdsong, and Otto put the muzzle of the P38 smack against her sweet head. And it wasn't even much noise, because the brains absorbed the sound, didn't they? Neither was the mess much bother because it sprayed out the other side.

And.

And.

Bang.

Grandfather was a credit to the Empire, the way he stood there empty-headed for a few moments before losing his decades-long battle against gravity and tumbling into the messy snow. Unseen, Grandfather's spirit fizzes away like tonic water. Tiny dot-sized bubbles bonding to make speck-sized bubbles rising to join up as itty-bitty bubbles that burst themselves into the world. What had once been Grandfather sprawls there just as dead as the best of them.

Here, a pink plastic something, curled like a cashew nut, lands at our feet. And here Otto snatches it up and snugs the bloody thing, still warm, into his own ear.

# 62

**FROM THE CITY SURROUNDING US COME SIRENS AND THE SMELL OF SMOKE.**
The cry of glass breaking. Gunfire. The pre-male rebellion!

Past Hyde Park we brake too fast, leaving two rubber skid marks smack into the doors of some French neoclassical blather, a great house rising up from the Victoria Memorial.

Near to Sir Richard's, we're at some great ancestral pile where Otto leaps from the auto and strides to a great carved-stone doorway. He lifts a fist and knocks his knuckles smartly against the grand wooden door. High in an upstairs window a light blinks on. Otto knocks once more.

To cut to the chase, we're at Buckingham Palace, aren't we? We hear footsteps approach on the other side of the door, and a muffled voice asks, "Who goes there?"

You see, Her Royal Highness is exceptionally bright for a royal, so when Otto knocks at the doors of the palace she doesn't readily open up. The sound of corgis barking reaches us from within. All the staff and guards have been mustered to fight the prison uprising, they have, but they've gone and forgotten to lower the Royal Standard. No, it just flaps away at the top of its pole over Buckingham Palace, the East Front, facing the Victoria monument, where Otto drops to his knees and uses his fingers to open the Letters slot in the door and peek inside. Through the slot, he calls, "Hello, mum!"

From the sound of it, the Queen is speaking into one cupped hand in an attempt to disguise her regal voice. Doing so, she says, "What's your business?"

In response, Otto calls, "Did you order chips to be delivered?" He winks at me, clever Otto, and shouts, "I've an order for skate and mushy peas, with four quid owing on the bill."

The grand old bird must be peckish because she calls, "Just let me get my handbag."

I've still not the foggiest notion what Otto's up to.

Through the door comes the clack and snap of bolts being thrown and locks unlatched until the door opens a crack to reveal a thin security chain still in place. A white-gloved hand emerges through this crack holding a few bills, and a plummy voice asks, "I've only some five-hundred-pound notes. I hope you can break that."

Otto takes the money and pockets it.

The gloved hand remains in the narrow opening, waiting palm up.

Otto says, "Well, I can't very well pass a big sack of chips through that small crack, can I?" He says, "Take off the chain, mum. I won't bite."

Here despite all rules of protocol, the white-gloved hand slips the chain off. The door swings aside to reveal a lovely older woman sporting the snowiest blue-white hair, with atop that a great blazing crown of diamonds and pearls with blazing at the top the bloodred boulder of a ruby known worldwide as the Black Prince's Ruby. Stuck on here and there are the Stuart Sapphire and the Cullinan II Diamond. Quite smart it looks, that crown.

It's Her Royal Highness Elizabeth II, isn't it? And here her plucky bird's eyes register Otto, and she must know his face, know it from that parade ground at Sandhurst where Otto's bare buttocks marched about to display that great toothy Jaws bite mark on his milky flesh. One gloved hand goes to cover her royal mouth in shock, and color rises in her powdered cheeks. In a clock tick she regains her composure and snaps, "Mind you, what about my chips getting cold!"

Nimble as a boy Jones or a Michael Fagan, Otto makes his move. Here it is he pushes his way inside, and HRH smacks him in one ear with her royal imperial scepter with the bloody big Star of Africa diamond, a 530-carat cudgel it is, that leaves a diamond-shaped welt upside Otto's poor head.

Not to be outdone, Otto says, "Sorry, Mum, but if you'll just give me what I want I'll be getting along."

By now I've moved into the palace alongside my brother. The Queen steps back, clearly itching to make a dash for it. Around all of us a veritable flood of Welsh corgis yap and scurry.

The Queen says, "I've a whole palace guard, I have!"

So as not to spook her, Otto holds up both hands, palms out. "Just hand over your debit card," he says in a calming voice.

I've no choice but to follow as the two of them edge deeper into the palace. The Queen slowly in retreat while Otto advances. It's nice if you've not been, Buckingham Palace. All great, grand drawing rooms lined with pillars and pilasters of carved lapis lazuli. Deep blue, they are, with loads of gilded what have you. All John Nash and Edward Blore, if you fancy that stuff. That scagliola colored plaster.

The corgis are a blasted nuisance as the three of us maneuver about the piano nobile. The Chinese Luncheon Room with its porcelain pagodas and lacquered glories swiped from the Royal Pavilion at Brighton. The coffered and bracketed all of it. The Rembrandts and Vermeers. Marble Hall and the Bow Room and the Kylin clock, if you go in for the frou-frou.

Here is all the gleaming, alarming mash-up of pomp and camp that constitutes Empire. Grandfather had walked these halls many a time.

At Otto's constant urging, the Queen digs a plastic debit card from her handbag and gives it over.

Otto pockets the card and says, "Now your PIN, if you please, Mum."

On the Minister's Staircase I suggest to Otto that we not brutalize the Queen. It won't do to turn public opinion against us.

Her Royal Highness says, "My PIN number?" She brandishes her scepter, ready to whack him again with that bloody big South African diamond.

"Yeah," Otto says, "for your accounts and whatnot. Your password. And you best not lie."

The Queen retreats step by step to the Blue Drawing Room and says, "You know very well that the Queen can't lie."

Otto says, "I know nothing of the sort, do I?" Advancing on her.

Here the Queen stands her ground. She pulls her royal self up to full height, steeling her spine. Her tone dripping with sarcasm, she says, "It's put forth in the Magna Carta, if you'd ever deign to read that document." As almost an afterthought she adds, "And my PIN is one-two-three-four."

The corgis crowd around our feet.

Aghast, Otto asks, "One-two-three-four? That's it?"

To which Her Highness responds, "I've not got to answer to the likes of you, have I?"

"Now just one more request," Otto says, "and we'll take our leave."

The Queen looks about for the best avenue of escape. Everywhere are gold-leafed pianolas and similar obstacles.

With more than a hint of menace in his voice, Otto says, "If you don't mind, I'll take your wee telephone now." Here the orange fire blazes up in Otto's eyes, so bright that it makes the rest of the palace look dark by comparison. The kind of fire, that if it ever got out of the stove it would burn all of us alive. And he says, "And I'll take the launch codes for all your nuclear warheads, Mum, if you'd be so kind."

Otto means to blow us all to bits. It's as Grandfather predicted. Otto means to spoil not merely the nest, but to spoil the whole world and everyone in it.

At this the Queen bolts. Quite the spry, old thing, she is. It's clear she's been biding her time and energy because now she's off like a shot. She tosses aside that great heavy crown and sprints like a gazelle toward the 1844 Room or the 1855 Room or some royal safe room. She's near to gone, and Otto's not given chase.

No, instead Otto gives out with a great, shrill whistle and shouts, "You forgot something, ducky!" He stoops to collect one lovely corgi dog and lifts it in his arms. A much-beloved, elderly corgi by the look of it. Otto cradles it and kisses its Welsh fur.

From a safe distance, Her Royal Highness ventures a backward glance. At the sight of Otto holding her treasured pet, she gasps, "No, don't hurt him! Not my precious Tamerlane!"

Otto will wring the dog's neck, just as he did the nanny's. It's certain.

Without raising his voice, he says, "Tamerlane will be fine, just so long as you hand over your phone. The application for launching nuclear devices. And the launch codes."

And with that we're sunk.

## 63

IT'S AFTER BUCKINGHAM PALACE WE STOP BY A BANK OF ENGLAND BRANCH.
At the ATM Otto inserts the Queen's card and punches one-two-three-four, and the machine dispenses us three hundred quid and the message that we can't withdraw more funds until the next day. Otto punches more buttons, and the machine tells us we have six hundred billion pounds available in our account—well, the Queen's account. Here Otto asks me, "At the rate of withdrawing three hundred quid per day, Cecil, how long will it take us to draw down all six hundred billion?"

As for me, I'm stymied. You see both of us are worthless at maths.

"Well," Otto says, "at least the old bird told us the truth."

## 64

**EVERYTHING IS WRONG.**

Everything spins out of control.

The day is dripping wet with great black clouds drooping down smack in our faces and bolts of lightning staggering on great legs across the horizon and claps of thunder to cover the screams of the set-upon. Still, weather is the least of our worries, isn't it?

Their faces painted with great smudges of Mummy's blue eye-shadow, Otto's phalanxes surge upon the village. Otto's pack of mad dogs runs down a great skinhead in red-laced boots, knocks him to the bricks, and has it off with him. All's the pity how he bellows until the attackers have a go on him from that noisy end as well. Otto's pride of pre-male lions sets upon ironmongers and fishwives alike and relieves them of their cherry trifles and figgy puddings. Nor are the tykes spared as our pre-male berserkers run them down and snatch away their Starbars and Turkish Delights. Our polyethylene terephthalate–deformed Saxons and Jutes, the mob gives chase after punters and yobs to have at any sugar and then to discard the rest.

Prey are appealing because they run. It's why tigers don't eat tigers, isn't it? Whereas Otto and his forces are as mean as cat's meat. Our eagles swoop down upon the baby sea turtles, and tackle the stampeding gazelles, and have it off in mindless acts of sexual deproduction at the bell end of a John Thomas.

Nobs and proles alike are compelled to surrender their marmalade tarts, and we requisition candied rose petals and boiled sweets, and when any rough-and-tumble type resists we overpower the man and have a messy go with him. And it's all-round madness. And I say, "Otto, stop! This is madness!"

Foot soldiers wield burny things—flaming torches—to set alight the houses and farms of the hormonally undisrupted. Our forces cart away a great plunder of sandwich cakes and pillaged blood puddings.

In that manner entire streets are laid waste to. Whole districts are emptied of their sticky buns, and our fey, coy, cloying soldiers of fortune are freed upon the populace. And it's here that a look gets on Otto's face like when Mummy said *chilblains* and Otto heard *chilled brains* and we'd all laughed with Daisybelle and our spotted pony and had not known how horrible and rotted out the whole of the world already was. Here Otto says, "Cecil, it strikes me that the revolution is now running under its own steam." He says, "Let's you and I pay a call on Mummy." Here, Otto says, "I must put a bullet into the dashing head of James Jr."

Everything is wrong.

Everything spins out of our control.

And here I say, yes, let's go see Mummy. But I propose we make a stop at one other place on our pilgrimage home.

## 65

OTTO WOULD HAVE US BURN DOWN AND NUCLEAR BOMB THE ENTIRE nation. When last seen, our chip-shop Digby was heading up a great column of troops marching to take Greater London. A born leader of men, he is. A Tiny Tim to the bone, yes, but he's always pictured something like tonight, some fine gentleman seeing the potential in him and giving him a chance, this Digby, and with that kind of a leg-up he'll for sure get his full measure and make his mark. And won't folks on his street be knocked back when they see him. The captain of an army. A world leader, could be.

For Otto and me, all roads lead back to that old hotel bang on the ocean. Back to the ghost forest, where a great tidal wave of sand has pulled a grave over Winnie-the-Pooh's Hundred Acre Wood. There, driftwood ghosts poke up out of the sand to spread stubby branches of broken bone. Where Daddy and the first Digby and some other unlucky punters stand buried upright as deep as a telephone pole is tall. Their mouths and lungs full of muck.

Otto wants to head home and put an end to James Jr., the surly usurper, the strapping usurper, only I sidetrack him to here.

Sickened me, dispirited me, I've no desire to make the whole world an extension of my damaged self. To date I've remained a rather background character in my own life. My opinions hardly qualify as my own because Otto has given them to me.

As Otto always says, "Things have to end badly, or else they'd never end."

Otto recites by heart the lines I hear by heart.

As Otto always says, "Most people are so stupid that I'd rather have it off with them than talk to them." Clever Otto.

So we've gone back to the ghost forest, where we march along in the footprints left by Daddy and so many other men. Otto says, "It's no use searching." As we trudge along he says, "Daddy's gone out to Australia, he has."

With every step we're backsliding down the steep face of the dunes. Otto says, "If you ask me, it's little James Jr. we ought to put an end to next." Mummy's strapping husband, and our half brother.

And here I say nothing, but only pull Otto along by one hand. It's less an act of murder this is than resignation. One of us must go. I rather hope with each step that it will be me who falls into a hidden pocket, a grave that closes over my head. Like Russian roulette it is, like navigating a minefield. Otto hasn't the foggiest notion what's at stake. He holds my hand and trudges along beside me and bangs on about being super predators and apex predators and having a go with other nations once we've overrun England.

All the pre-males of the world, all the wee house pets, we'll have it off with all the dik-diks, young and old alike. We'll have everything that's lovely and delicious. And what we can't have we'll spoil. Where our fate actually lies I've no clue so I steer our walk this way and that, between the bone-white barren trunks. If one step sinks deep, deeper than the last, I hold my breath ready for the plunge to my death. Only when the earth holds firm do I breathe out.

With every next step one of us will perish. I'm quite ready to go into the ground, into the red dirt with Daisybelle and our spotted pony. If you must know, I'm somewhat bored of this kill-or-be-killed, this eat-or-be-eaten state of things. And sopping up the world's problems with my liver. With the only reward being an endless go at spotted dick and inebriated skinheads.

Not that I lay the blame on Otto. As a big brother he's done his best. Misguided Otto, well-meaning Otto. All we've had to go on were the nature films. Those, and the blue movies that young Grandfather, skinny Grandfather made to teach human toilet and rusty trombone to the feeble, fey pre-males of 1969. Those, and Sir Richard's whispered lessons about the Law of the Jungle.

You see, Otto and I are both stumbling along, mired in loose and shifting sand and headed in no real direction. Just wandering in the blind hope that something will turn up.

And here it is. Otto is no longer the taller of us. In size at least he's no longer my big brother. Otto has shrunk. With but one footstep he's dropped down to the size of a small boy. A boy not half Otto's age. The sand rises up around his waist as he sinks into some hidden pit, and Otto says, "I've found it, Cecil."

I ask what he's found, and hold tight to his hand.

Otto sinks to his armpits and says, "I've got there at last, haven't I?"

And tugging to keep him aboveground, I ask where he's got to.

Otto says, "It's the kangaroo's pouch, isn't it?" He says, "Cecil, you must let go of my hand. You see this is how Australia works. And if you hold fast to me then we'll both be lost."

I brace my feet against the sliding sand of everything and clasp his hand in both of my own and pull to keep him with me.

Here a look gets on Otto's face like got on the tutor's face when he plunged into the secret lake. Bliss, it was. Blissful. With his free hand he's punching buttons on the Queen's phone. Here the sand pours in to cover his scalp. The launch codes.

In moments, the sky will be crisscrossed with the vapor trails of intercontinental ballistic missiles. Yet slowly Otto, the weight of my brother, pulls my hands, then my arms, underground, dragged down by the sinking whole of him until my face is pressed into the dirt and I'm forced to turn my head to one side and breathe sideways as if doing the Australian crawl.

My hands feel the pulse in Otto's, a heavy, heaving throb as blood pounds in his fingers. And here I feel something sharp. Deep inside the earth, hidden where I can't see, clashing sharp stones attack my buried fingers. Stones grind at my knuckles and snip away the skin and muscle, but I still hold fast even as Otto sinks away, pulling me until sand pours into my own mouth.

All the while the stones like teeth inside the world nip and gnaw at my thumbs and fingers, making my grip slick with my own blood. It's Otto's mouth, dingo Otto, kiwi-bird Otto, biting and chewing to save my life. He's eating my hands so the rest of me isn't dragged into the underworld. Still I hold on to him, until I don't, until first one hand loses Otto's, then my other, and my brother is swallowed whole.

For the longest time I lie there with my arms buried, rooted and bleeding into the earth. For all night, and then into the next morning when the sun burns through the early fog. Yes, the sun actually makes an appearance in my rainy, wrecked life, and quick enough all the events of that previous day are lost to me.

## 66

**OLD NANNY SITS IN OUR KITCHEN SHINING A SPOON, SHINING AND RESHINING** it until Mummy's monogram is fairly worn off. It's our last spoon it would seem. Here a look gets on her face like the look on my own face reflected upside down in the bowl of the spoon.

You see, along my journey home I came across our things—one of Mummy's shoes for instance—dropped in the mud beside the lane. Then the drawing-room settee sitting a ways off in a field as if it were a silly cow. Our velvet settee, up to its ankles in wet grass. Distressing little exhibits such as the clock from our third-floor landing, now set atop a stone wall like an owl, or the firedogs from the library. This last item I found beside the Crossroads well. By Tishingbeck I stumbled upon a stuffed panther, our panther, propped against a stile. Following that I came upon our stuffed jaguar. Followed by the mattress from the nursery bed, stained with the bloody shape of Daisybelle's red dying. Then the library vitrine, looted of its fingers. Our lovely things had somehow escaped the house to wander the countryside, hadn't they?

None of this had boded well. And I'd quickened my pace and pressed the buttons of my wee telephone but only succeeded in reaching a stranger, someone named Voicemail who asked that I leave a message, which I did not. To suffer the loss of my brother and the loss of my tutor had taken the stuffing out of me, still I soldiered on. At home, cook would have a lovely quince jelly and mutton, and I could retreat to the nursery with Mummy and confess to her the fate of Otto. And here along the road I almost near to stepped on a book, *The Erosion Process and Behavior of Resultant Sedimentary Materials,* and my heart skipped.

The ruin that greeted my return was not our lovely crenellated, ancestral pile with mullioned windows and gargoyled niches. A thin ribbon of smoke rose from but a single chimney pot. Gone were the library windows, and the curtain within hung ragged and stained. Likewise, the whole of the north tower stood as a brittle shell with burnt-out casements and charred, tumbled-down timbers and beams within.

Some great conflagration had befallen the place. Littering our lawn and garden were teacups and bibelots and taxidermized grizzly bears, and the sod itself was churned to mud by footprints too many to count. The grand front doors stood open, and the disarray continued within, our lovely oil paintings cut from their frames and absent. Smoke scented the air, and a veil of ash dusted the all of it. The floors crackled, gritty with broken glass and crockery.

I shouted for Mummy but got no reply. I shouted for a footman to receive me, but none were forthcoming. To mount the stairs and survey the wreckage of the upper floors, that effort was beyond me. Belowstairs I found nanny set on a stool, polishing her spoon. I asked after the rest of our silver, not to mention our *objet d'art* and tinned meats.

"Gone," nanny fairly crows. "Sacked, Master Cecil, the whole of it!"

I ask who's undone our lives.

"'Twould be easier to say who *wasn't* here," laughs nanny. The shrill keening laugh of someone half mad. "Why, every tradesman in the village was here, Master Cecil, weren't they? Looking to kill the monster, they was!"

Fussbudget nanny, fretting nanny, here a look gets on her face like when she'd asked after my red backside, and she says, "Master Cecil, what's become of your hands?"

You see my hands, the state of my hands had slipped my mind. The skin was all over teeth marks like the great Jaws bite marks on Otto's buttock at Sandhurst. And I've a finger off and hardly hands at all, seeing how they're so swollen and stiff with dried blood and sand, and here nanny sets aside her polishing and draws me a bath next to the kitchen fire just as in the old days. Our kitchen remains surprisingly intact. She removes my trousers and jumper and settles me into the warm water and has at me with a soft flannel while I toy with the lovely cake of lavender soap that floats between my hairy knees.

As nanny scrubs away she says a lunatic woman had popped round asking about Daddy, a demented woman brandishing a handgun, and when the footman barred the doorway she'd shot him in the arm and crashed her way inside and had a row with Mummy and made off with James Jr., hadn't she?

"Not that the daft chippy was alone," says nanny. "A mob of mad-men she'd brought with her." They'd set about drinking the Domaine Leroy Chambertin Grand Cru 1990 and downing the lovely pills left over from the one governess. Even before the villagers had arrived these madmen had pulled down the bed curtains and begun to drag away the tapestried everything of our heritage. What they hadn't made off with they'd smashed.

Hardly had the crazed mob departed when an army of village ale-wives and barmen and local toughs had come up the lane waving pitchforks and pikes to do battle with the nursery monster.

"By then," says nanny, "your poor mum was beside herself with fear." Mummy had tossed through the cabinets in search of her Wal-ther P38 and found it missing, hadn't she? As the shouting crush had surged through the house Mummy had fled higher and higher until she'd been stranded atop the roof of the north tower, where at that point the house had been put to the torch. A tiny flame put to the tasseled fringe of some velvet swag made a bigger flame that wicked upward to an embroidered valance to make an even larger flame that licked across the domed and frescoed ceiling, to consume chariots and cherubs depicted in the style of Constable. All of this Capability Brown. All of our pompous tapestry horsehair.

Mummy had stood at the parapet wall and shouted coarse in-vectives as she'd endeavored to topple various gargoyles onto those below.

"A credit to the Empire, your mum was," says nanny. "A great lady right up to her end."

By now the bathwater has gone pink with blood from my knackered hands. A look gets on nanny's face when she sees all my Welsh hair has grown back. Keeping me smooth is rather a lost cause.

What the lunatics hadn't spirited away from this accursed house, the villagers had carted off. And as she'd watched them Mummy had railed from her tower. The chauffeur and cook and maids had all given their notice at that time and fled without references, taking with them only the clothes on their backs. Here nanny falls silent so I coax her to go on.

"Oh, Master Cecil, don't make me give an account of the ordeal!" cries nanny. "Not of your poor besieged mum high upon that flaming tower!" She lifts her apron to her eyes and begins to boo-hoo. It takes little effort to picture Mummy outlined against the sky and set upon from all sides by fiery conflagration.

Old nanny says, "Your mum cursed even the flames that destroyed her!" Here nanny's boo-hooing overwhelms her.

Poor nanny. The old thing is so useless that here my heart swells on her behalf, and I ask her to bring me pen and paper so I might make provisions for her future upkeep. She's to always have a home in this half-burned house. With her future livelihood secured, the question of my own future arises.

Mopping her eyes with the hem of her apron, she says, "Perhaps, Master Cecil, you and Master Otto could go in search of your father." Bonkers nanny, dotty nanny. Let her have her second childhood here among the broken teacups and ghosts. It's best not to strip her of her illusions.

As for myself, I ask nanny to teach me. How to bathe. How to best cut a steak. Despite my gnawed hands I must learn to do for myself. I must kill that always-moving part of myself that all young people need to kill. That reckless, restless me who I don't want to be anymore by old age.

HERE MORE THAN ELSEWHERE IN THIS CHRONICLE I FEAR STRIKING A FALSE note. That fear aside, we must happen across some element of the sublime. The divine, no less.

You see, servants might always be telling you what to do. And tutors tell you what to think. But elder brothers, they tell you who you are. So while I might feel utterly bereft and rudderless at this point, it's within the realm of possibility that my rudder to date has been barnacled and worm eaten and has misguided me. You see Daddy left Otto at a very precarious time, so Otto grew very quickly to become a toddler's version of a powerful man: heartless and silly, with an appetite only for having it off with great numbers of nameless goes. It follows that Otto raised me as he'd been forced to raise himself, didn't he?

To date I've been as much Otto's toddling bairn as Mummy's. And while I ought to feel a great timidity, stripped as I am of Otto and Mummy, Daddy and nanny, Daisybelle and Grandfather, instead I feel a faint prickling in my solar plexus.

At this, perhaps we'd best go back as far as the very beginning and make an entirely new start.

Did I let on about the clock? Our kitchen clock, it is. Trusty clock, dusty old clock. It's been stopped since the day Daddy took a powder. Here I open the case and use the key to wind the lovely old thing. Where I place the hands doesn't signify. What matters is that it's tick-tocking. What matters is that we've come unstuck in time.

**YOU'LL BE PLEASED TO HEAR THAT AUSTRALIA ISN'T AS HORRID AS WE'RE LED** to believe. On the contrary, Otto would fancy the skies, a great wide-open sky every day and not the droopy, drippy sky of Buckinghamshire. What's more, it's not littered with dead kangaroo babies. I've seen quite enough people and animals done in, thank you very much. The tutor by water. Otto by earth. Mummy by fire.

The Australian Outback spreads out around me, not altogether horrid and inhospitable. And, no, the world isn't all Winnie-the-Pooh, but I take exception to Sir Richard's truck about Survival of the Fittest. As of late I haunt the Outback, and when I see a pink joey clinging to a mummy's fur coat I'll walk right over, I will. It's not so much as a booger stuck to the mummy's fur coat. A nasty bit of pink snot. And I'll pluck it up and stuff the baby kangaroo into the pouch. A job done properly.

In another clock tick I'll see another and save it, too. In a pillow-talk voice I whisper, "Let's just put this baby joey where he belongs." At that I'll stuff the pink thing into its mummy's pouch.

Otherwise, I clap my hands to drive off the dingoes and the blood-thirsty kiwi birds. In April I shall journey to the Galápagos Islands where I'll wave a stick to ward off the meat-eating seabirds and save the tiny baby turtles, and the predators will simply have to settle for a plant-based meat substitute, won't they? Something with the satisfying mouthfeel of baby peccary. In November I'll be in Africa to tell the cheetahs that eating newborn dik-diks is terribly bad form, and to drive off the cheetahs if need be.

I've still got the Queen's debit card, haven't I?

You see I'm finished with wishing for a better world. It seems I must pitch in. And here's another fey, weak, feeble pink joey I must pluck and stuff in a pouch. And here's another. And here a dingo is watching me, and a look gets on the dingo's face just like the look that got on Sir Richard's face like got on Grandfather's when he talked about Marilyn Monroe. In the kindest tones he'd say, "I show you the world as it is, my boys."

It's all well and good, having it off with a lot of homicidal maniacs and convicts, this is Australia after all. But one must make an effort, mustn't one, to bring about a better world.

The nuclear missiles have yet to launch. It would appear that Her Highness had fibbed about her launch codes, an untruth I hope the Empire can forgive her.

And here I'm plucking another joey and stuffing it. And here I'm stuffing another joey into a pouch full of warmth and milk. A person's life must be given over to something, because the only people afraid of dying are those who've never lived.

And here I'm snatching a baby kangaroo from the red dust and brushing it clean and stuffing it into the applicable pouch. This I do without pause. I might not be happy here, but I'm too busy to take note of my unhappiness. It's a busy place, the Outback. A great dirty machine, Otto once called it. But once I arrive, I've kept no memory of our world. Not forever, but for now.

# ACKNOWLEDGMENTS

In closing, we have read the preceding, and it left us rather deflated. It's not terribly clever, even by American standards, is it? Why the author would have you believe all manner of rubbish, such as the idea that Australia and Austria are entirely different nations. While as learned people know for an iron-clad fact that the matter is simply American v. British pronunciation, similar to aluminum v. aluminum and tomato v. tomato. What's more, we suspicion that all the heavy lifting of this dodgy tome was done by Scott and Tim and Cameron. That's not to forgive Sloan and Dan and Maria for their part. And no small measure of the devilish effort was contributed by writers in the so-called author's workshop and his peers on Substack.

May all of the co-conspirators find themselves in kangaroo heaven supping on iced meringues and pumpkin spice lattes, but not for a very, very long time.

Sincerely,
Cecil

## *ABOUT THE TYPE*

This book was set in ITC New Baskerville, which was designed by John Quaranda as a late twentieth-century interpretation of John Baskerville's work. Baskerville was known as a writing master and printer in Birmingham, England, and was especially popular for the masterpiece folio Bible he produced for Cambridge University.

# ABOUT THE AUTHOR

For several years, people have brought me books to inscribe for their spouse or sibling or child. When I inquire why the reader in question isn't there to ask, the person says, "Because they're dead."

In each case the young person has overdosed on drugs, and the surviving friend or relative wants to bury the book in the casket with the beloved's body. I scribble something, and they thank me. After that I go to the hotel and drink myself unconscious.

For a long time I've wanted to write a book about the pain of addiction, both the pain of the addicted and the pain of those close to them. That's the engine behind *Not Forever*. Given the choice, most people are not going to read a book about pain, but I would like to share my intention. "Having a go" and "lemon syllabub" are all metaphors, duh. Not to mention the way thirty years can vanish, and one finds himself still a child who's wasted his life.

Thank you for reading this novel. If you read it a second time, please keep this note in mind.

The Author.